DARKANGEL

BOOK 1 OF THE WITCHES OF CLEOPATRA HILL

CHRISTINE POPE

DARK VALENTINE PRESS

DARKANGEL

ISBN: 978-0615984407
Copyright © 2014 by Christine Pope
Published by Dark Valentine Press

Cover design and book layout by Indie Author Services.

To learn more about this author, go to
www.christinepope.com.

To Erik, for going on this crazy journey with me

DARKANGEL

CHAPTER ONE

Number Forty-Four

My Aunt Rachel paused at the doorway to my room. "He's here," she announced—unnecessarily, since I'd heard the doorbell just a few minutes earlier.

"Okay," I replied, and didn't bother to keep the reluctance out of my voice. Neither did I bother to turn away from the table where I sat, which functioned as both a computer desk and dressing table. At the moment my laptop was closed. I should have been primping in front of the mirror, but really, what was the point?

Up until that moment my aunt had worn her usual cheery expression. But I saw her mouth compress slightly, even as she gave my jeans, black T-shirt, and black cowboy boots a sideways glance. "Angela, it might help if you at least looked as if you were making an effort."

I lifted my shoulders. "What difference does it make? If we're fated to be together, then he really shouldn't care what I look like, should he?"

"That's not the point—" She broke off, really looking at me this time, instead of my outfit. Voice gentler, she said, "He's nice-looking, this one."

Their looks generally weren't the problem. My aunt knew I hated this ritual, knew how much I hated not being free to make my own choice, and so I got the impression that she quietly filtered out the candidates who were awkward or plain or had acne or whatever. Even so, a depressing number of hopeful young men had passed through our door in the months since I'd turned twenty-one.

Forty-three, actually. The one waiting for me downstairs would make forty-four. That was a hell of a lot of blind dates.

"I'll be down in a minute," I told her.

Another one of those pauses, and then she nodded. But, since she was my Aunt Rachel, she couldn't seem to keep herself from adding, "Just a little lip gloss, dear," before she turned and went back down the stairs, silver bangles jingling, skirt swishing. Unlike me, my aunt dressed in a jumble of multicolored broomstick skirts and ethnic jewelry, alternating from tanks and tees in hot weather to long-sleeved T-shirts and sweaters in the winter. Her attire wasn't really that unusual for this part of the world, which had more than its fair share of New Age practitioners of various persuasions.

The difference between all those New Age types and my aunt—and everyone in my family, actually—was that we really *were* witches.

Scowling, I opened the little carved box from India that I used to store my meager supply of cosmetics. A tube of soft peach-colored lip gloss stared up at me, but I ignored it and instead took out a tube of Burt's Bees lip balm and applied some of that instead. After all, what was the point of putting on gloss when it was just going to get kissed off in a few minutes anyway?

Rubbing my lips together, I went down to meet the latest candidate.

His back was to me when I entered the living room. All I saw was someone tall, with dark hair, and for a second my heart leapt. *Maybe it's finally him....*

But then he turned toward me. Dark eyes met mine, and my heart fell, just as it had every other time the candidate was someone tall and dark-haired, but also definitely not the man who had been haunting my dreams for the past five years.

My aunt smiled at the stranger, then at me. Deep down, I had to admire her for being able to summon a real-looking smile after all these disappointments. "Angela, this is Alex Trujillo."

"Hi," I said, and managed a smile of my own. I had a feeling it wasn't quite as believable as my aunt's.

"Hi," he said.

I could tell he was looking at me but trying not to *seem* as if he was looking at me. By that point I was more or less used to it, even though I didn't like it very much. These encounters never lasted long enough for me to ask what the young men were looking for, precisely, although I had a feeling most of the time they'd been expecting more from the McAllister clan's *prima*-in-waiting. My friend Sydney had tried to tell me more than once that I could be beautiful if I just worked at it a little, which made no sense to me. Either you were beautiful, or you weren't.

Judging by the studiously neutral expression on this Alex Trujillo's face, I guessed he thought I fell in the second category.

"Well, I'll leave you two to get acquainted," my aunt said, and disappeared down the hall that led to the kitchen. Some truly amazing smells were drifting through the hallway and into the living room.

Poor Aunt Rachel. Every time we went through this whole song and dance, she had a big meal going, just in case *this* candidate would turn out to be the one and so would need to stay for dinner. Good thing her "friend" Tobias came by regularly to eat with us, or there would've been a heck of a lot of roasts and chili and tamales piling up in the freezer.

You'd think after doing this forty-three times, I'd be a little better at it. I cleared my throat and said, "So, um, Alex…where are you from?"

The first five or six times I'd tried poking around on Facebook and using Google to dig up as much background information about the candidate as possible, wanting to be forearmed. Then I realized if I already knew everything about the guy, we wouldn't have anything to talk about. So these days I just went in blind and hoped for the best.

Alex shifted his weight from one foot to the other. With the exception of my cowboy boots—he was wearing black Chucks—we were dressed a lot alike, both in jeans and black T-shirts. His skin was warm olive, and Aunt Rachel was right…he was good-looking. If it weren't all so awkward and strange, I wouldn't have minded kissing him, even if he wasn't the man of my dreams.

Literally.

"Tucson," he said at last.

Which meant, despite his last name, that he was part of the de la Paz clan. Maya de la Paz was the *prima* of that clan, which counted both Tucson and Phoenix as part of their territory. Compared to that, we McAllisters, with our little corner of northern Arizona, were pretty small potatoes. This was the first time a de la Paz had been offered as a candidate, and I wondered why they'd bothered at this point. Alex had to be a more fringe relation…or maybe not. The McAllister clan was not as powerful as the de la Pazes, but then again, I wasn't just any witch.

I was the next *prima*.

"So you're one of the de la Pazes?" I asked, even though I already knew the answer. "And Maya de la Paz is your…?"

"Grandmother," he supplied at once.

A direct relation, then. Interesting. Probably I should have known that, but trying to keep track of all the twigs and branches in my own family tree was work enough without delving into those of the other clans. Aunt Rachel reveled in that sort of thing, and kept detailed lists and charts. Handy, I supposed, when so many in a clan were related to one another in some way.

Not that witches and warlocks couldn't marry outside their clans, of course. It was good to bring in fresh blood—or else I wouldn't have Alex Trujillo standing in front of me right now—but there were still a lot of third and fourth cousins married to one another even so. And now that I thought about it, I seemed to recall a McAllister marrying into the de la Paz clan a few generations back, so Alex and I still might be related, if only tangentially.

But I knew I was letting my thoughts wander so I wouldn't have to think about the task at hand. This would be a lot easier if we could both share a drink or two first and get a little tipsy, let our guards down a bit. Custom dictated, however, that we go into this clear-headed and wide-eyed. Otherwise, our reactions could be clouded by the alcohol, and that wouldn't do at all.

"So she's okay with this?" I asked. Probably not all that tactful, but I couldn't think of anything else to say.

A lift of the shoulders. Nice, broad shoulders. Although our conversation was limping along, I couldn't help wishing this encounter might have a different conclusion. He really was awfully good-looking....

"Of course," he said immediately. "It's a big deal, to be the consort of the *prima*. Even from a clan—" He broke off then, as if he'd just realized he was about to stick one of those size-twelve Converse high-tops right in his mouth.

"Even from a piddly little clan like the McAllisters that lives in the middle of nowhere, right?"

"I didn't mean that."

I was pretty sure he did. I let it go, though. Kissing a next-to-perfect stranger was hard enough without getting into an argument beforehand. "It's okay," I said. "I know we're not much compared to the de la Pazes. But we like it that way."

Alex nodded. "It is pretty cool up here. I've never been to Jerome before." His dark eyes fastened on mine, and he moved a few steps closer. A new warmth in his expression made an excited little shiver go down my spine, even though I knew this wasn't going to end the way he wanted it to. "I think I could get used to it here."

Another step, and another, and then he was standing right in front of me. He smelled good, too, of some citrusy aftershave or cologne, something fresh and clean.

"You could?" I managed.

"Yes," he replied, then reached up and took my face in his hands, fingers warm and strong against my cheeks. He pressed his lips against mine, and…

…and nothing.

I'd known that was what would happen, but even so a sharp wave of disappointment washed over me. It didn't matter that he was gorgeous and smelled good and seemed more or less friendly. Whatever it was—whatever that spark was that should flare into a raging fire once a *prima* kissed her intended consort—well, it just wasn't there. He wasn't the one.

For a second or two he continued to kiss me, as if he thought I was on a delayed-reaction fuse or something. But he could kiss me for the next ten years, and it wouldn't make a speck of difference.

Gently as I could, I pulled away. I didn't say anything at first. Then, "I'm sorry, Alex."

His dark brows pulled down as he frowned, but then he gave a philosophical lift of the shoulders and stepped back a little. "My *abuela* warned me that this wasn't a sure thing."

I forced a chuckle. "Oh, she did?"

"Angela, you're sort of legendary. Forty-three candidates—forty-four now, I guess—and not one suited you?"

"It's not as if I have a choice—"

"Oh, I know." To my surprise, he bent down and kissed me again, only this time on the cheek. "It's sort of like buying a lottery ticket for us candidates, I guess. We all know the odds aren't very good, but we all hope that we might be *the* one." He grinned, a flash of white teeth, and said, "*Hasta luego,* Angela." Then he went out the door that led to the hall, and from there to the front door.

Well, technically, it was the back door, as our house was a two-story apartment above my aunt's store, and so the private entrance was off the alley and not the main street, but still. Either way, he was gone. *Adios,* number forty-four.

I had no idea who number forty-five was going to be, but I had a feeling he couldn't possibly be as cute as Alex Trujillo.

———

Aunt Rachel appeared a minute or so later, wooden spoon dangling from her hand. "No?" she asked, in weary but unsurprised tones.

"Nope," I replied. It bothered me that it still hurt so much. By this point, shouldn't I have gotten numb to the whole process?

But I hadn't. Each time the hope would surge, even though my mind always told me the new candidate couldn't be the one, because he wasn't *him*.

Since she was my Aunt Rachel, she didn't sigh. Maybe she allowed herself the smallest twitch of her mouth, or lowering of her eyebrows, but that was all. She gave tilted her head to one side, appearing to consider my expression. "There's still time, Angela. No need to worry."

"Who's worried?" Before she could reply, I added, "I'm going upstairs. Unless you need me to help with dinner?" That was the last thing I felt like doing at the moment. Even so, I didn't hesitate to ask, since that was what I was expected to do.

I'd gotten really good at doing that, what was expected of me.

My aunt shook her head. "No, sweetie, I'm fine. You take some time for yourself."

I murmured a thank-you and fled upstairs. Most days my room felt like a refuge, a place I could go to escape the weight of all those expectations. Today, though, it felt more like a cage, even with the breathtaking view that looked out over my hillside town, perched on Cleopatra Hill, and down into the Verde Valley, past the red rocks of Sedona, and all the way to....

It was a clear, cool day in mid-October, with visibility of fifty miles and more. Much more, actually, as I could see Humphreys Peak in Flagstaff, nearly a hundred miles away. On days like this, it seemed as if I could almost reach out and touch it...if I were crazy enough to do such a thing. Flagstaff was forbidden territory.

Flagstaff was where the Wilcox clan held sway.

I didn't have any time to think about the Wilcoxes, though, or their myriad sins, because right then my cell phone rang. For a second or two I considered ignoring it, even as I wished we were back in the summer's monsoon season, when my cell phone tended to crap out any time we had a decent thunderstorm. At least when that happened I didn't have to make a conscious decision to avoid looking at the caller ID so I could let it roll over into voicemail without feeling guilty.

But since I had a fairly good idea of who it was even without glancing at the display, and since I knew she'd only keep calling until I picked up, I decided to forestall the inevitable. After grabbing the phone, I went and settled on my bed. I knew this was probably going to take awhile.

"Hi, Sydney."

No preamble, just a drawn-out, "Sooooooo?"

"So nothing," I replied, and kicked off one, then the other of my cowboy boots. I might have been twenty-one, legally an adult and able to drink and vote, not to mention being the clan's next *prima*, but Aunt Rachel would still give me hell if I put my boots on the expensive embroidered duvet cover she'd gotten me for my birthday last year.

A groan. "Not again!"

"Yes, again." I wiggled my toes, and wished I'd grabbed a glass of water or iced tea from the kitchen before I came upstairs.

"Was he cute?"

"What difference does it make?"

"Was he?"

I knew she'd keep asking until I told her everything. "Yes, he was cute. But it doesn't matter, because he wasn't—"

"Yeah, I know. The mystery man. The man of your dreams. The one beside whom all others pale. The—"

"Okay, I get it." Sometimes I really wished I'd never told Sydney about *him*. But weren't you supposed to be able to tell your best friend everything?

She knew about me…knew about the McAllisters. Her family had lived in Cottonwood almost as long as the McAllisters had been in Jerome, and they were some of the few whom we trusted with our secrets. Long-timers around here, they knew about my clan, about its traditions…its powers. Well, its purported powers, anyway. There hadn't been a public display for more than eighty years, not since the time Henry McAllister caught a recently laid-off miner attempting to steal the contents of his cash register. The miscreant was held upside down, suspended in midair, until the sheriff came to claim him. Spectacular, sure, but the clan elders made it clear that such exhibitions of power would not be tolerated.

Fly low and avoid the radar—that's our motto. Attracting attention was not a good thing. And so, I more or less confided in Sydney, knowing that she came from people who knew how to keep their mouths shut. In her case, this was something of a miracle, since she seemed able to rattle on at length about pretty much any other topic.

"Who'd believe me anyway?" she'd asked once, and I'd had to shrug and smile. This part of the world had a high-per-capita instance of psychics, witches, energy healers, you name it. Calling us out as witches would have earned a yawn at best. Most people didn't realize that there were witches...and then there were *witches*.

"So what now?" she asked. "Does your aunt have the next one lined up yet?"

"I don't think so. I mean, how many guys can there be who are my age and from a suitable clan? She's already had to cast pretty far afield." As far as California, and Oregon, and Colorado. Not New Mexico, though. The clans there were connected with the Wilcoxes. I shivered, then added, "I'm sure she'll be on the phone tomorrow, though, scraping the bottom of the barrel."

A little pause. "Well, since you're not getting bonded to your soulmate after all, you want to go to Main Stage with me tomorrow night? I've heard the band is supposed to be pretty good."

"Who's playing?"

I could almost see her shrug. "I don't know their name. Does it matter, as long as it gets you out of the house?"

"True that." It would be good to get out. And Cottonwood was safe territory. I didn't have to worry about anything strange happening down in Cottonwood. "Dinner first?"

"Drinks and dinner. They have got the cutest new guy working at the Fire Mountain tasting rooms...."

Envy surged through me. How I wished I could go out and flirt and look at good-looking guys, maybe give my phone number to someone who seemed particularly interesting. That was never going to happen, though. I was the next *prima* of the McAllisters. I was supposed to meet my soulmate, get married, and use my powers for good, an agenda that didn't exactly lend itself to casual hook-ups. As usual, I'd have to settle for living vicariously through Sydney.

"Okay." I knew arguing was pointless. She might not be a witch, but Sydney did have an almost magical talent for getting her way.

"Real clothes," she said in warning tones. "*Girl* clothes."

"Yas'm," I replied. "I'll meet you in old town at…?"

"Seven. Don't be late." She hung up then, and I hit the "end" button on my phone and tossed it onto the coverlet.

I doubted that a girls' night out would magically heal all my woes, but I figured I had to start somewhere.

———

Dinner that night, though excellent, was more than a little subdued. I guess it helped that Tobias was there; he chatted with Aunt Rachel about preparations for the upcoming Halloween festivities—Halloween was a big deal in Jerome—had a second and even a third helping of ranchero beef and rice and cowboy beans, and generally acted as if nothing untoward had happened earlier that afternoon.

I did like Tobias; he was the latest in a long string of my aunt's "friends," although since the two of them had been seeing each other for almost four years now, I'd begun to wonder if they had plans to make things more formal. Probably not; Aunt Rachel had always said she'd never get married, that she was too set in her ways to disrupt her life by having a man underfoot. There'd never been the barest trace of accusation or even regret in her tone when she made those comments, but I still couldn't prevent the stir of guilt that went through me whenever I heard them. Would she have felt that way if she hadn't gotten stuck with me from almost the time I was born?

The subject of my mother didn't come up much…or rather, Aunt Rachel gently headed me off at the pass whenever I tried to go down that road. No one came out and said it directly, but it was pretty clear to me that my mother was supposed to be the next *prima*, and she just couldn't handle the pressure. Took off about a month after her twenty-first birthday, after going through a couple of candidates who obviously didn't appeal to her. No word, no nothing, until she showed up a year later with a two-month-old daughter in her arms.

If there had been recriminations, I wasn't told of them. No, my aunt had taken her wayward sister and her infant daughter back into the house as if nothing had happened. This I heard from my Great-Aunt Ruby, the current *prima,* who had apparently taken pity on me and given me a few bare facts. Not many, but she claimed she didn't have a lot she could tell me. My mother hadn't said anything about my father, except that he was a "civilian," as we liked to refer to those not in the witch clans. She said briefly that she'd gone to California, that she'd wanted to see the ocean, and that was the end of her revelations.

And then she'd left Aunt Rachel watching me one night, and had gone off to party and drink at the Spirit Room bar down the street, and ridden away on the back of some guy's Harley after they'd had a few too many beers and whiskey shots. The winding two-lane road up to Jerome could be icy and treacherous in February, and they had crashed. Neither of them had been wearing a helmet.

I didn't really mourn her. How could I? I'd never even known her. All I had was a few photographs in one of Aunt Rachel's albums. Maybe I looked a little like my mother—same oval face, same full mouth and arched eyebrows. My hair was darker, though, my skin paler. Did I resemble my father at all? Impossible to say.

"...going to the Halloween dance?" my aunt was saying.

I blinked. "What?"

She smiled, then repeated, "Are you and Sydney going to the Halloween dance?"

"I think so. That is, we've talked about it. She's excited, since this is the first year we'll be able to go."

Every year on the Saturday closest to Halloween, a benefit dance was held at Lawrence Hall here in Jerome. The gathering was strictly twenty-one and over, and so neither Sydney nor I had been able to go before this year. Even being *prima*-in-waiting wasn't enough to get the organizers to break that rule. In the past I'd helped with the decorating, partly because it gave me a chance to get a peek at what it might be like to actually attend, and partly because, as the next *prima,* I was sort of expected to pitch in and help out.

True, Sydney was more excited about the whole thing than I was, but I suppose part of that was simply realizing that I'd thought I would have met my soul-mate by now, and would have someone to go with besides Sydney. It would still be fun. I'd heard great things about the dance at what we locals referred to as "Spook Hall."

More on the "spooks" later.

"It's a great party," Tobias said. "I keep trying to get your aunt to go, but she keeps trying to fob me off with nonsense about it being for the kids or something. Which is b.s., and you know it, Rachel. At least half that crowd is over forty."

She shot him a mock-irritated glare and shook her head. "We can discuss that later. I don't even know what I'd wear."

"Well, you've got two weeks to figure it out," I told her, and helped myself to some more sweet potatoes.

"I vote for a cheerleader costume," Tobias put in with a wink.

"Are you kidding? With these thighs?"

"I happen to like your thighs."

I cleared my throat. "Um, I'm trying to eat over here."

They both laughed, and Aunt Rachel tipped a bit more cabernet into my wine glass. Another part of being a grown-up, I supposed. Oh, she'd let me taste wine before, saying it couldn't hurt for me to familiarize myself with the selections from the local wineries, since they were such a big part of the local culture. However, it wasn't until I actually turned twenty-one that she got formal about it and let me have my own glass with dinner. A stickler for proto-col, that was my aunt.

But the silly banter did what I was sure my aunt intended it to do—get my mind off Mr. Number Forty-Four, and thinking about something fun to look toward, rather than the way the calendar was inexorably moving toward December and my twenty-second birthday. Well, all right, the conversation got my mind off that for a few minutes.

Later, though, as I sat in front of my mirror and brushed out my hair, all the worries and doubts began to seep back in. No, the world wouldn't end if I weren't safely paired off with my soulmate before December twenty-first, but it wouldn't be good, either. It had happened a few times in the past, for various reasons, although never to the McAllisters. A *prima* who entered her twenty-second year without a consort found her powers greatly reduced.

Aunt Rachel had never been able to explain that very well to me, except to say that there was something about the bond a prima and her consort shared that strengthened the magic within her, enhanced it somehow.

"And what happens if *the* prima is gay?" I'd asked, thinking the whole setup seemed positively medieval. Maybe it was. We didn't know for certain how far back some of these traditions went, only that we'd been following them for generations, had brought them over to America when the first group of McAllister witches emigrated here from Scotland sometime in the late eighteenth century.

My aunt had shot me an irritated look. "I have no idea. It's never happened before. Not that I've heard of, anyway."

Something in her tone told me I should drop it, so I did. Not that I was gay…I was inexperienced, but I knew who I was attracted to, and it definitely wasn't other girls. But it had seemed a logical enough question to ask.

I'd also wondered why, since my mother had blown her chance at being *prima,* someone else in her age group hadn't become the heir apparent… even her own sister. That was a question I didn't dare ask Aunt Rachel, but I'd broached the subject to other relatives, such as my cousin Rosemary, and she'd only waved a vague hand in the air and said, "Oh, there is only ever one in a generation. That's why it's so important to keep you safe."

And when I pressed as to what would happen if there was no one to inherit, she flashed me a look of genuine horror and shook her head, saying, "It would be the end of the clan."

I must have let out a shocked sound, because she hurried to add, "But that will never happen to us, Angela. You are here, and you will find your consort and inherit Aunt Ruby's powers when the time comes. Everything will be fine."

At the moment, I wasn't sure if everything was really going to be fine. While we certainly didn't indulge in pyrotechnic magic battles—that whole "fly low and avoid the radar" thing—it still wasn't good for a clan to have a weak *prima*. That made the clan vulnerable to more subtle forms of attack. Such attacks had happened before, in other clans, and there was no reason to think the McAllisters would be immune if the worst happened and I turned twenty-two before making that oh-so-necessary bond with my consort.

I couldn't let that happen. What was wrong with me, that not one of the more-or-less eligible young men I'd met had lit that spark in me, had made me know then and there that I'd met the person I'd spend the rest of my life with?

Aunt Rachel kept insisting there was nothing wrong, that it would all work out in the end, but I wasn't so sure. Only two months to go, and I was still as single as I'd been on my twenty-first birthday.

And the clock kept ticking down. I might have magic running through my veins, but no witch in the world could stop the inexorable march of time.

CHAPTER TWO

Meeting Mr. Wrong

OF COURSE I DREAMED OF *HIM* THAT NIGHT.

His face was never distinct enough that I would be able to pick him out of a lineup. Tall, yes, and with sooty dark hair, almost black, longish and pushed back from his brow. Eyes green, but not my brilliant emerald, a shade that invariably had at least one person a week asking me if I wore contacts. No one else in my family had eyes that shade. A gift from my unknown father? Maybe. But the stranger's eyes were darker and cloudier, like deep nephrite jade, or the layered and shifting hues of moss agate.

We never interacted in these dreams. I would see him standing at the end of the street, or across a crowded room. In my dream I would begin to run toward him, but it was as if my feet were mired in quicksand and I couldn't move. Or suddenly the street would impossibly lengthen so it seemed as if a mile separated us instead of only a few yards. Either way, I could never reach him, could never get close enough to see his face clearly.

This time I was running, pounding down Main Street, in a spot as familiar to me as my own face. He stood at the far end of the road, just before it curved past the fire station, his profile to me. And he didn't move, actually seemed to be getting closer...and then from the clear sky snow started to drift down, blanketing the pavement, covering everything in a blurry veil of white. I slipped and fell to my knees, wincing in pain, and began to slide down the street away from him, moving faster and faster, screaming, knowing the ice would kill me just as it had killed my mother.

I sat up in bed, cold sweat gluing my T-shirt to my body, hands trembling as I grasped the covers and pulled them closer to me, trying to erase some of the chill of that nightmare. That's what this one really had been, the first of the dreams I could call a nightmare. The others had been frustrating, had made me wake almost shaking with need, but not like this.

What had changed?

Shivering, I got out of bed and went to the little altar I had set up on top of my bookcase. Time to light the white candle, to summon the protection of the light. Since no one was watching me, I didn't bother with matches, but only touched the tip of my finger to the wick. "Spirits of air and light, I summon you," I murmured, and the candle instantly came to life, a warm glow filling the room and sending the shadows away, bringing with it the comforting scent of vanilla. Somehow that didn't seem to be enough, however, and I grasped the chunk of iron pyrite that sat on the altar, holding it, allowing its protective influence to surround me and fill me, and keep me from harm.

That was a little better. I still felt cold, though, so I shoved the pyrite in the pocket of my yoga pants, then went to my dresser and pulled out a beat-up old sweatshirt with the legend "Jerome, the Wickedest Town in the West" written on it. I pulled the sweatshirt over my head and made myself take a deep, calming breath. Nothing here could harm me, especially not the lingering dregs of nightmare. Our property, and indeed Jerome itself, was ringed with circles of quartz, charged with powers of protection during rituals shared by all the members of the clan. No one who intended me any harm could intrude here.

That was one of the reasons my world was so narrowly focused. Here in Jerome I was safe, and in Cottonwood down the hill as well, although that town was too large to have the protective circles built there. But it was still within our sphere of influence, and negative forces would have a difficult time gaining a foothold there. The farther afield I went, the more problematic the situation, although Prescott and Payson were still more or less safe as well. Even so, I never went to either of those towns unless accompanied by my aunt, and on longer journeys, such as our semi-annual trips to Phoenix to stock up on things we simply couldn't get locally, it wasn't just Aunt Rachel who came along, but Tobias and Margot Emory, the youngest of the clan elders and the one best-suited to handle a long drive.

They weren't being unnecessarily paranoid. Years and years ago, when Great-Aunt Ruby was the same age I was now, a *prima*-in-waiting on the cusp of coming into the fullness of her powers, the Wilcoxes had tried to kidnap her, to have her bond with their own *primus*. Such a pairing would have made the Wilcox clan immeasurably powerful...if it had worked. She'd sensed their ill intentions and sent out a warning. This had happened on Samhain Eve all those years ago, and we thought maybe the Wilcoxes had chosen that day because of the dark power that surged around Samhain. Thank the Goddess they hadn't been successful.

Things had been more or less quiet since then, but we'd never let down our guard. Not when the Wilcoxes were involved.

Another shiver passed over me, and I reached into my pocket and wrapped my fingers around the chunk of iron pyrite. A small tingle went up my arm, as if the stone was telling me that it was here for me, was lending its powers of defense to those of the quartz crystals embedded in the very foundation of the building, to the prayers of protection my aunt offered up every evening to the Goddess and the Triple God and all the smaller, yet still powerful, entities who inhabited the very trees and stones and streams of our mountain town.

I had to hope it would be enough.

Fridays were always fairly busy in Jerome. People came to spend a long weekend, or drove in from neighboring towns to shop and eat and sightsee. So I knew that sitting in my room and brooding over my failure with Mr. Number Forty-Four was not an option. Probably just as well. At least by working in the store I could keep myself occupied until it was time to go out with Sydney.

The shop had once been a general store, but over the last fifteen years my aunt had transformed it into an eclectic space filled with Jerome-related memorabilia, local pottery and baskets, some antiques, books, music, and jewelry. My jewelry, to be exact.

I was about twelve when I first started playing around with stones and settings. It was easy enough to pick up those sorts of things in Jerome, a place inhabited by artists and artisans. Luis Sandoval, a local designer, though not a member of the clan, began to show me how to work with metal—how to use a soldering torch, to set stones, to twist pieces of delicate wire to make intricate and unique settings. Once I'd mastered those skills, I began to experiment with creating pieces based on the resonances of the stones they contained, of making them harmonious as well as beautiful. After that I also began to make talismans, some of which were purchased by tourists who had no idea of their real power, only that they were somehow attracted to them.

Two or three days a week I would work in my studio—well, a converted spare bedroom—and create new pieces to sell in the shop. Friday through Sunday I helped out behind the counter. Working weekends all the time wasn't much fun, but I owed my aunt that much. Besides, the shop closed at six unless there was a special event going on that would keep people around later at night, so it wasn't as if being there Saturdays and Sundays seriously impinged on my social life.

Not that I really had much of a social life.

That Friday was especially busy. October in our part of the world was generally mild and lovely, a good time to sightsee and go antiquing and visit the wineries. I didn't have much of a chance to chat with my aunt that day, which maybe was just as well.

Telling her about a new and somehow frightening twist in my dreams of the mystery man would only make her that much more worried. And what could she do about it? She was a powerful witch in her own right, and had kept me safe for more than twenty years, but even she didn't have the ability to prevent the dreams from forming.

So I smiled at the tourists, and pulled earrings and pendants and the odd talisman out of the showcases as requested, then escaped at noon to grab some lunch. At twelve-thirty my aunt went to get some lunch, then came back at one, just as we always did. Something in her features seemed troubled, as if she'd seen worry surface in my expression, despite my attempts to act as if everything was fine. Luckily, she didn't ask any questions. Maybe she would later; the store was way too public to be discussing anything remotely sensitive, and she knew it.

It seemed that she didn't want to do anything to upset my evening out with Sydney, though. We went home, made a few comments about it being a good day, and then she headed to her own room to primp a little before Tobias showed up to take her to dinner. That was their own ritual—she might cook for him the rest of the week, but on Friday nights he always took her out. Most of the time they stayed right here in Jerome, although occasionally they'd head down into Cottonwood or even Sedona if they wanted something different.

I changed out of my T-shirt and Levi's into a tighter pair of jeans and a slinky dark green top that Sydney had picked out for me as a birthday present last year. My footwear consisted of cowboy boots and work boots for the winter and flip-flops for the summer, so I had to make do with cowboy boots, but at least they were pointy and shiny black and looked good with the jeans tucked into them. Some turquoise jewelry, some lip gloss, and I had to admit I didn't look half bad. Not runway-model material, that was for sure, but going out on the town in Cottonwood wasn't quite the same thing as going out in New York or L.A.

Or so I supposed. It wasn't as if I'd actually been to either of those places, and I guessed I never would.

"I'm leaving," I called out as I descended the stairs. "Taking the Jeep!"

"Don't be too late," was her reply, but she didn't emerge from her room.

Considering the shows at Main Stage didn't even start until nine-thirty, that was a silly request, but I thought I knew what she was trying to say. *Be careful, be vigilant, don't get a wild hair about driving off to Sedona or anywhere except Cottonwood or maybe Clarkdale.*

Like I would. It might have been tempting, but I knew better than to go outside the immediate area without backup. That would change once I had found my consort, but until then my world would have to remain as closely guarded and circumscribed as that of the most sheltered nunnery-raised medieval princess.

I went out the back door to the carport where the Jeep waited. My aunt and I shared it, since it was silly to have two cars when we walked to work and only went down the hill for groceries about once a week. Even so, I always experienced a fleeting sense of freedom when I was able to get away alone, to drive down the winding highway into Cottonwood, even if it was only to get gas or pick up some extra toilet paper or whatever.

The sun had gone down behind Mingus Mountain by the time I pulled into an open space on Main Street in the old-town section of Cottonwood. There weren't too many of those parking spaces left; the tasting rooms stayed open later on Fridays and Saturdays than they did the rest of the week.

I found Sydney leaning up against the bar in the Fire Mountain Winery tasting room, a position guaranteed to give Anthony, the object of her interest, a really good look at her cleavage. It was working, too; I noticed how he kept having to jerk his eyes upward toward her face. Just past her were a couple in their thirties with a selection of the winery's offerings in front of them. The woman didn't look too thrilled with Sydney or Anthony at the moment, and I hoped Sydney's flirting wouldn't get him in trouble with his manager.

"Hey, *chica*," she said, and waved for me to come stand next to her at the bar. "Nice top."

"Yes, it is," I said coolly, and turned toward Anthony. "Hi, Anthony—a glass of the Fire, please."

"You got it," he replied, clearly glad to have something to distract him from Sydney's rack.

"You trying to get that boy fired?" I asked in an undertone, and she just grinned.

"Of course not. I'm just trying to get him to ask me out."

"You know, *you* could ask *him*."

"Hell, no. I'm too old-fashioned for that."

Since I couldn't really think of an adequate retort, I settled for sending her a disbelieving stare, at which she only smiled more broadly.

Anthony came back with my glass of wine, giving me the perfect opening. "Hey, Anthony," I began.

"Yes?"

"What time do you get off work? Because Sydney and I are going over to Main Stage after dinner tonight. Want to come hang out?"

Sydney raised her eyebrows and gave me her best "oh, no, you didn't" stare, even as Anthony replied,

"We close at nine, so I should be able to make it by nine-thirty."

"Perfect," I said. "Meet us there?"

"Sure." He was trying hard to sound casual, but I could tell he was looking forward to it.

At that moment the man from the couple next to Sydney waved Anthony over, so he was spared having to make any other comment.

"What the *hell?*" Sydney whispered fiercely.

"Well, he's too shy to make the first move, and you're just being stupid with that whole 'old-fashioned' thing, so I took care of it for you."

"Oh, really? And what if he thinks he's going there to meet you and not me?"

"He isn't," I told her. "He didn't look at my chest once."

She shook her head. "You're impossible."

It was my turn to grin. "Well, I try to be."

———

We went out for pizza at Bocce after that, and had a few more glasses of wine. Well, Sydney did; I nursed one all through dinner, knowing we'd have more once we were at Main Stage.

"I figured out the perfect costume for you for the dance," she announced midway through demolishing a piece of pesto chicken pizza.

"What is it?" I asked in guarded tones. Visions of the cheerleader costume Tobias had suggested to Aunt Rachel danced in my head.

Either Sydney didn't pick up on the wariness in my voice or, more likely, she simply decided to ignore it. "You know how my friend Madison does all that crazy ballroom dance stuff? Well, she can only wear her costumes once or twice, and then she usually sells them on eBay to get rid of them. But she said I could have a couple if I wanted."

"Aren't those things really skimpy?"

Sydney let out a sigh. "Jesus, Angela, you're worse about that stuff than Melanie Baxter, and she's *Mormon*."

Maybe that was true, but I just didn't feel comfortable letting it all hang out, as it were. Talk about old-fashioned, but there it was. Still, I knew Sydney was trying to help me out, so I asked, "Okay, what are the costumes?"

"I'll take the skimpy one. I think she used it for a rhumba or something, but since it has sparkly fringe all over it, I think I can turn it into a flapper dress. But the other one she wore when she was dancing a pass double, or *paso...paso....*"

"*Paso doble*," I supplied. She shot me a look of surprise, and I added, "*Strictly Ballroom* is one of Aunt Rachel's favorite movies."

"Oh. Okay, so anyway, it looks like a Spanish fla-menco dancer's dress or something. It's long. Yes, there's probably some boobage involved, but that's historically accurate, isn't it?"

Maybe. I didn't know for sure, since historical costume was sort of outside my field of expertise. I could ask Maisie about it, I supposed. Maisie was the "spook" of Spook Hall, one of Jerome's most famous ghosts. She didn't like to come out when the tourists were around, but Monday mornings were pretty quiet in Jerome, so I could talk to her then.

I just lifted my shoulders, so Sydney plowed ahead. "And we're all more or less around the same size, so it'll work out perfect. You'll need better shoes, though," she added, with a dark glance toward the cowboy boots hidden under our table.

"I'll figure out something," I said, making a mental note to dig through Aunt Rachel's collection to see if she had anything that would work. It wasn't that I couldn't afford to get myself some shoes for the occasion…more that I really didn't see the point for something I'd only wear once. Jerome's uneven streets and steep hillsides made most "girly" shoes even less practical than usual.

She nodded, and we went on to talk about her cosmetology course—she'd be finishing in the spring—and whether she should get her own place once she was working full-time, or whether she should hang on at her parents' house and save up for a while first. This whole conversation made me a little sad, partly because I was limping my way through an online bachelor's degree in communications at the University of Phoenix and not enjoying it very much, and partly because Sydney, for all her outward craziness, had a pretty clear plan for what she wanted to do with her life. Finish her certificate, get some experience at a local salon, and then open her own place, preferably in much ritzier Sedona, where she could earn a lot more.

Whereas I...well, I couldn't even do the one thing that was expected of me, and get a consort in place before my next birthday.

I must have let out a sigh, because she stopped abruptly and laid an encouraging hand on my arm. "It will be fine," she said. "I know you're bummed because it didn't work out with this last guy. But you know, I've been thinking about it, and maybe you guys have been going about this all wrong."

"How so?"

"Well, your aunt is doing all this work finding guys from other clans or whatever, but maybe that's not where you should be looking. Maybe the answer has been under your nose all this time."

"If you're suggesting Adam—" I began in warning tones, and she shook her head at once.

"I'm not stupid. Of course I know he isn't the one, or the guy, or whatever you call him."

"The consort," I said wearily. Stupid name, really. Made me sound like the Queen of England or something instead of some girl from Jerome, Arizona.

Anyway, Adam McAllister was my third cousin once removed. Or maybe it was twice removed. I could never keep that stuff straight. He was two years older than I, and had been convinced from the time he was seventeen and I was fifteen that we should be together, despite overwhelming evidence to the contrary. That is, I wasn't attracted to him, and even if I were, it didn't matter, because he'd goaded me into a "test kiss" not long after my eighteenth birthday, and absolutely nothing happened. Definitely not consort material.

"Right, the consort." Sydney finished off the rest of the tempranillo in her glass and looked wistful for a second or two, then perked up, as if realizing more would be on the way once we got to Main Street. "Anyway, you've been hiding yourself away... barely even *talked* to a guy during high school...just because you thought this mythical person was going to show up and put the glass slipper on your foot or something. But maybe he's actually right here in Cottonwood!"

"I doubt it," I replied. "The *prima* almost always marries someone from her own clan, or at least a clan her own is connected to by marriage or treaty. They don't go around marrying...." I trailed off; I didn't want to insult her by calling anyone not in one of the witch clans a "civilian."

"Normal people?" she finished for me. "But you said 'almost always.' So there've been exceptions, right?"

"A few. But it doesn't happen very often."

"It doesn't have to happen often, just *now*. So maybe that's why you haven't met him, because you've been looking in all the wrong places."

It didn't sound right, but I didn't know for sure that she was wrong, either. And at this point I was willing to try just about anything. The regular process sure wasn't working for me.

"Okay," I said, and finished my wine as well. "I'll give it a try. Let's go to Main Stage and see if we can find my Prince Charming."

———

At first glance, Main Stage seemed about the last place where I would bump into the man of my dreams. Not that there was anything wrong with the club itself; it was actually pretty classy inside, with its dark walls and low couches and tall vases filled with tree branches accented with white fairy lights. It was definitely not a crummy cowboy honky-tonk or anything like that. But face it, with a population of barely 12,000 people, Cottonwood didn't exactly boast a large pool of possible candidates.

Even so, I couldn't help scanning the crowd there, trying to see if there was anyone who remotely fit the bill of prospective future consort. Not anything too promising at the moment; I saw a few hipster-looking guys nursing cheap beers, and the requisite number of barflies sitting at the counter. You'd think they were too old for a place like this, but I supposed Main Stage was just another stop on their tour of the local watering holes.

I let out a sigh, and Sydney poked me in the arm. "Oh, come on—the band doesn't start for another twenty minutes, and I bet that's when people will really start showing up. Let me buy you a drink."

"You don't have to do that—"

"I know I don't *have* to. I *want* to. You can buy the next round if you want."

"All right," I replied, and followed her over to the bar.

Of course the men sitting there gave her the hairy eyeball, despite most of them being old enough to be her father. She ignored them, and asked the bartender for a couple of glasses of wine. Usually when we went out, Sydney stuck to mixed drinks, but since we'd already had wine with dinner, she appeared to be playing it safe. I had a feeling she didn't want to repeat the experience of her own twenty-first birthday, when she'd mixed everything but the kitchen sink and then spent half the night throwing up all those mojitos and martinis and beers and tequila shots.

"Here," she said, and handed me a glass. "I see a free table over there—let's snag it before it gets too crowded in here."

I nodded and headed for the table in question. It had four chairs around it, which I guessed we didn't need. I draped my purse's strap over the empty seat next to the one I took, and Sydney sat down next to me.

"To fate," she said, and lifted her glass.

"To fate," I repeated, although I wasn't sure if fate had been particularly friendly to me lately. Still, I supposed it never hurt to offer a libation to the gods and hope they might be listening.

The wine wasn't as good as what we'd had with dinner, but it would do. At the rate Sydney was gulping hers, she'd be done before I got halfway through my own glass.

"Hey, there's Anthony!" She set down her wine and started waving. "Anthony! Over here!"

So much for her irritation at me inviting him along. I looked where she was waving and saw that Anthony wasn't alone, that he had someone else with him, a guy around my age, maybe a few years older.

Tall…dark-haired…. I couldn't see the color of his eyes because of the dim lighting in the building, but even so my heart began to beat a little faster. No way it could be this easy….

"Hi," Anthony said as he approached the table. "This is Perry. I figured you wouldn't mind if I brought a friend, so we wouldn't turn out lopsided."

"No, that's great," Sydney said at once, giving me a significant look. "I'm Sydney, and this is Angela. Hi."

"Hi," Perry said, his gaze shifting toward me.

I found my voice. "Hi," I replied. "Um, let me get that purse off that chair—"

"It's cool," he said. "Looks like you two have already got your drinks, so my man Anthony and I'll go get our own and be back in a few."

"Okay," Sydney and I said together, and the guys grinned and then headed off toward the bar.

Once they were gone, she turned to me. "Oh. My. God. It's like he was served up on a platter for you."

It sort of felt that way. "He seems nice," I said cautiously.

"'He seems nice.' For fuck's sake, Angela, he is totally hot!" She tossed a lock of perfectly streaked dark blonde hair back over her shoulder. "I'm kind of jealous."

"Anthony is very cute, too," I pointed out. Most of the people who worked at Fire Mountain Wines were Native American, and so was Anthony, although I didn't know which one of the local tribes he was from. Yavapai, maybe.

"Oh, I know." She drank some wine. "You know me…I'm always distracted by the new and shiny."

"Well, I'd say Anthony falls in that category, considering you haven't even gone out with him yet. Give him a little time before you dump him and break his heart."

"I would *not*—" she began fiercely, but had to stop as the two guys approached. They were both carrying bottles of beer, but a local brew from Oak Creek Brewery in Sedona, not the cheap stuff. I had to approve.

Perry and Anthony sat down, and although I was feeling sort of awkward and tongue-tied, not sure what I should say, they both started talking about the band, how they'd gone to high school with the drummer. As I'd guessed, they were local but several years older than Sydney and I. Maybe I should've remembered them from school, but, as Sydney had pointed out, I'd kept my head down through high school and had barely talked to guys in my own class, let alone an exalted upperclassman. And although she'd been far more popular, even a popular freshman generally didn't hang out with the seniors.

Slowly, though, I got drawn into the conversation, drinking wine, sharing some laughs about Cottonwood High, until the band went on stage and it got a little too loud to talk. They were good, too, a crazy fusion of bluegrass and punk that somehow seemed to work. I finished my wine, and Perry offered to get me another one. Even though I knew I should be pacing myself, I told him sure, that sounded great. Anthony went along with him to get refills for himself and Sydney.

"Aren't you glad you didn't stay home and sulk?" she half-shouted at me.

I nodded, since I didn't feel like having to scream my reply. But that seemed to satisfy her, since she nodded in return, smiling, a smile that only widened as the guys returned with the next round of drinks.

And that was how the night went, alcohol flowing, music pounding. It felt good to get lost in it, to get carried away by the false euphoria all that alcohol brought. I suppose that was why I didn't question him when Perry suggested we step outside to get some fresh air, even as Sydney giggled at me from within the curve of Anthony's arm as he nuzzled her neck.

It had been a mild day, but nights got cold fast in the high country, and I shivered as we went outside.

"It'll be warmer in my truck," Perry said, and I nodded. Sure, why not?

He had a big Ford F-250. I climbed up into the cab and shut the door behind me. The temperature in there was marginally warmer than outside, but I didn't have much time to point out that fact. The second we were alone, Perry sort of launched himself at me, pulling me against him, pressing his mouth against mine. He tasted of beer, which I found I didn't mind as much as I thought I would. And although I didn't feel any of the roaring heat of a consort match in our touch of lip on lip, I still thought I liked him kissing me, his hands tangling in my hair.

I wondered if this was how my mother had managed it. Had she gotten herself numb with alcohol, gone out and met some halfway presentable guy and surrendered her V-card, as Sydney put it, so she wouldn't have to be burdened with the weight of being the McAllisters' *prima?* I had no way of knowing, of course, since she was gone before I could ask her a single question or even say my first word.

Maybe that was what I should do—let this Perry, whose last name I didn't even know, push me down on the bench seat, pull down my jeans and take my virginity away, take the responsibility of being *prima* from me as well.

His eyes glittered in the lights along the side of the building that illuminated the parking lot. I saw that they were blue, pale blue, not deep green, and something in my stomach twisted then, telling me this was wrong, all wrong, and I pushed against him, trying to wriggle away from the hands that were gripping my arms. He was strong, fingers browned and callused. Maybe he worked in construction, or maybe at one of the ranches on the edge of town.

"What's the matter?" he asked, voice coaxing. "You don't want to do it here? That's okay...my place isn't far."

"No—no, I can't. I shouldn't be here." I struggled against him, and those rough hands only tightened on my biceps.

The pale eyes narrowed. "What kind of bull-shit is this? You let me buy you drinks all night, and then you won't even give me a little something in exchange?"

I wrenched an arm free. "You want me to pay you back? I've got money inside, in my purse."

"That's not what I want," he growled, and began to haul me toward him by the one arm he still held.

Not thinking of anything except the need to get away from him, I cried, "Blessed Brigit, give me the strength to be free!"

White-hot light shot from my arm, striking Perry in the chest. He slumped backward against the driver-side door, eyes wide open, mouth slack. Half sobbing, half gasping, I hurled myself out of the truck and ran back inside, ignoring the curious stares of the small clumps of people who were standing out in the parking lot and smoking. The music had started up again, and the beat pounded against my eardrums as I pushed through the crowd and came back to the table, where Sydney and Anthony were busily sucking face.

"I have to go," I gasped, and yanked my purse off the back of the chair where it had been hanging by its strap.

Sydney pushed herself away from Anthony and fixed a bleary gaze on me. "You what?" Her eyes tracked past me and seemed to notice I was alone. "Where's Perry?"

"He's, um, out in his truck." Well, that was true enough.

That seemed to satisfy her. "Oh, okay." Then she focused on me again. "You sure you're all right to drive?"

I was pretty sure I wasn't, but I also knew I couldn't stay here. What if Perry was dead? No, I couldn't believe that. I'd struck out in self-defense, but not with the sort of focused intent that actually killing someone would require. He was just uncon-scious. He'd wake up in a few hours and feel like crap. That's all.

Or so I tried to convince myself, in my less than lucid state.

"Oh, sure, I can drive," I told her. "Anyway, I know that road so well I could drive it asleep and blindfolded. I'm fine."

"Okay," she replied, sounding dubious, but since she was in even worse shape than I, obviously she wouldn't offer up any more protests.

"Call you tomorrow," I said. "'Bye, Anthony."

"Mmm...'bye," he replied absently, and returned to burying his face in Sydney's neck as she giggled and reached for her wine.

That was my cue to leave. I went back outside and hurried over to the Jeep. Part of me wanted to stop at Perry's truck and make sure he was okay, but I'd already attracted enough attention. I just wanted to go home and forget this evening ever happened.

Since he was parked in the space closest to the driveway, I did get close enough to see that the windows of his F-250 were starting to fog up. That had to be a good sign. At least it meant he was breathing.

Thus reassured, I turned left on Mingus Avenue and headed back up to the highway. The speed limits around here were low enough that I didn't feel too challenged, even though I had to keep blinking to prevent the streetlights from blurring around me, obscuring the road ahead. That wasn't the alcohol, though.

Those were tears.

Biting my lip, I maneuvered the Jeep around the last traffic circle before 89A headed up into the hills. Off to my right I could see the glaring white lights of the Clarkdale cement plant, but then they were obscured by the black bulk of the mountain as the road began to twist its way up toward Jerome.

I slowed down; there wasn't anyone behind me to care that I was going at least five miles an hour below the speed limit. These roads didn't get patrolled that often, except during the holidays or when Jerome hosted a big event such as the Halloween dance. I figured I could make it home safely as long as I maintained my death grip on the steering wheel and kept every ounce of focus on the road.

The curve for the final approach up into town appeared a few yards ahead. Standing in the middle of the road was a dark figure—a man in an overcoat, as far as I could tell. Adrenaline surged through me, and I jammed on the brakes, screeching to a stop as the acrid scent of burning rubber hit my nostrils. I blinked, and he was gone.

Oh, Jesus. Had I hit him? Hands shaking, I put the Jeep in park and got out, tottering over the uneven asphalt to the spot where I had seen the man standing, sure I would find a crumpled body in the roadway, blood…something.

But there was no one. A cold wind blew from the northeast, pulling at my hair, biting through the utterly inadequate pashmina shawl that had been a Yule gift from my Great-Aunt Ruby. I stumbled over to the side of the road, wondering if maybe the man had jumped out of the way and was lying in the brush there, but again nothing. The road was utterly deserted, lifeless and without movement, except for the tire smoke swirling in front of the Jeep's headlights.

I knew I couldn't keep standing there. Even though by then it was almost two in the morning, someone might still come up the road to Jerome, whether that was their destination, or whether they'd be heading up and over Mingus Mountain on their way to Prescott.

So I got back in the truck and drove off, still shivering, wondering who I had actually seen...or what.

CHAPTER THREE

Hamburgers and Hauntings

"YOU WERE OUT VERY LATE LAST NIGHT," AUNT RACHEL SAID the next morning over breakfast.

I pushed my eggs around on my plate. "The band didn't start until almost ten."

She lifted an eyebrow but said nothing, and instead sipped at her green tea.

Strange that I didn't feel more hung over, considering how many glasses of wine I'd consumed the night before, but maybe that jolt of adrenaline as I was driving home had shocked the alcohol right out of my system. Nothing strange had happened after that, though; I'd maneuvered the Jeep up the final curves of the road before coming into Jerome proper, then turning down the side street that allowed access to the carport behind our building. All had been quiet and dark as I crept inside, as I had expceted it to be. My aunt often stayed up until midnight, since the store didn't open until ten, but two o'clock was kind of extreme even for her.

My brain also kept picking at the little problem of Anthony's friend Perry, slumped over in his truck. I thought he was *probably* all right, but I didn't know for sure. And even though I kept checking my phone, I hadn't heard anything yet from Sydney. Normally that wouldn't have bothered me too much, since she tended to be a late sleeper even when she wasn't up until all hours the night before. Now, though, I kept wondering why she hadn't called...and being half-way glad. If something catastrophic had happened, surely she would have texted or called or emailed. Something.

"You're very quiet," my aunt said.

"Just tired, I guess. I'm not used to staying up that late."

Her hazel eyes regarded me carefully. I hated it when she looked at me like that, as if she were trying to unearth whatever secrets I might have buried in my soul. But she was a witch, not a clairvoyant, and so she couldn't really do that. I hoped.

She seemed as if she were about to reply, but just then we heard the buzzing of the door chime, the one at the back entrance, not the main shop. Her gaze flickered up to the clock above the doorway. Nine-thirty. A little early for visitors, but maybe Tobias was stopping by for something. No, that wasn't right. Aunt Rachel had given him a key more than a year ago. He always gave a quick knock to let us know he was there, and then opened the door with the key.

Not that we witches generally needed keys, but it felt more polite to do it that way than just come barging in.

"I'll get the door," she said. "You go ahead and finish your breakfast."

After setting her napkin down on the kitchen table, she got up from her chair and headed down the short flight of stairs that led to our apartment's private entrance. I heard her open the door and greet someone, followed by the rumble of an unknown man's voice. Then she said, "This way," and mounted the steps, someone larger and heavier obviously behind her.

She came into the kitchen, a man in the dark blue uniform of the Cottonwood police department a few steps behind her. I swallowed. This couldn't be good.

I'd never had a run-in with the Cottonwood police before, not even a parking ticket. I knew Deputies Sandoval and Murphy with the Yavapai County sheriff's office, since Jerome was in their patrol area, but the grim-faced man staring down at me was someone I'd never seen before.

Pushing away my plate, I got to my feet. "Officer?"

He took a small pad of paper out of his pocket, along with a ballpoint pen. "You are Angela Diane McAllister, currently residing at 129B Main Street, Jerome, Arizona?"

"Yes," I replied past the lump in my throat. Part of me wanted to point out that it was sort of obvious that was my residence, since we were all currently standing in it, but I resisted the impulse. There were still a lot of things I didn't know about how the world worked, but even I knew that smart-mouthing a police officer was generally not a good idea.

"And were you at Main Stage in Cottonwood last night between the hours of 10 p.m. and 1:30 a.m.?"

I nodded miserably.

My aunt spoke up then. "What is this about, Officer?"

His gaze barely flickered away from me as he replied, "Ma'am, we have a report that this young lady assaulted a young man in his vehicle. Bruised him up pretty bad, although the hospital says none of his ribs were cracked." The policeman's dark eyes narrowed. "You want to tell me about that?"

"Yes, Angela, tell us about that," Aunt Rachel said, her voice sharper than I had ever heard it.

I took in a breath, expelled it, then said, "Look, I know it was stupid to go with Perry to his truck, but he got totally out of control. I had to defend myself."

"And do you have any evidence that your assault on Perry Haynes was in fact self-defense?"

Actually, I did, although I'd tried to cover it up by wearing a long-sleeved shirt, an embroidered tunic from India that I'd picked up in Sedona a few years ago. I pushed up the bell-shaped sleeve hiding my left arm, revealing an angry ring of bruises, purple and dark red, on my bicep.

I heard my aunt gasp, even as the officer said calmly, "Both arms?"

In grim silence I let the one sleeve drop and pushed up the other so he could see that the marks were in fact on both arms, although the bruises on my right arm were placed a little lower.

Without saying anything, he put the pad of paper back in his pocket. After a slight pause, he asked, "Do you want to press charges?"

I blinked. "Do I—?" Then I shook my head. "No. It was just a stupid misunderstanding. He got rough because he'd had one too many beers, and I guess I pushed back on him harder than I thought I did. No harm, no foul, right?"

For a few seconds he was silent. "You are within your rights to press charges, Miss McAllister."

"No, really, that's all right. I'd rather just forget it happened."

"That's your prerogative. In the future, you might want to consider how much you have to drink…and who you're drinking with." He inclined his head toward my aunt. "Ma'am. Sorry for disturbing you. I'll let myself out."

His heavy tread moved down the stairs. Less than a minute later, I heard the sound of the door closing, not slammed, but with a solid *thunk*.

Aunt Rachel stared at me, arms crossed over her chest. Normally I would have described her looks as softly rounded, still very pretty, with her lively hazel eyes and full mouth that always seemed on the verge of smiling. No hint of a smile there now; her lips were pressed together in a thin line.

I didn't want to meet her angry gaze, but I wasn't a child she could punish.

I was the next *prima*.

"It was just a misunderstanding," I said at last, my voice quiet. "Perry had too much to drink, and I guess he got the wrong impression from me. He—"

"And just how did he get that impression? Because you spent the night drinking with him, went with him to his truck? What did you think was going to happen?"

"I don't know," I replied, a sulky note slipping into my tone despite my best efforts to keep it away. "I guess I didn't think it would go that far. I thought—"

"I think it's pretty clear that you didn't think at all. Angela, you cannot put yourself in such situations. Think of what could have happened—"

"What, that I might've lost that precious virginity you all've been hiding and hoarding like it's gold bars at Fort Knox?"

She went still then, hand reaching down to grasp a fold of the lively broomstick skirt she wore, as if by doing so she could prevent herself from letting go an outburst she might regret later. After a visible pause, she said calmly, "We only want what's best for you. We want you to be safe."

"Maybe so, but you have to stop treating me like a child! I'm not a child—I can vote and drink and do everything an adult is supposed to do…except make my own decisions about my future." My voice was rising, and I knew I should try to control it, but I was tired and my head ached, and I just wanted to say what I felt for once. "I couldn't even go to the college I wanted to, because oh, no, that's in Wilcox territory. Everything I do is managed and bounded in this little box here in Jerome. I can't go shopping by myself… to the movies by myself. Goddess, I'm surprised you even let me go to the bathroom by myself!"

With that parting shot I turned and stomped up the stairs, then marched into my room and slammed the door. An empty act, really, since we had to open the shop in less than ten minutes, and as angry as I might have been, I wasn't going to make my aunt try to manage the store on her own. Not on a busy Saturday on the sort of mild October weekend that brought up all the day-trippers from Phoenix and beyond.

And isn't that you, I thought then with some spite. *You can't even make a grand gesture without worrying about how it's going to affect someone else.*

It was going to be a very long day.

———

We maintained a frosty silence for most of the morning. Then I saw a flash of bright blue as someone snagged the prime parking space in front of the store, and realized it was Sydney in the Ford Focus her parents had bought her as her high school graduation present.

Uh-oh, I thought, and risked a quick glance at Aunt Rachel just as Sydney came inside, string of temple bells jingling from the front door as it closed behind her.

Once again I saw that thinning of my aunt's mouth, but she said pleasantly enough, "Hi, Sydney. What brings you up here today?"

Sydney shot an anxious glance in my direction. "Um, I was wondering if I could borrow Angela for lunch? I know she usually only gets a half-hour, but—"

"It's fine," my aunt replied, although her voice sounded strained. "I'm sure you two have a good deal to talk about."

Sydney's expression clouded, but I didn't give the exchange a chance to go any further, instead slipping out from behind the jewelry counter and saying, "Sounds great. I'm starving—let's go up to Haunted Hamburger, okay?"

I took my friend by the arm and steered her back out of the store. Once we were a few paces away, she said, "Oh, my God, Angela, I am so sorry—"

"Not here," I broke in. Not that the patio of the Haunted Hamburger would be much better, but I had to hope that anyone overhearing us there would probably be tourists who had no idea of what was really going on.

At least she got the hint. "Okay."

We walked down the street for a block and then cut up to the next street by using the stairs located at the park. Jerome was like that, built in terraces on the side of Cleopatra Hill, and although you could go the long way around if you didn't want to take the stairs, why bother?

The place was crowded, but we were able to get a table out on the patio. Normally the view out over the Verde Valley was enough to distract me for at least a minute or two, but I had more important things on my mind right then.

"Oh, God, Angela, I had *no* idea that Perry guy was going to be such a douche! He came pounding on Anthony's door at, like, eight in the morning, saying he was going to have you arrested for assault or something, and—"

"You spent the night at Anthony's house?" I interrupted.

Red flared along her cheekbones, underneath the pink blush she was wearing. "Well, I really wasn't in any shape to drive, and he said I could crash, so I went home with him, and, well, you know how it is."

No, I don't, I thought wearily. All I said, though, was, "So Perry showed up this morning—"

"Yes, banging on the door, saying how he'd spent all night in his truck and almost froze to death or something, which is just stupid because it wasn't even close to freezing last night, and that you'd assaulted him, and please, the guy has to have sixty or seventy pounds on you, so how could you have done that?"

Since she'd paused to take a breath, I said, "Well, I sort of did, but only because he wouldn't take no for an answer."

Her blue eyes widened. I didn't talk much about spells and powers and all that around Sydney, mostly because those exact details were something we witches preferred to keep private, and partly because I didn't want to scare her off by revealing too much. She thought the whole "McAllister witch" thing was pretty cool, but probably because she didn't have the whole story. Maybe an eighth of the story, if that.

"So you, what"—her voice lowered—"put the whammy on him or something?"

That word made me laugh, despite the situation. "No, I just…called on someone to give me the strength to fight him off. And according to the police, he's bruised, but that's about it, so he doesn't have all that much to complain about, considering…"

I hesitated, then looked around at the crowded tables to either side. One family was arguing whether to continue up the mountain to the hiking trails and picnic area or to go over to the Tuzigoot Indian ruins, and at another table a mother kept telling her daughter that no, she wasn't getting soda, so it was milk or nothing. Obviously they weren't paying any attention to the two girls at the far table having a *sotto voce* conversation, probably about boys or something equally uninteresting. So I pushed up one sleeve and showed her the band of bruises around my arm, then just as quickly tugged my sleeve back down.

"Holy shit, Angela, he did that to you?"

"I told you he wouldn't take no for an answer."

The conversation was interrupted then by Eileen, the waitress on duty that day, coming out to take our orders. Since I'd been to the Haunted Hamburger hundreds of times, I already knew what I wanted and ordered a barbecue burger and fries, along with an iced tea. Sydney shot me an envious look but still only ordered a charbroiled chicken salad.

After Eileen had left, Sydney remarked, "It is so not fair. You must have the metabolism of a hummingbird or something."

"Or something," I replied with a shrug. My mother had always looked thin in the few pictures I had seen of her, so maybe that was where I got it from. At least I had something of a chest, despite being thin, although nothing as eye-catching as Sydney's curvaceous frame.

"Anyway," she plowed on, "you said 'according to the police.' Did you a file a report on him?"

"No, he tried to do that to me. But once I showed the officer the bruises Perry left behind, they dropped the whole thing."

"You should've had him arrested."

"What's the point? I think he learned his lesson, and we're all about not attracting attention, you know? Bad enough that it went there at all."

Her mouth drooped. "I am so, so sorry about that. Anthony seemed like a nice guy. Who knew he'd be friends with such a dickbag? I won't see him again, if that's what you want."

At once I shook my head. "Why would I want that? Do you like Anthony?"

"Yes. I mean, I think so. He was super nice to me last night, and he's, well—"

"I don't need to hear the gory details." I tried to keep my tone light, but I didn't know how successful I was. Despite my best efforts to suppress it, a flicker of jealousy licked through me. It was so easy for her. Meet a cute guy, go out, spend the night. No baggage, unless you wanted there to be. I knew there was more to it than that, but seriously, I was kind of tired of feeling like the last virgin in the Verde Valley.

"Okay," she said at once. "I just mean that we've been friends for a long time, and if it was going to be weird for you—"

"It's fine. You've been wanting to go out with Anthony for a while now. I hope it works out. Just don't ask me to go on a double date with you guys and Perry."

She actually laughed at that, and a short time later Eileen reappeared with our food and drinks—apologizing about the wait for the tea, but that things had gotten a little crazy in the kitchen. I assured her it was no problem, and she told us thanks before hurrying back inside to pick up another order.

For a few minutes both Sydney and I were silent as we plowed into our food. Yes, my aunt had fed me a decent breakfast that morning, but all the stress and nervous energy that followed the police officer's visit had pretty much burned up any calories it had provided. Even though I felt like inhaling my burger,

I tried to keep my chewing to a more or less decorous pace.

After we both slowed down a bit, Sydney gave a furtive look around and asked, "Is *she* here?"

"'She' who?" I returned, although I knew exactly what she was talking about.

"You know. The *ghost.*"

There was a reason why the Haunted Hamburger was called that. Many of the buildings in Jerome had their own resident spirits, and the restaurant was no exception. Four ghosts actually haunted the property, two of them tradesmen who'd been killed when the scaffolding they were working on collapsed, one a miner who'd had a heart attack and died there purely by accident. Then there was Edith, the "she" Sydney was asking about. Edith had lived in the flat on the second floor and killed herself when her fiancé confessed to her that he'd been visiting some of the prostitutes down on Hull Avenue. Needless to say, she was not a very happy ghost.

"Well, this is her home," I pointed out. "So she's always here."

Sydney shot a furtive glance over one shoulder. "Okay, but is she *here* here?"

"She's not out on the patio waiting to steal one of your croutons, if that's what you're asking." I paused and looked up toward the second story of the building. A pale face glimmered behind one of the windows and disappeared. "I think she's upstairs, so you don't have anything to worry about."

A lift of her shoulders in a shiver. "I still don't know how you can stand seeing them. I mean, doesn't it freak you out?"

Good question. I'd started seeing the ghosts soon after my tenth birthday. In fact, at first I hadn't even realized that the kindly Chinese gentleman I was talking to down in the alley actually was a ghost until my aunt had come outside to put out the trash and asked me who on earth I was speaking to.

The truth came out then, and that was when Aunt Ruby declared that I was in fact the next *prima*, and this great talent only proved it. All *primas* had some kind of talent that tended to manifest itself around that age, although I really didn't see what good there was in being able to talk to dead people.

I sort of got the impression that Sydney thought my life must be like that scene out of *Ghost* where Whoopi Goldberg's character was surrounded by specters wherever she went. It wasn't like that at all, though. They approached me if they had something to say—like my first encounter with Mr. Hong outside the English Kitchen. I'd been playing in the street, and he came out to scold me for not being careful, warning me that I could get run over by a car. Over the years I'd interacted with most of them, although some, like Edith here, were quite reclusive.

Every once in a while I could pry some information out of the spirits if necessary, but most of them, with the exception of Maisie, weren't all that chatty. Even she hadn't really approached me until I hit junior high. I think before then she'd thought I was too young to bother speaking with. True, talking to her could be entertaining, and since neither she nor any of the ghosts were gruesome in appearance—they just looked like regular people to me, albeit in wildly outdated clothes—I didn't see much in them to be afraid of.

Not everyone had the same opinion of them, of course.

I popped a french fry in my mouth and chewed it carefully before answering Sydney's question. "No, it really doesn't freak me out. They're just…a different kind of people who live in Jerome, I guess. They can't hurt anybody. Not really," I added, since some of them did like to play pranks on both tourists and residents. But slamming doors or stealing hammers didn't exactly qualify as *Exorcist* material. No matter how many times I pointed that out to Sydney, though, she never seemed to quite grasp it.

"If you say so." But she still looked up at the window, although it was empty now, reflecting nothing but blue sky with a few high, thin clouds.

"Anyway," I said, since I thought staring up at Edith's window was kind of rude, and would probably only result in the ghost moving elsewhere even less to Sydney's liking, "I think it's a good thing that the next big event is the dance here in Jerome, since I have a feeling my aunt isn't going to be too thrilled about me making any solo expeditions to Cottonwood any time soon. You might have to bring the dresses here for me to look at instead of me going to your house, but let's see how it goes."

"No problem. Maybe on Wednesday? I should be able to pick them up by then, and I don't work on Wednesday." She worked part-time at a beauty supply store in town.

"Sounds great," I replied, and we ate and talked about the dance some more. Sydney didn't give me any flak about taking orders from Aunt Rachel, even though I was an adult and not some high school kid who could still get grounded. Even though my best friend didn't completely understand what was at stake, she knew my aunt and liked her, and understood that Aunt Rachel wouldn't clamp down for no reason. It had been a close call last night.

Too close.

I came back from lunch a little before one and took over at the store so my aunt could go get her own lunch. She gave me a piercing look before she left, but I didn't get the impression that she was still angry with me…more like worried, or even afraid. Afraid of what, I wasn't sure. After my experience with Perry the night before, I certainly wasn't eager to go back out and test any boundaries.

She only stayed away for a half-hour, which was good, since the tourists were definitely out in force that day. Not that I minded; they kept me busy, and when I was busy I didn't have much time to think. The money was nice, too, of course, although none of us really needed it. Our homes had been paid for long ago, and the family sat on wealth that had been carefully accumulated during the boom years and then invested just as carefully in the leaner times that followed, when the mine was shut down and most of the non-witch population of Jerome moved on to greener pastures. The clan elders watched over the investments and made quiet payments to all the clan's members. Of course we were free to earn what we liked on top of that—and we did—but basic survival was never a worry.

As we were locking up, Aunt Rachel said, "I had planned to go over to Tobias's tonight, but—"

"You should go," I told her. "I'm not going any-where, believe me. Well, maybe up to Grapes to get a pizza if we're not having dinner at home, but that's it. I'll watch some Netflix or something."

Her brow puckered a little at that. She was not a fan of television—we didn't even own one—but she couldn't really keep me from streaming videos on my computer. That is, *she* couldn't. The connection up here wasn't always the best. But the weather was clear, so it should be all right. And if not, I had plenty of books to read. Books had been my companions through most of my youth, until I was finally allowed to have a computer when I entered eighth grade.

"All right," she said at last. "But I'll just be down at Tobias's, so…." She trailed off and gave me an uncertain look, as if she wasn't quite sure what sort of catastrophe might befall me but wanted to make sure I knew she'd be around to help head it off if necessary.

"And I've got Floyd Barnett on one side and Cousin Rosemary on the other, so unless you know something and I don't, and Armageddon is set to happen tonight, I really think I'll be fine."

A smile then, albeit a weary one. "You're right, of course. And you know how to take care of yourself, but after last night—"

"I still took care of myself. I just did it in a way that the Cottonwood P.D. didn't appreciate very much." *And did it while practically blind drunk,* I thought, but I knew better than to say anything else.

"True." She reached under the counter and pulled out her purse. "You can finish locking up?"

"Sure thing." I'd done it many times, but tonight her allowing me to manage the important task of

securing the store seemed to take on an extra signif-
icance, as if she was trying to show that she still did
trust me, despite my foolishness at Main Stage the
night before.

She nodded and headed toward the back of the
shop and the rear exit. Tobias's combination house/
studio was at the extreme southern edge of the town,
right before the houses petered out and the highway
took over, but I knew she'd walk it anyway. Everyone
walked in Jerome. Why do anything else when the
place was less than half a mile from end to end?

We'd locked the front door promptly at six, so all
that remained was for me to empty the cash register and put the money and credit card receipts in the
safe. Twice a week we'd go down the hill to deposit
the cash at the Wells Fargo in Cottonwood, but we
wouldn't be doing that again until Monday.

This wasn't the first time I'd been left alone in
the store at the end of the day, but for some reason
a flicker of unease passed over me, a chill, although
I knew that, unlike many of Jerome's buildings, the
one that housed both the store and the two-story
apartment where Aunt Rachel and I lived was free of
any ghosts or spirits. Although the frightening memory had danced in and out of my thoughts several
times during the day, I'd never had a real opportunity
to mention the dark figure I'd seen in the bend in the
road the night before.

To be perfectly truthful, I'd begun to wonder if I'd imagined the whole thing. Sydney had once told me a story about her older brother, who was attending Arizona State University, driving home slightly wasted from a party one night and hallucinating a wall stretching across the freeway. The shock had kept him awake and alert the rest of the drive home. Maybe my brain had done the same thing to me, inventing someone standing in the road to keep me from falling asleep at the wheel.

Never mind that I hadn't felt sleepy at all, charged up as I was from the confrontation with Perry.

Well, talk it over with Aunt Rachel tomorrow, I told myself. *You're certainly safe here, so don't worry about it. Just get that money put away so you can go get a pizza before they get too crowded.*

That sounded sensible enough. I gathered up the money bag and stack of receipts, and headed back to the storeroom, which was also where we kept the safe. Even with my own no-nonsense words ringing in my head, I still made sure to flick on the lights in the back of the shop as I went. All right, so I turned them on with a quick impulse from my mind, rather than my finger. There wasn't anyone around to see what I was doing. Besides, my hands were full. And I did the same thing with the lock to the storeroom door, opening it without a key and letting it swing inward.

The storeroom wasn't all that large, maybe ten by fifteen feet, with boxes stacked neatly against the wall and a couple of forlorn mannequins set in one corner. In the winter we'd pull them out when it was time to display the handwoven shawls and cloaks that went over big as holiday presents, but in the meantime they'd been stuck back in here with the rest of the display items we weren't currently using. Their blank eyes seemed to watch me as I bent down and entered the combination to the safe, then set the money bag and stack of rubber-banded receipts inside.

So now I was letting a couple of pieces of fiberglass get to me? I shook my head at myself and closed the safe, then straightened up before heading toward the open door. For a second I thought I saw a shadow moving outside in the hallway, and again a shiver traced its way down my spine. Then I realized it had to be someone walking down the sidewalk outside the shop. The sun was just beginning to go down behind Mingus Mountain, and the light was chancy, uncertain.

You're being just a bit too jumpy for a girl who talks to ghosts, I chided myself before I exited the storeroom and closed the door behind me. It would lock automatically; we had keys, of course, but Aunt Rachel and I rarely used them—mainly if there were enough customers in the shop that they'd notice something strange if we went in the room without unlocking the door first.

I kept my purse on a shelf under the counter, so I retrieved that and double-checked to make sure the front door was locked as well. Of course it was, so I threw my purse over my shoulder and began to walk toward the short hallway that led to the rear entrance. Once again I thought I saw a shadow move against the wall, tinted golden with the last rays of the sun.

Without stopping to think, I turned around. A dark figure stood in front of the door to the shop. It was about the size and shape of a tall man, although I couldn't see any details. Not like any ghost I'd met so far in Jerome—they all tended to look to me the same way they must have in their previous lives. And then I felt it, a wave of cold, of malice, as it waited there, seeming to watch me, though it had no eyes.

Still, I'd been talking to ghosts since I was a child, and although this apparition looked like none I'd ever seen before, I thought I should at least attempt to make contact. "Who are you?" I asked, making sure my voice was calm, steady.

Nothing. It stood there, the air around it feeling twenty degrees colder than it should have. I was surprised that frost didn't start forming on the shop window behind it.

Fine. I'd try another tack. I stared at it, trying to look more or less where its eyes should be. "What do you want?"

For a few seconds it did not respond. Then one shadowy arm lifted, and it was as if a finger pointed directly at me. The reply came in a whisper, soft and chilling as the rustle of leaves in a graveyard.

You.

CHAPTER FOUR

A Binding

I DIDN'T STOP TO THINK. INSTINCT TOOK OVER, AND I WAS bolting toward the back of the shop, running down the corridor, until I reached the back door and flung it open, then slammed it behind me. Yes, I know—some way for the next *prima* of the McAllisters to act. But I'd never seen or heard of anything like that before, and had no idea of how to fight it or dispel it. The smartest thing seemed to be to put some distance between it and myself.

Once I was outside, I felt a little bit better, and retained enough presence of mind to lock the door before I hurried down the smaller, less-traveled street that backed up to our building, then cut back up to Main. Although most of the stores closed at six, there were still a good number of people out and around, either on their way back to their cars or heading for an early dinner. As soon as I had people around me, some of the cold and dread seemed to leave me, although my hands were still shaking.

No thought now of getting a pizza to go and taking it back to the apartment over the store. I knew I should probably high-tail it down to Tobias's place and get my aunt, tell her what had just happened, but I hated to bother her, especially after the run-in we'd had this morning. Besides, I was supposed to be the next *prima*—shouldn't I be trying to figure these things out on my own? Aunt Rachel would find out soon enough; she might be spending the evening with Tobias, but she wouldn't stay over for the night. She never left me alone, not for that long.

So I continued walking up toward Grapes. I still needed to eat, one way or another, and better to do it in a familiar place surrounded by other people.

As I'd feared, the restaurant was crowded, but a group was just being seated outside as another party was leaving their table, and so I was able to snag that one. Normally I would've just sat at the bar and not kept a whole table to myself, but I wanted to snug in against the wall and feel something solid at my back. And apparently Linda, who was tending the bar and also doing traffic control, saw something in my face, because she didn't even suggest that I not take that table.

"Rough day, huh?" asked Tina, the server who came up to check on me.

I knew her, of course, just like I knew everyone in Jerome, but she felt a little closer than some because she'd babysat me from time to time back when I was in elementary school. Neither she nor Linda were part of the clan, although as long-time residents, they knew about the McAllisters. Like Sydney, though, they could be trusted to keep our secrets. A quiet vetting process went on in our town every time a house or apartment became available. We made sure that no one moved in whom we couldn't trust. It was a quiet spell, but an effective one, the charm that brought sympathetic souls to us.

"Rough day," I echoed. "Yeah, you could say that. A glass of the Plungerhead, please?" I hadn't bothered to look at the menu; I could probably recite it by heart at this point.

"Got it. Know what you want to eat?"

I shook my head. "Not yet. Pizza, yes, but I haven't decided which one."

She shot me a reassuring smile, then said, "I'll get that wine for you right away."

Goddess knew what was on my face right then, but I didn't much care. It just felt good to be there, surrounded by familiar smells and friendly faces. About half the crowd was made up of tourists, but everyone seemed to be having a good time, so the energy was good...a far cry from what had been emanating from that entity back at the shop.

Another shiver, and I clenched my hands on the tabletop. No ghost like any I'd ever seen, but maybe the ghosts themselves would have some input. Normally I wouldn't bother Maisie on a Saturday night, since she didn't like crowds. In this case, though, I didn't think I had much of a choice. I would have to try coaxing her out, see if she'd heard anything.

Felt anything.

I crossed my arms and wished I'd brought a jacket. Not much chance of that happening when I was bolting from the store like a frightened hare. Anyway, the chill moving through me right now didn't have much to do with the air temperature, although I knew it would get cold outside damn quick once the sun was down. That walk over to rustle up Maisie would not be a comfortable one...and it would only be colder when I walked down to Tobias's house.

But I wasn't completely unprepared. Aunt Rachel had taught me a long time ago to always carry a scarf or wrap of some kind in my purse, so I reached in and pulled out the same pashmina I'd worn the night before. The bright emerald green wasn't the best match with the pale blue top I wore, but I wasn't trying to impress anybody.

I heard the door to the restaurant open, but I didn't bother to look up. No, I stared down at the chipped polish on my nails and vaguely wondered when I'd have the time to take it off, and then tried to figure out why I even cared. I had much bigger things to worry about at the moment.

Someone approached my booth and sat down without so much as a by-your-leave in the seat opposite me. I looked up, frowning, a frown that only deepened when I saw who it was. Adam McAllister, my third-or-fourth cousin, someone I really didn't feel like dealing with at the moment.

"Hey, Ange," he said. "Word on the street is that you've been looking for love in all the wrong places."

I blinked at him. "What?"

"I heard about your little 'incident' at Main Stage last night."

Damn. I'd almost forgotten about my scuffle with Perry in the parking lot the night before. "How the hell did you find out about that?"

"Alicia's working dispatch for the Cottonwood P.D., remember?"

Oh, right. Adam's big sister had gotten a job as a dispatcher for the police department about six months ago. It was a little out of character for a McAllister, since we tended to be artsy types who stuck around Jerome, but she wasn't a very strong witch. On the other hand, she was a hell of a gossip.

Working as a dispatcher was probably her dream job, since she got to hear everybody's business firsthand.

And obviously she'd heard all about my business last night. Sigh.

"It was just a misunderstanding," I said, and hoped Tina would come by with my wine soon.

"Must've been some misunderstanding, with him ending up in the hospital."

At least one wish was granted, because Tina did appear with my zinfandel, which she set down in front of me before sending a quizzical glance in Adam's direction. Naturally I'd said nothing about someone joining me...because I had no idea somebody would.

"A Corona for me," Adam said, and I had to keep myself from rolling my eyes. Typically tone-deaf of him to order a beer in a restaurant called "Grapes."

Maybe it would've been polite to wait until he had his beer before I drank any of my wine, but the hell with that. It wasn't as if I'd invited him to sit down or anything. So I picked up the little carafe Tina had brought me and poured about a third of it into my wine glass, then took a good swallow. Much better.

"Is there a point to all this, Adam?"

"I just don't know why you'd bother to pick up some civilian down in Cottonwood when you've got me right here."

I really did not need this right now. "I wasn't 'picking up' anyone. He's a friend of the guy Sydney was with. That's all."

"'All' doesn't usually end up with someone in the hospital and the Cottonwood P.D. paying you a visit."

"He got a little handsy, okay? Nothing I couldn't handle."

"I guess so." He grinned, and I really wished it was permissible for the future *prima* to sock someone in the jaw.

That wouldn't be dignified, though—and would definitely bring down Aunt Rachel's wrath—so I settled for asking in acid tones, "Is that the only reason you've invaded my space, or did you have some other reason for dropping in without an invitation?"

He shrugged. "It's a public place."

"The restaurant, yeah. Not the booth I just happen to be sitting in."

"Okay, you got me." He opened his mouth, as if he were about to say something else, but Tina arrived with his Corona and set it down in front of him.

"Ready to order?" she asked.

"Prosciutto and mozzarella for me," I told her.

"Italian meat," Adam said with a grin.

She shook her head slightly and headed back to the kitchen. I would have been even more annoyed by him ordering something besides just the beer, but I'd known I was doomed from the minute he sat down in my booth.

"So you were saying," I prompted.

He was in the middle of taking a swig from his Corona, and so I had to wait until he swallowed the beer. "I went by the shop first, but you'd already closed up."

"You did?" Despite my better instincts, I couldn't help asking. "Did you…notice…anything?"

"What was I supposed to notice? You weren't there. I'd already thought about getting a pizza to go, so I came up here and saw you through the window. And here we are."

Yes…unfortunately. In a way it was funny, because a lot of girls back in high school had had their crushes on Adam, and yet all he cared about was pursuing me, even though it was hopeless. We had no connection. It didn't matter that he was good-looking, with his thick brown hair and gray-blue eyes and nice strong chin. He wasn't my match, my soulmate, my other half. And I really wished he would figure that out once and for all, and leave me the heck alone.

More importantly, though, he'd gone by the shop and hadn't sensed anything, seen anything out of the ordinary. He wasn't an overly strong warlock, but normally he was sensitive to places, air currents, weather. If a weather spell needed to be cast, he was often the one to do it. Wouldn't he have been able to feel something terribly not right about the store if there really was some malignant presence lurking around the place?

I couldn't think of the right way to ask him, though. If I told him what had really happened, then he'd probably try to get all manly and protective, and that would almost be worse than the ghostly figure I'd seen.

No, scratch that. A guy trying to protect you when you really didn't want to be protected wasn't exactly on a par with some vaporous apparition reaching toward you and saying that it wanted you.

Maybe I shivered. Adam set down his beer and stared at me, eyes narrowing. "Are you okay? You look like you've seen—" He broke off, but I knew what he'd meant to say.

You look like you've seen a ghost.

Well, hey, that was nothing new. That was just something Angela McAllister did. I wished that was all I had seen. A ghost was fine. But this?

Not fine at all.

I took a few more swallows of wine. "It's nothing."

Adam was a lot of things, but stupid wasn't one of them. His gaze sharpened. "You don't look like it's nothing. What's going on?"

It would probably get out sooner or later anyway. We McAllisters didn't keep a lot from one another. "I saw…something."

"Saw what?"

"I don't know what it was. I've never seen anything like it. And I've seen my share of strange things."

"True." He shifted in his seat, and for a second or two I was worried he would try to reach out and touch my hand where it rested on the tabletop. He appeared to resist that impulse, though, and said, "But it scared you."

I didn't like to admit it, least of all to Adam, but he'd already seen the truth in my face. "It did. I had to get out of there. So I came here."

"What did you see?"

For a few seconds I didn't say anything, only ran a finger along the wood grain of the table. Even thinking about that shadowy apparition made a wave of cold move over me, a chill that had nothing to do with the warm, friendly surroundings in which I sat. "A shadow. It was standing in front of the door to the shop. I could feel it watching me. I thought it had to be some sort of spirit, even though I'd never met one like that before. I asked it who it was, and it didn't say anything. Then I asked what it wanted, and…" I paused again, and swallowed. "…And it told me, 'you.'"

Even Adam seemed shocked by that revelation. "Damn, Angela, you need to tell someone. Someone besides me, I mean."

"I know. I will. It's just that my aunt is over at Tobias's place, and I didn't want to bother her...."

"I don't think she'll mind being bothered." He hesitated. "I'll walk you over there, if you want."

Never did I think I would be so relieved by Adam McAllister offering to accompany me somewhere. But there were lots of dark and shadowy places between here and Tobias's house, and I forced myself to admit that I'd feel a whole lot better about the whole thing if I didn't have to walk it alone. "Okay," I replied. "I'd like that."

He grinned, and for a second I wished I hadn't agreed to him coming along after all. But then Tina showed up with our pizzas, and for a minute or two everything seemed normal and prosaic, just Adam and me dishing ourselves a slice, doling out the parmesan and the red pepper flakes. I knew better, though. There wasn't anything normal about any of this.

Still, now that I knew what I was doing after this, I felt a little better. I had no idea what Aunt Rachel was going to say, and it seemed as if my plan for talking to Maisie would have to be shelved for a while. She wasn't going anywhere, though, and I could always try to scare her up—so to speak—the next day.

Whether she'd have anything useful to contribute, I couldn't begin to guess.

The sun had long disappeared by the time Adam and I emerged from the restaurant. I pulled my wrap around my shoulders in a futile attempt to stave off some of the brisk wind blowing outside. At least it was coming from the south. Although I knew the Wilcoxes had little to do with it, a north wind, the kind that blew down from Flagstaff, always put me on edge. An ill wind, as Great-Aunt Ruby liked to say.

Adam noticed the somewhat flimsy pashmina, and I worried that he might try to make the gallant gesture of offering me his jacket. Something in my expression must have warned him off, though, and so he kept silent, walking next to me as we headed down Main Street. It was too early for that night's band to have started up at the Spirit Room, but the street in front of the bar was already lined with Harleys, and people hung around outside, chatting and smoking. Their presence comforted me, although I knew the crowds would thin out as we wended our way down the hill.

As they did. By the time we passed the Ghost City Inn, Adam and I were the only people on the sidewalk. Down here I could feel the wind even more strongly. The stars glittered against the black sky, and a thin moon had just begun to rise above the mesas to the east. It would be full on Halloween, I realized.

All around me were buildings and trees and cars I'd seen hundreds of times, and yet somehow now seemed foreign, unfamiliar. Part of me wanted to draw closer to Adam. I told myself that was foolish, for several reasons. I certainly didn't want to give him the wrong idea, and of the two of us, I was the far stronger witch. Having him come along had been sort of silly, in that respect, although of course the two of us working together would be more effective than even me casting a spell of protection alone.

He was silent, as if realizing I really didn't want to talk, and I felt a rush of warmth toward him then, that despite his usually irritating ways he understood my need for silence, my need to have someone walk with me through the darkness. For a second or two I found myself wishing things could be different. I was so very tired of having to look for someone who seemed to not even exist.

Tobias shared studio and living space with three other artists in a renovated commercial building on the edge of town. Each flat had its own entrance and kitchen and studio, so although they shared common walls, they were still very private. His was the one on the south side of the building—"I like the light"— and faced out over the lights of Cottonwood. In the daytime you could see the line of the Verde River from here, but now of course all was dark.

From the other side of the building I heard music and the sound of people talking. Susan Callery lived over there, and I'd heard her mention a small opening she was having, if I wanted to stop by. Between the mess at Main Stage the night before and my latest spectral sighting, I'd forgotten all about it.

Adam and I made our way down the winding path that led to Tobias's front door. Wind chimes jingled in the darkness, and I saw the prayer flags hanging from the trees outside his windows fluttering in the night wind. Out here, though, it seemed less oppressive, instead wild and free, and I felt my spirits lift a little.

As we approached the door—a massive thing of local twisted juniper, lovingly polished—I could hear laughter from within, and a pang went through me. I wished I didn't have to disturb my aunt on her night out, but I certainly didn't want to go back to the apartment without reinforcements that were somewhat more substantial than what Adam could offer.

So I raised my hand and knocked, then waited for a minute until Tobias opened the door. He held a wine glass in one hand and blinked down at me, his gaze traveling over to Adam and then back as if he couldn't quite figure out what was more strange—that I should be there at all, or that I was standing there with Adam McAllister next to me.

"Angela?" Tobias said at last.

"Hi, Tobias," I replied, attempting to sound breezy and probably failing miserably. "I need to talk to Aunt Rachel. Is that okay?"

He blinked again, then seemed to recover himself. "Of course, of course. The two of you come on in."

We both went inside, and waited as Tobias shut the door. The place was laid out with a small entryway, and then opened into a large combined living room/dining room/kitchen. The remains of dinner seemed to still occupy the dining room table, and off to my right I saw Aunt Rachel sitting on Tobias's large leather couch. A fire flickered in the freestanding fireplace near the far wall.

As soon as she saw us, she set down her own wine glass on the coffee table and got to her feet, her expression understandably puzzled. "Angela?" Her gaze flickered to Adam, and she frowned. She knew I wouldn't have dragged him down here without a very good reason. "What's the matter?"

"I—" Now that the time had come to explain what had happened, words seemed to fail me.

"She saw something, Rachel," Adam supplied.

Her hazel eyes widened. "Saw what?"

Tobias moved past us to stand near Aunt Rachel. "It couldn't have been good, to have you come walking all the way down here."

I found my voice. "No, it wasn't. It—there was something in the store, something…evil. Dark."

The lighting wasn't all that good in there, since the only real light on was the overhead fixture in the kitchen. Candles flickered on the dining room table and on the coffee table in the living room, and by their uncertain light I thought I saw her turn pale. But her tone was firm enough as she asked, "Do you know what it was?"

"No." I pulled the pashmina a little more closely around my shoulders, as if it could do anything to rid me of the pervasive sensation of cold that seemed to take over whenever I thought of the dark shape I'd seen in the store. "But…it wasn't the first time I'd seen it."

"What?" came in unison from both my aunt and Adam, and then they stared at one another in confusion.

Might as well come clean. The only way to attempt to figure out what was going on was to use all the available facts. "I saw it last night as I was driving home. It was standing in the last bend before the road curves up to town. Since it was so dark, I thought it was a person. I thought I'd hit somebody.

But when I got out, no one was there. And then today...." I trailed off, and swallowed.

"Today?" my aunt prompted.

"It was after you'd left, right after I put the money and the receipts away. I think maybe it was waiting."

"Waiting for what?"

"For me to be alone."

She watched me carefully, gaze fixed on me, as if we were the only two people in the room, as if Tobias and Adam didn't exist. "Go on."

"It was standing in front of the window. It was shaped like a man, but it had no detail...only shadow. And when I asked it what it wanted, it said it wanted...me."

Silence then, as she watched me, and Tobias watched her, and Adam stood beside me, not saying anything, either. I think he knew he'd done what I'd asked of him, and now it was time for the more important players to step in.

At last she said, "This is not good."

"I didn't think it was," I replied.

"Tobias, would you come up there with us?" she asked him, and he nodded grimly.

"I wouldn't let you go back without me."

After that he went and got his coat, and Rachel's as well, and we all went back outside. He didn't bother to lock his door. Jerome was sort of like that; the only reason we locked up the shop was all the merchandise inside, and the fact that it was right on the main drag.

Tobias and Aunt Rachel took the lead, with Adam and me bringing up the rear. Maybe I should have volunteered to go first, but I wasn't feeling very brave at the moment. They wouldn't have allowed it, anyway—their duty, as they saw it, was to protect the next *prima*.

We came up the back way, along Hull Avenue. As the three-story building loomed over us, black against black in the night, I swallowed. No, I didn't really feel anything back here, except the heebie-jeebies I was giving myself, but it was so very dark. We had a light we usually kept on at the back entrance, but of course I'd run away so quickly that turning it on had been about the last thing on my mind.

Aunt Rachel fished her keys out of her purse and unlocked the door. As she did so, I heard her murmuring under her breath, a spell of protection, of light. I guessed that was why she used her key—she wanted to save her energy for the protection spell. And the hallway lights did blaze forth as the door opened before us, showing the same short hallway I'd walked down thousands of times, with its scuffed tile and the warm sienna paint we'd applied two summers ago.

"Do you feel anything?" she asked Tobias.

He put his hand against the doorframe. Solid, natural materials were his strength—wood and stone, clay and tile. He shook his head. "No."

Apparently heartened by this reply, she stepped inside, with him following so closely they appeared joined at the hip. Adam and I followed. I put forth a mental plea for strength and vision, and sent my own questing tendril of thought down the corridor, out into the main shop space. I felt nothing, sensed nothing.

Then again, I hadn't sensed much until I'd seen that…thing…standing right in front of me.

The lights in the store turned themselves on at my aunt's silent request. Everything looked perfectly ordinary, perfectly normal, from the display of wind-chimes in one corner to the table loaded with books on local history in the other.

Aunt Rachel stopped in the middle of the space, eyes shut, and turned slowly with her arms out-stretched. This was something I could sense—the ripples of power moving out from her, the glow of her spirit as it attempted to find something wrong with the very fabric of the world. Her talent had always been order, knowing when the peace and calm of the community were somehow being disrupted. It was a quiet strength, but an important one.

At last she opened her eyes, but I saw no relief in them. She was frowning, and I saw her teeth worry at her bottom lip. "I felt it...very faint, but some-thing...wrong. Distorted, cold. Hungry."

That last word sent another shiver through me. *Hunger.* Yes, that was something I'd sensed from the apparition, although at the time I'd been too scared silly to stop and really identify it.

"What now?" Tobias asked briskly, as if he real-ized I didn't know what to do next. I might be the next *prima,* but I had no experience with this sort of thing.

"We'll check the apartment, just to make sure, but we need to have the coven here to cleanse the place, to lay down the spells of protection again. Something got through, although I'm not sure what and not sure how."

"All right," he said. "Let's send out the call, then."

This was something we could all do together. In unspoken accord, Tobias, Aunt Rachel, Adam, and I all stepped closer to one another and joined hands, Adam's strong and cool in my right, my aunt's fin-gers warm and reassuring in my left. The energy surged up and out, calling to the coven, broadcasting our need.

Brothers and sisters, come to us now. Come for the cir-cle—your strength is needed!

There were just shy of 450 people living in Jerome, and a little more than half of them were part of the McAllister clan. Of those we only needed a fraction, of course. Many rituals were performed with as few as three or seven. For the greater workings, we would need to combine the powers of twenty-one. That, I knew, was how many would answer tonight's call, and I also knew they would be the strongest, the best suited for this sort of ritual.

Cousin Rosemary was there almost at once, since she lived in the apartment over the tea shop next door. Aunt Rachel had just pulled the white candles out from underneath one of the counters when there was a knock at the back door. Tobias went to get it, since I could tell my aunt didn't want me out of her sight, and Adam sort of shifted from one foot to the next as if not sure exactly what he should be doing. I wondered if he would end up participating at all, as protective magic was not his strongest suit.

"Goodness, what is it?" Rosemary asked, emerging into the main shop space and blinking at all of us. She always reminded me a bird, light and fluttery, with her pale hair and big green eyes. She was five or six years younger than Rachel, but somehow seemed older, as if she'd embraced a little too much the whole idea of being a solitary witch. It didn't take much mental effort to imagine her stirring a cauldron, although we McAllisters actually weren't that big on potions.

"An incursion," my aunt said briefly, setting a container of pink Himalayan salt next to the white candles. "We'll need to cleanse the whole building and set up new wards."

"Oh, my!" she exclaimed, and despite everything, I had to stifle a laugh as Adam sent me a sideways look. Cousin Rosemary did tend to act like she'd just escaped from a Harry Potter novel or something.

After that there wasn't much time for conversation, as more people converged on the shop—Allegra Moss, who had a sculptor's studio across the street from Tobias, and Efraim Willendale, who ran the tiny post office, and Wyatt McAllister, owner of a B&B a few doors down from the stately Victorian where Great-Aunt Ruby lived. So many of them, all surrounding us with their strength, until the magic number of twenty-one was reached. Well, twenty-two, counting Adam, but he wasn't going to be participating.

"What about Great-Aunt Ruby?" I asked. Usually she would take part in something this important.

My cousin Dora, who lived with Ruby, shook her head. "She's been feeling a little tired the past few days, so I thought it better if she sat this one out."

At that reply I couldn't help feeling a little guilty. When was the last time I'd gone up to visit my great-aunt? Had to be almost a week now. I'd spent way too much time wrapped up in my own problems.

Aunt Rachel also looked rather grim, but then she shook her head, as if reminding herself to focus on the task at hand. After pulling out a soapstone incense burner and some cedar incense, she said, "Angela, you'll need to lead the ritual, as you're the one who saw the entity we're protecting against. We're all here to support you."

I'd guessed she would ask that of me, but it didn't make this any easier. Even with all of them there, I couldn't help feeling alone. I would have to put myself out in front of everyone and hope that whatever it was had long gone.

There wasn't much I could do except nod, however. I picked up the candle and sparked the flame with my thought. It lit at once, its glow steady and calming.

"Goddess, we ask that you lend us your strength, and aid us in cleansing this house of whatever evil spirits might have visited here. Let this pure white fire dispel the shadows, and bring peace to this place."

An icy breath seemed to pass over me, and the candle flame flickered wildly. At once I heard the echoing murmur from the coven.

"Bring peace to this place."

Warmth began to return, and the candle stilled. I moved to the front door and repeated my plea to the Goddess. From there I moved clockwise around the room, although the coven members stayed more or less in the center of the space. Not that it would have been all that easy for a crowd that size to follow me everywhere, what with all the table displays and bookshelves that filled the store.

I moved down the hallway to the stairs opposite the storeroom door, and hesitated. Were they all going to follow me upstairs to the apartment?

Apparently they were, although they had to straggle their way upward in ones and twos, a line that stretched almost all the way back to the first floor by the time I reached the second story. I felt nothing up here, not even the hint of a chill I had sensed before the power of the light pushed it back, but of course I wasn't about to take any chances. Clockwise again, moving from the living room to the kitchen, and then to the funny little cubbyhole off the dining room that my aunt used as a workspace for drying flowers and herbs. From there we climbed yet again, to Aunt Rachel's room and my own bedroom, past the inadequate little bathroom we had to share. All the while I focused on the power of the white light, of how it sent the darkness away from every corner, every cubby.

Then it was all the way back to the ground floor again, and the ritual repeated with the burning incense and the purifying power of air, then finally with spring water poured from one of the bottles we always kept under the sales counter, mixed with the pink Himalayan salt, bringing the strength of earth and the balance and clarity of water to all the spaces in the building. As I worked, I could feel the energy of the coven humming along with me, lending me the power necessary to perform the ritual and make it a lasting one, something that would maintain its protection for months and even years.

At last we had made all the circuits. I took up the bowl with the spring water and salt mixture, then went to the front door and traced the form of a pentacle there with my index finger.

"Peace and purity dwell here now," I said. "Nothing of ill will may enter. So the Goddess wills it, and so it will be."

"And so it will be," the members of the coven repeated.

For the barest second I almost thought I heard the sound of faraway laughter, mocking and cold. But then it was gone, and I told myself it must have been the wind. After all, around me was only warmth and light and the reassuring presences of the people who stood a few feet away. My coven.

My family.

It seemed I was safe now. But even then I wondered whether it would be enough.

CHAPTER FIVE

Speaking With the Dead

THEY ALL DISPERSED AFTER THAT, TALKING QUIETLY. ADAM was watching me with something like awe, which I didn't really understand. After all, he'd seen me work magic before. But then I realized this was the first time I'd actually led such a large group, been the one to direct all that energy. In the past, Great-Aunt Ruby would, as *prima*, have been the one to take on such a role. There was power in me, of course, although it was nothing compared to what it would be when she passed the strength of the *prima* to me and I had found my consort.

Cousin Dora had said Ruby was too tired to perform the task today. Was she really too tired, or was this her way of telling me it was time I stepped forward and showed everyone that I really was capable of taking on the mantle of *prima?*

I didn't know for sure; my great-aunt was eighty-eight years old, and if there's one thing you've earned at eighty-eight, it's the right to be tired. Even so, I couldn't help wondering.

Aunt Rachel began taking the items I'd used in the ritual and putting them back in their places under the counter. As she worked, however, she looked from Adam to me and back again, her gaze thoughtful.

"Thank you, Adam," she said after an awkward pause. "I think Angela's pretty tired after all that, so…."

He wrenched his eyes away from me. "What? Oh, yeah, I guess I should get going, too."

"Thanks, Adam," I added, realizing I was sort of falling down on the job here. However I might feel about his unwanted intentions, he'd certainly come to my aid tonight, and the very least I could do was express my gratitude…even if he might prefer that I express it a little bit differently than with a simple "thanks."

"No problem," he replied, too casually. Then he said, in a quick undertone clearly intended for my ears only, "You know I'd do anything for you."

He left after that, hurrying to the back door, since of course the front was still locked. For a minute or two after he left, neither Aunt Rachel nor I said anything.

Finally, after closing the little storage area under the counter and locking it, she asked, "Is that going to be a problem?"

"What?" I blinked, then realized what she probably thought the "problem" was. "You know there isn't anything between Adam and me."

"I thought I knew that...until I saw the two of you show up on Tobias's doorstep."

"He saw me at Grapes and basically invited himself to sit down with me. But he was the one who convinced me to go to you and tell you what happened, and yeah, I was glad to have him walk with me. After what I saw, I was kind of spooked, you know?"

Her expression gentled. "I do know. I only felt traces of...whatever it was...and that was enough for me." She came out from behind the counter and moved toward me, pulling me into a quick, fierce hug before she let me go. "I won't lie and say I'm not worried, but things do seem quiescent for now. Still, Angela, if anything like this happens again, come to me at once. I don't care if you have to pull me out of bed with Tobias. Understood?"

My cheeks flamed at the thought of having to interrupt my aunt having sex with her boyfriend. "That's a mental image I didn't need."

She shot me a warning look.

"Okay, okay. I know. I guess I wasn't thinking clearly. Too many things coming at once, I suppose."

Surprisingly, she didn't offer any more remonstrances, but only nodded. "Well, I think we'll both feel better after a good night's sleep. The house is cleansed, and safe. There isn't anything here that need worry you."

I still wasn't completely confident on that point. Voicing my misgivings probably wouldn't be all that productive, though, so I allowed myself to nod and then said, "You're right. I'm going to get ready for bed."

Never mind that it was barely nine-thirty on a Saturday night. Right then I only wanted to sleep. I didn't even want to dream of him. My thoughts were roiling enough as it was.

———

My Great-Aunt Ruby summoned me the next morning.

I say "summoned" because that's what it felt like—a summons to the royal presence. I was sure she'd heard about all the events of the day before… and maybe my run-in with Perry at Main Stage on Friday night, too. Part of a *prima*'s responsibilities included keeping tabs on her clan members, especially the girl who happened to be the *prima*-in-waiting.

Since I'd gone to bed so early the night before, I was up before eight on Sunday, and had toast and instant oatmeal before Aunt Rachel had even come downstairs. She wasn't much of a morning person, and since the store didn't open until eleven on Sundays, she tended to sleep in then even more than usual.

Nothing so prosaic as a text or email or even a phone call to let me know Great-Aunt Ruby wanted to see me. No, I heard her voice in my head, saying, *Angela, I want to see you.* That was her particular power, to be able to reach out to any of us mentally whenever she needed. I thought it was probably a little more useful than being able to talk to ghosts.

At any rate, I didn't dare ignore that voice. And I also took a little more care than usual with my appearance that morning, ditching my jeans and cowboy boots for one of my few skirts, a long sequined piece from India, and a pair of ballet flats. Nobody in their right mind wore heels in Jerome, unless their plans only included walking a few steps from their car to a restaurant or something.

The air was cool that morning as I let myself out, the sky dappled with clouds. I didn't see a lot of people out on the streets yet; most shops in town didn't open until eleven or twelve on Sunday, and while there were a few places that offered breakfast, the tourists generally came up for lunch or dinner. I paused for a minute or two on Main Street, letting the wind ruffle my hair, breathing in deeply and feeling the air currents as they moved and shifted around me.

No sign of the shadowy presence that had manifested itself the night before. Not even an echo of that unearthly chill, or the laughter I thought I'd heard but must have imagined. It was just a clean, bright Sunday morning, the sun warm but letting me know the seasons were shifting, and winter wasn't far off.

I shook my head, then began the climb up to Great-Aunt Ruby's house.

The large Victorian house she occupied had once belonged to one of the mine's overseers. How exactly it came to be the residence of all the McAllister *primas* since then was somewhat murky. I don't want to say that long-ago overseer was exactly coerced into giving it up, but I had gotten the distinct impression that he'd sold it for a song without recalling exactly why he'd been willing to let go of his beloved home for so little.

When I was younger, my great-aunt frightened me a good deal, not simply because she was the *prima* and therefore in charge of the whole clan, but also because she had seemed so very old to me. My grandfather was the youngest of Randolph McAllister's four children, and Ruby the eldest, with almost fifteen years separating them, so she was much older than my grandparents would have been…if they were still alive.

Another tragedy there, since Grandpa Logan had tried to break up a bar fight years before I was even born, and gotten a knife between the ribs in thanks, and my grandmother had sort of withered away after that. She'd never been a very strong witch, according to Aunt Rachel, who seemed disproportionately disapproving, considering Grandma Irene was her own mother. But maybe Rachel was still hurt and angry, since my grandmother had passed away when her two daughters were only in their teens. No wonder my mother had grown up to be such a wild child.

At any rate, Great-Aunt Ruby had always seemed as if she came from a generation even further removed than that of my grandparents or other people their age. Her own two sons were still in Jerome, of course, Lionel a noted sculptor and Joseph the chief of the fire department, but even they didn't seem to be quite the same force of nature she was.

Eventually I made it to the front steps of her house. Up until even a year ago, my great-aunt had managed all the hills in Jerome without batting an eye, but time seemed to be finally catching up to her. I paused for a second or two to catch my breath, watching the clouds move against the blue sky. The red rocks of Sedona to the north and east seemed to almost glow as the fast-moving shadows passed over them.

I wouldn't let my gaze move any farther than that. After last night, the last thing I wanted was to be looking into the dark heart of Wilcox territory. That seemed to be inviting more trouble than I already had.

The rosebushes on either side of the walk up to the front door still had a few blooms, but the grass in the tiny pocket handkerchief lawn was already starting to appear yellow and tired. As always, though, the rest of the place looked immaculate, the paint in its shades of ivory and blush and terra-cotta gleaming. Not every house in Jerome was maintained quite so well, but the *prima* had to keep up appearances.

Just as I approached the front door and raised my hand to knock, it swung inward. I didn't see any sign of Cora, who lived here and acted as a sort of nurse/ companion, but that didn't surprise me too much. Great-Aunt Ruby did like her little theatrics.

"In the sitting room," came her voice from within the house, so I stepped inside and shut the door behind me.

"Coming, Aunt Ruby," I replied, and made my way to the chamber that was her favorite, in the octagonal tower on the southwest corner of the house.

It didn't really surprise me that it was her favorite room, since it provided staggering views across the

Verde Valley and into Sedona, and southward along the Black Mountains. From here I could see the line of cottonwoods following the path of the Verde River. Those trees were just beginning to burst into their autumnal finery of bright yellow; the lighter patches seemed to gleam like flame amongst the dark green of the leaves that hadn't yet turned.

My great-aunt sat in an imposing chair of about the same vintage as the house; I guessed she liked it because it looked like a throne. Her gaze seemed to be fixed on the landscape outside the windows, but she turned her head slightly as I entered the room, and pointed a wrinkled hand at a smaller chair just to her right.

"Sit down, Angela."

I did as she requested, of course, glad I'd decided to put on that skirt and those ladylike shoes. The world had changed a lot since Ruby was a girl, and she'd changed with it...just not to the point where she was happy seeing the next *prima* of the McAllisters wearing faded jeans and cowboy boots that needed resoling.

At first she didn't say anything, but only looked me up and down, as if recommitting my features to her memory. Then, "I heard you did well last night."

"You did?" I asked, surprised. I'd been worrying that she would take me to task for not going to Aunt Rachel about that apparition or entity or whatever it had been first thing, rather than attempting to fortify myself with some pizza and wine beforehand.

"Yes. It isn't an easy thing, to hold the energies of that many people in your hand, to use them to strengthen and guide you. That was the work of a true *prima*."

"But...I'm not the *prima*."

"Yet," she said crisply, and fastened me with a pair of blue eyes that were still very sharp, despite their faded color. I don't know what she saw, but she sighed then and glanced away, her gaze once more returning to the landscape of golden fields and purple-hued mountains miles beyond the windows. "Angela, my time is coming soon. I can feel it."

Cold began to work its way down my spine, even though the room was quite warm—warmer than I would have usually preferred, especially after my hike up here. This wasn't how it was supposed to be. There was supposed to be a long time after the *prima*-in-waiting found her consort before she had to take over as the clan's new leader. It was only because my mother had refused to do her duty that so many years separated my great-aunt and myself. "Don't say that, Aunt Ruby—"

"I *will* say it," she interrupted. "I am eighty-eight years old, child. Being a witch does not make one immortal."

I didn't reply to that, only clasped my hands between my knees, knowing I wasn't going to like what was about to come next, and also knowing that I had no choice but to listen to it.

She nodded, but I didn't know if it was in approval of my silence, or because she was mentally going through what she meant to say next. "It's been hard. I lost my Pat fifteen years ago, and oh, how I wanted to go with him. You'll understand, when you find your consort."

If *I find him,* I thought. I doubted she wanted to hear that...then again, maybe she knew I was thinking it. Contrary to popular belief, being a witch doesn't necessarily make you psychic, and anyway, that wasn't Great-Aunt Ruby's gift. However, she of course knew all about my failure to find my own match, and it didn't take a mind reader to figure out I was feeling a little disheartened by the whole process.

Bony fingers tightened on the carved arms of the chair. "But I held on, because I knew you weren't ready. How could you be, at that age? So I've been waiting this whole time, waiting to see if you would be able to manage when the time came...and I think you will be." She shook her head, correcting herself. "No, I *know* you will be."

"How can I, when I can't even find a consort?" I argued. Her talk of the "time coming" and all that was frightening me more than I wanted to admit, even to myself. She couldn't go before I found my match. I'd be vulnerable.

I'd be alone.

"You will. The more difficult the search, the stronger the bond, when it comes." Her expression grew dreamy, and beneath the lines and the fine, paper-thin skin I could see a ghost of the beautiful young woman she'd been so many years before. "How they came to court me, back in the day, and I wouldn't have any of them. Just like you, Angela. My mother despaired and my father blustered, but I hadn't a care in the world. I knew he'd be there when I needed him. And so he was—Patrick Lynch, come up from Payson on business, not thinking of anything except selling some cattle. Certainly not thinking he'd be the consort of the McAllisters' *prima*. But I was down in Cottonwood, shopping with my mother, and there he came walking along the street, and I knew. I knew the second I laid eyes on him. Just as you'll know, Angela."

I nodded, albeit sadly. I wanted to feel that conviction. I wanted to look up and suddenly meet those cool green eyes I'd seen so many times in my mind, and know the doubt and worry were over at last. How I wanted that more than anything in the world. Wanting something, though, wasn't quite the same as actually getting it.

"Why, you're seeing him already in your dreams. He wants to come to you, just as you want to come to him."

"Well, he's taking his sweet time," I remarked, my tone a little more acid than I'd intended. Her brows lifted, and I hastily added, "I know, I know. These things happen as they're meant to be. But I barely have two months left."

"A lot can happen in two months, even though it might feel like an eternity to you. The worst thing you can do is allow yourself to become discouraged. That only leads to a lowering of your spirits, and that makes you vulnerable." Her mouth tightened. "And that is the thing this clan needs the least."

Something in her tone told me she was making an oblique reference to the spirit or entity I had seen. "Did you—did you feel it?" I asked.

She didn't bother to inquire what I'd meant by "it." A nod, and she replied, "Faintly. I was sitting here, napping a little, I suppose." Another pursing of the thin wrinkled lips. She didn't like to admit to any weakness, even something as harmless as taking an afternoon nap. "It felt to me like a cold draft blowing through a crack in the wall. Then it was gone, and until Rachel sent out the call to the coven, I thought I must have imagined it."

"It is—it is gone, though, isn't it?" Even though I could sense no trace of that malevolent presence, it still nagged at me, as if it were hiding somewhere just out of range.

"As far as I can tell. It was a good cleansing. I sense no negativity here now...unless you want to count the drivers going over the mountain cursing as they have to slow down to ten miles an hour to get through town."

That remark made me smile. I guessed she'd made it on purpose in an attempt to banish my lingering worries. "So what should I do?"

"As you have done. Be vigilant, of course, but don't let yourself worry too much. Everyone is here for you, and will be, no matter what happens."

I regarded her steadily. "And you, Great-Aunt Ruby? Will you be here for me, too?"

She didn't blink. Those blue eyes were sharp as a hawk's. "You've got to take off the training wheels sometime, child." Then she made an impatient gesture with one hand. "That's enough for now. You go—your aunt will need you at the shop. It's almost eleven."

If it had been anyone else, I might have tried to argue, press her for more details...plead with her to hang on until I'd found my consort. Maybe she would, and maybe she wouldn't. But that time would be of her choosing, and none of mine.

I got to my feet. "I'll talk to you again soon," I said firmly.

"I'm sure you will," she replied, tone neutral.

After bending down and giving her a swift kiss on the cheek—the expected farewell—I went back to the front door and let myself out. A cloud moved over the sun in that moment, and I barely kept myself from flinching. Heck of a way for the McAllisters' next *prima* to act...jumping at shadows, always looking over her shoulder.

Shaking my head at myself, I went down the hill to my aunt's store.

I didn't look back.

As Sundays went, it was busy but not horribly so. Enough to keep me somewhat occupied, but not so much that I couldn't keep worrying at the nagging problem of the unwelcome spirit who'd shown up here the day before. Yes, everyone seemed to think it was gone, and I'd have to accept that for now, but the one topic people seemed to be avoiding was the question of what it actually had been. Maybe no one really had a clue, and so didn't want to profess their ignorance. It made some sense; in Jerome, I was the ghost girl. And if I didn't know what that thing was, how could I expect anyone else to figure it out?

I decided I'd better go directly to the source.

We closed the shop at five, and Aunt Rachel went upstairs to check the roast she'd left cooking in the crock pot all day. Tobias would be coming for dinner, as he did every Sunday, but we wouldn't be sitting down until six-thirty. I had some time.

Except for the few tourists staying at the local hotels and B&Bs, and a few stalwarts who remained behind to squeeze one last dinner out of their week-ends, Jerome tended to clear out on Sunday evenings. I slipped down to Hull Avenue and around the corner of Spook Hall, a place where Maisie tended to hang out...if you could call what a disembodied spirit did "hanging out."

"Maisie," I whispered, as the sun began to drop behind Mingus Mountain and the shadows length-ened. "I need to talk to you."

Nothing at first, which didn't surprise me. It was quiet down here; the wine tasting room a few doors down had already closed, and the hall wasn't hosting any events that day, so there wasn't anyone else around. I leaned against the cold cement wall and waited. True, Maisie had much more time on her hands than I did, but acting impatient or agitated was the surest way to keep her from appearing at all.

At last I saw her shiver into existence a few feet away from me, her form slowly becoming more substantial as I watched. She wore a simple white high-collared blouse and dark skirt, and looked a lot more respectable than most people might think a mining town prostitute should. Then again, she may have decided she didn't want to spend eternity wandering around in a camisole and corset. Her curly blonde hair was pulled up into a loose knot on the top of her head, although a few tendrils waved around her face, and moved in a breeze that had little to do with the wind currents in Jerome at that time of day.

She showed no surprise at seeing me. "Angela."

"How are you today, Maisie?"

Her mouth quirked, and she raised an eyebrow. "'Bout the same as always, I reckon. What did you want?"

"Can we talk a bit?"

Her lopsided dimple deepened. "Sure. Not like I have anything else I need to do right now."

This sort of an exchange had turned into a ritual for us. It had always seemed sort of rude for me to jump right into asking her for what I needed, and so we always shared a little banter to get things started. "Let's go down to the stoop."

About halfway down the side of the building was a raised area outside one of the exits. I settled myself on the edge, but Maisie remained standing. I'd actually never seen her sit down, but I didn't know if that was personal preference or because she really couldn't sit.

I settled myself in place, and she watched me from a few feet away. It always startled me how much she looked like a regular girl, even in her 1890s getup. If someone had seen her, they'd probably think she was just a local historical reenactor of some sort. There really was no way to tell that she'd died only a few feet from this spot almost a hundred and twenty years ago.

As far as I could tell, though, I was the only one who could actually see her. Anyone passing by would see me standing there and talking to myself, but that sort of behavior was mostly ignored in Jerome.

"So, Maisie," I began, then hesitated. There really wasn't an easy way to ask the question. "Did you feel...or see...or hear...anything strange late yesterday afternoon?"

She'd been staring past me at the square, stolid bulk of Lawrence Hall, but her gaze sharpened at once. "Laws, yes. I was wondering if you were going to come poking around and asking about that."

I should have been relieved at a chance to clear up the mystery. Somehow, though, I wasn't sure I wanted to hear what she had to say. "So you know what it was?"

"Now, I didn't say *that*. I just said I felt something strange."

"What did you feel?"

"Cold. I shouldn't feel cold...I don't feel anything at all, most days, although every once in a while I fancy I can feel the wind on my face. My imagination,

I s'pose, but there it is." A frown pulled at her fair eyebrows, at skin that would never see a line or wrinkle. I always had to remind myself that Maisie had been younger than I was now when she died.

"I felt it, too," I told her, and tried to repress a shiver, not all that successfully.

She shot me a curious glance. "And you don't know what it was, neither?"

"That's why I was asking you. I thought you might know something more because you're a, well—"

"'Cause I'm a ghost."

"Well, yes."

Her shoulders lifted. "Never felt nothing like it before, that's true. It wasn't one of *us*."

By "us" I knew she meant the thirty-odd spirits who'd made Jerome their permanent abode. I'd already guessed that much, since I knew all of them as well as I knew the members of my own family, or the residents of the town who weren't McAllisters but were trusted with our secret.

"But do you—do you think it was a spirit who used to be someone?"

"I *am* still someone."—Somewhat indignantly.

"I know. I'm sorry." I sighed, and ran a hand through my hair. Or rather, I attempted to and was stopped by a tangle. My hair tended to drive me nuts, since it was halfway between wavy and curly, and could never make up its mind what it wanted to be. "I just meant the spirit of someone who died."

"Not like any I've ever met, that's for certain." I'd never thought I'd see a ghost looking scared, but at the very least she looked troubled, if not downright frightened. "I didn't like it. See, we all know each other here, the good and the bad. We rub along. But this—" Another shake of her head. "I'm glad you made it go away."

"So it is gone."

"Far's I can tell. And I think I'd feel it if it was still here."

That was something. Not much, but better than nothing.

"Thanks, Maisie." I pulled my cell out of my jeans pocket to check the time. Six-ten. Aunt Rachel would want me back home to help put the finishing touches on dinner. "You'll tell me if you feel any-thing else strange, won't you?"

"If you come and ask," she said.

That was ghosts for you. Always wanting it done their way.

"Sure," I replied. "You take care of yourself."

"Bit late for that, I think," she said tartly, and disappeared.

Since there wasn't anything left for me to do, I began to walk up Hull Avenue toward the back entrance of my building. Even as I went, my mind worried at the problem. So it wasn't a ghost. Other types of spirits existed, dark entities whose purpose was anything but benign. They had their counterparts on the light side, but of course what I'd felt was definitely not good. And if one of those dark, inhuman presences had somehow decided to make me its prey, it might require more than a cleansing ritual and a charmed pentacle on the door.

Suddenly the shadows of the buildings around me felt too black, and I found myself hurrying home, hurrying toward the safety, however spurious, of my aunt's house.

CHAPTER SIX

House Arrest

He came to me in my dreams that night. Another change, because this time he stood beside me, although for some reason I still couldn't look up into his face. But he held my hand in his, the two of us standing there in the soft twilight as snow began to fall all around us. I wasn't cold, even though I was wearing only a flannel shirt and jeans and boots, no jacket or gloves or hat. His fingers were warm in mine, strong and welcome, and I squeezed them slightly, as if even in my dream I had to reassure myself that he was real.

Something in the air seemed filled with anticipation, as if I knew at any moment he would pull me into him, would cup my face in his hands and bring my lips to his, so I'd know at last I'd found him, found the one I'd been waiting for all these years. He shifted, and in my dream I smiled, knowing what was going to come next.

Only as he moved, he became shadowed, as if his whole body had turned to black, had turned as featureless and frightening as the figure that had stared at me in the shop the day before, and the fingers holding mine were no longer warm, but deathly cold. In my dream I tried to wrench my hand away, but he was too strong, and not only held on to that hand but grasped the other, pulling me against him, the chill of his body leaching into mine. Then we were falling to the snow, a weight as cold and heavy and black as the depths of the ocean on top of me, holding me down, smothering my heat with his ice, and though I pushed and pushed, I couldn't get away, couldn't take a breath, couldn't force one scream....

"Angela! *Angela!*"

My aunt's voice, and her hands on my shoulders, shaking me awake. I blinked, and saw her worried face peering down into mine, outlined by a yellow rectangle of light—the open doorway to the hall, with the overhead fixture bringing welcome illumination to my dark room.

"What was it?" she asked, voice urgent. "A nightmare?"

I wanted to say it was only a nightmare, but I couldn't say for sure. Mine was not the gift of seeing visions, or the future, but all witches had flashes of precognition from time to time. I didn't want that to be the case here. I wanted it to be only a nightmare, only a horrible dream put together from my worries and fears and the frightening experiences of the past few days.

"I...don't know," I said at last.

"Tell me," she said, and I knew from her tone that she wouldn't let me get away with any evasion.

So I told her everything I remembered, no embellishment, no speculation, just the bare bones of the dream. That was enough; her face, pale already without its daytime makeup, went even whiter.

"It got through," she murmured. "Even through all the wards we set up...."

"It was only a dream," I said, but the protest sounded halfhearted even to me.

"We don't know that for sure." She reached out and touched my hand where it lay on top of the embroidered bedspread. "You're like ice."

That was true enough; shivers still wracked my body. "What should we do?"

"Bring in reinforcements," she said immediately. "You'll have to be watched around the clock."

As much as the dream had bothered me, that idea upset me even more. Wasn't my life circumscribed enough? Was I now going to have some kind of McAllister version of the Secret Service dogging my every step?

Yep, that was about the size of it.

Margot Emory, one of the clan elders, and Boyd Willis, a warlock noted for his strong spells of protection, and Henry Lynch, one of Great-Aunt Ruby's grandsons, all set up camp in the living room that night, watching over me, watching over the house, making sure that no trace of evil or ill will could enter. And the next morning another group of three took over, only to be replaced by yet another trio the following evening. They attempted to stay out of the way—well, as much as they could with my aunt worrying about what she should cook for them all—but it was trying, to say the least.

I retreated to my studio and tried to concentrate on twisting wire and setting stones and choosing gems for the next round of pendants and earrings and talismans after the ones I was working on were done, but I had a hard time focusing. More than once I clipped a wire in the wrong place, or placed a stone crooked so I had to pry it out and start all over again, but I supposed it was good I had something to occupy myself. And in an odd way the very presence of the stones reassured me, the quiet strength of garnet, the gentle warmth of rose quartz, the serene coolness of jade. I took solace in their touch, and thanked them for their beauty as I set them in shimmering silver and vibrant, glowing copper.

Late on Tuesday afternoon, Sydney texted me. *R U coming 2 try on dresses tomorrow?*

I really, really hated text-speak, even though I supposed it made sense in a twisted sort of way when you were trying to save time and effort. Even so, I always replied using proper sentences. *I'm under house arrest. Can you come up here?*

Her reply came back almost at once. *No prob. See U @ 4. Dinner @ Grapes?*

Okay, I texted back. I had to hope that the restaurant was close enough to home that I could go out to eat with a friend without having to drag my bodyguards along.

She showed up around four-thirty the next day, a garment bag slung over one shoulder. I'd given up on my jewelry for the day and was pretending to make myself useful by dusting some of the more obscure corners of the shop, but I had a feeling Aunt Rachel saw right through that tactic.

When Sydney came in, I gladly abandoned the feather duster. "We're going upstairs to try on our stuff for the Halloween dance," I told my aunt.

That day's "bodyguards" were sitting at a table off to one side, pretending to browse through books on local history. They'd all looked up as soon as Sydney came in, but since she was clearly not a threat, they turned back to their books, ignoring us. Well, ignoring her, anyway.

Aunt Rachel smiled at Sydney and said hello, but couldn't spare much more than that, as she was in the middle of showing a turquoise cuff to a husband and wife at the time. Taking advantage of her distraction, I all but dragged Sydney upstairs.

"Who were those dorks?" she asked, jerking her chin over her shoulder as we climbed the stairs. "And what's this about house arrest?"

I really didn't want to go into the whole thing. "Let's just say things get a little weirder the closer I get to my birthday without a consort."

"O-kay," she replied, drawing out the second syllable as a means of registering her disapproval. "You're not going to have to drag them along to the *dance,* are you?"

"I don't know," I said. "I hope not. But I have a feeling they'll be there, only not so obvious. Kind of like Secret Service guys in black tie at a White House function or something."

"Are they going to wear those little earpieces?" she asked with a giggle.

I didn't want to explain that witches really didn't need that sort of thing. "Probably not. Anyway," I added, hoping to distract her, "let's take a look at these dresses."

That did the trick. She went over to my bed and laid down the garment bag as I shut the door, glad that the watchdogs didn't insist on being as close to me as Secret Service agents were to the President. It was enough for them to be in the building, keeping the wards strong, continually checking for any whiff of something that didn't belong. So far they hadn't sensed anything at all. Whatever was trying to come after me seemed to have backed off for the time being. Or maybe it was just playing with us, waiting to see if we'd get lax after a while.

If that was its game, it obviously didn't know the McAllisters very well.

"Okay, so, here's the one I brought for you," Sydney said, pulling out a long red dress with intricate flounces along the bottom, all edged in black sequins, and with red and black beading on the bodice. It was low-cut, but I'd already resigned myself to that. *Please* tell me you found some decent shoes."

In silence I went to my closet and produced a pretty pair of black leather Mary Jane–style pumps. They were my aunt's, but she and I wore the same size, and she was all too happy to let me borrow them. Actually, I think she was just as tired of the cowboy boots as Sydney was.

"Oh, those are pretty good," she said, eyeing them critically. "Go ahead and try it on, then."

I took the dress from her and used the standing mirror in the corner as a sort of screen as I pulled off my jeans and flannel shirt. One look at the bodice of the dress told me I couldn't wear a bra with it—there were cups sewn into the gown itself—and so I reluctantly unhooked my bra as well before climbing into the dress and sliding it over my hips and all the way up. The zipper would've been impossible to manage by myself...if I weren't a witch. It glided up smoothly, pulling the gown closely against me. It was snug but not too tight. Even so, I knew it showed off a whole hell of a lot more than I was used to.

After taking a breath to fortify myself—and realizing that those cups in the bodice were a lot more padded than I'd expected—I emerged from behind the mirror. "Is it okay?"

Sydney's eyes widened. "Okay? It's...way more than okay." She got up from the bed, where she'd been fussing with her own short, sparkly dress, and came to stand next to me. "That's spectacular." Then her eyes lit up, and she hurried back over to her purse, rummaged through it, and pulled out a tube of lipstick. "Put this on."

I took the lipstick from her and spread a thin coat over my lips. It was dark red, almost a perfect match to the dress. With it on, and with the bodice of the gown cut low over my breasts, I almost didn't recognize myself. My eyes glowed green in contrast to the red of the gown and the ruby of my lips.

"See?" she demanded in triumph. "I always knew you could be beautiful if you just put a little effort into it."

At any other time I would have protested, but now, with that familiar-yet-strange face looking back at me from the mirror, I thought Sydney might have a point. I put the cap on the lipstick and started to hand it back to her, but she shook her head.

"No, you keep it. I have a feeling you don't have anything that color, right?"

That was a joke. My entire lip collection consisted of my Burt's Bees balm and a single tube of peach lipgloss that got worn maybe twice a month, if that. "Thanks," I said.

She looked over my reflection, then gathered up my unruly hair and twisted it into a quick knot low on the nape of my neck. "We'll do your hair like this, and then a red flower…."

"Aunt Rachel has some dangly gold earrings I can borrow, too."

"Perfect! No one's going to recognize you."

"Well, especially with a mask on," I pointed out.

Her face fell. "Are we really going to wear masks? I hate those things. It always feels as if my lashes are jamming into the eye holes."

"It is a Halloween party, you know." Then again, I didn't know for sure if everyone wore masks to the dance or not. Maybe I'd bring one along and see what other people were doing. I mentioned this to Sydney, and she brightened a little.

"Okay, that I can work with." She turned away from me and held up the shimmering gold dress she planned to wear. "What do you think? Not as spectacular as yours, but...."

"It's gorgeous," I said truthfully. "And it'll look perfect with your hair."

She ran a hand over the beaded fringe and nodded. "I found this awesome pair of gold heels to go with it, too. I just have to hope that I won't break my neck walking down the street in them. I swear, I don't think there's one level sidewalk in this town of yours."

"Probably not." There didn't seem much point to staying in the red dress any longer, now that we'd determined it fit, and so I moved back behind the mirror to take it off. "I still can't believe Madison was okay with just giving these away."

"Well, I *might* have offered to give her free highlights for the next couple of months in exchange...."

I stuck my head out from behind the mirror. "That was generous. What can I do to chip in?"

"Nothing," she said blithely. "It's good practice for me. I don't mind."

Past experience had taught me that it was no use insisting, so I only said, "Okay, but let me get dinner at least," before going back to getting the dress off and putting it back on its hanger. As quickly as I could, I slipped my bra back on and pulled on my shirt and jeans.

"Deal." I heard the bed creak a little as she shifted on it. "Hey, Anthony has next Saturday off, and he and a couple of friends—*not* Perry—are taking their four-wheelers up to Crown King. Want to come?"

Crown King was a ghost town about seventy miles south of Jerome. Well, not completely a ghost town. A few people still lived there, and even more had summer homes on the mountaintop, but the place's biggest claim to fame was its saloon...and the bragging rights of driving over more than twenty-five miles of dirt road to get there. I knew a few people who'd made the trip, and it always sounded like a lot of fun, but it would've been a stretch at the best of times, and I knew it sure wasn't going to happen now, not with the whole McAllister clan watching my every move.

"I don't think so," I said slowly, and came out from behind the mirror, dangling my boots from one hand. "But you guys have fun."

For a minute Sydney didn't say anything, only watched me carefully, blue eyes scanning my face, looking for what, I didn't know. Then she said, "Are you going to tell me what's really going on?"

I gave her as guileless a look as possible. "Nothing is going on."

She crossed her arms. "How long have we been friends?"

"About seven years now, I think."

"And have I *ever* let slip any secrets about you? Told anyone the truth about your family?"

"Well, no," I replied, not sure where she was going with this.

"Then *why* won't you tell me what's wrong? I can tell something isn't right. You've got those people who look like refugees from Hogwarts camped out in your aunt's store, you seem all jumpy, you won't come up to Crown King even though technically it's still in your 'safe zone,' whatever that means. So why don't you trust me to tell me what's going on?"

Her tone was hurt, and I really couldn't blame her for that. She was right—she really had kept her mouth shut all these years, been a better friend than I probably deserved. A lot of people probably wondered why we were friends at all, since we were so different. Back in the day, I'd wondered the same thing, although at the time I'd thought she just wanted to take me on as a project. After all, the first thing she ever said to me, when she approached me on a cool

October morning all those years ago, was, "Nineteen ninety-three called. It wants its shirt back."

Okay, I had been wearing a flannel shirt, along with my favorite faded Levi's and a pair of well-worn boots, whereas she'd had on a denim mini-skirt, tight top, and wedges. I must have looked like a total hick to her. Cottonwood High was a small pond, but even it had its hierarchy. Yet somehow Sydney had seen something in me that she found interesting. True, I knew she was safe to be friends with—the charm that made sure only congenial souls resided in Jerome also ensured that members of the clan only made friends with those we could trust. Still, she'd stuck by me through everything, and I knew she'd defended me to some of her other friends from the more popular crowd.

"I do trust you," I said finally. "I guess I just didn't want to drag you into this."

"Into what?"

"We don't know for sure. But it's not good." Quickly, I told her about the dark presence in my aunt's shop, the nightmare, the need for increased vigilance. "None of us really know what's going on," I finished. "But we have to be really careful, so that means I can't even go into Cottonwood without some kind of escort. I'd love to go with you guys to Crown King. But I just can't."

Through all this, Sydney's expression had grown steadily more troubled. "I'm sorry," she said quietly. "I had no idea. But can't you guys, I don't know, call in reinforcements or something?"

It would take way too much time to explain to her the alliances and hierarchies of the clans, how we were more or less friendly with the de la Pazes, or the Cortez family farther out to the west, true, but that didn't mean we wanted to reveal any weakness to them. Admitting we were up against something we couldn't handle was not something any of us wanted to do. Not yet, anyway. Not until all other resources had been exhausted.

I shook my head. "It's usually every clan for themselves. It's our problem, so we have to take care of it on our own. And it's gotten better—I mean, since we stepped up the protection here, I haven't had any more bad dreams or seen or felt any other dark presences. Maybe what we're doing is enough. Even so, we don't want to take any chances."

"I can see why," Sydney replied, and shivered. Then she added, in a too-hearty tone, "Well, it's a good thing that the dance is right here in Jerome. They can't keep you from going to that, can they?"

That worry had been hanging out in the back of my mind, but since no one had said anything to the contrary, I guessed that the dance was still considered safe enough. "No. I'm not saying we won't have the Hogwarts contingent hanging out and keeping an eye on things, but if I can't be safe at Spook Hall, a block away from where I live, then I can't really be safe anywhere, can I?"

"I guess not." She reached out and touched a strand of the beaded fringe of her Halloween dress, running it between her thumb and forefinger. "I don't know how you do it, though."

"Do what?"

"Keep on acting normal, as if you don't have this horrible *thing* hanging over your head. I'd never want to leave my room."

I shrugged. "Because I don't have any other choice."

———

Despite everything, the next two weeks practically flew by. There were no more incursions—no dark shapes skulking around town, no nightmares to wake me, gasping, from sleep. I also didn't dream of *him* at all, but I was willing to accept that loss for the time being. Maybe his absence from my dreams meant he was finally going to make a real-world appearance.

The days grew colder, the leaves on the trees changing in earnest now, bright yellow for the cottonwoods in the river bottoms, flame orange and red for the oak and sumac around town. I'd always loved the fall, loved to watch the blaze of color around me and in the valley below. Now, though, despite no further incidents, I found myself watching the shadows more closely, looking over my shoulder more often. My aunt probably would have applauded my caution, but I hated it. I didn't want to live that way.

And somehow—driven by desperation, probably—she managed to dig up two new candidates to make their attempts at the ritual kiss. No go for either one, of course. The second one came by two days before the Halloween dance, and I found myself even more irritated than usual by my failure.

"Can you wait until after the dance for the next one?" I'd demanded irritably, almost as soon as he left. I did allow myself a moment of guilt; the poor guy had driven here all the way from California. Not that I had much control over the situation, so my guilt was probably misplaced...and that made me crabbier than ever. "I've got enough on my mind as it is."

"We can't afford to wait, and you know it," Aunt Rachel had said in imperturbable tones, as she continued to fold T-shirts and tidy up the display a rowdy group of college kids had wrecked.

Maybe they'd just picked up on my vibe... the whole time that group of laughing guys and girls were in the store, I'd watched them in some envy, wishing I could be that angst-free and oblivious. Hell, I wished I could just go to college like a normal person. But one of them had been wearing a Northern Pines University sweatshirt, which meant they had to have come down from Flagstaff…and which meant they were students at the last college I could ever possibly attend.

"I know we can't afford to wait," I told my aunt. Then, wanting to change the subject, "So are you and Tobias coming to the dance after all?"

"I think so," she'd replied. "It's probably best if there are as many of us there as possible…in case."

In case dark vaporous figures started oozing out of the walls or something, I supposed. But, depressing as the situation was, better that than the alternative. All I could do was hope we wouldn't have such a huge McAllister contingent there that they'd max out the occupancy of the place, thus defeating any chance of dancing with someone I hadn't known since I was in diapers. Bad enough that Adam had already announced his intentions of accompanying Sydney and me to the dance. Anthony was working at the wine tasting room until eight that night and had promised to come up to Jerome as soon as he could, but he still wouldn't be able to get to the dance much before nine.

Sydney didn't have a problem with Adam because she'd always thought he was kind of cute, and I hadn't quashed him because he had helped me a lot the day I saw the apparition—and afterward, too, mostly by backing off on his declarations of undying love for me. At that point I had to take what I could get.

Great-Aunt Ruby had called me into her presence several times, wanting a progress report. Not that there was much to tell her, since nothing had really happened. But she wanted to know the details of the warding spells we kept refreshing at twelve-hour intervals, wanted me to tell her if I'd noticed anything unusual about any of the tourists who'd visited the shop. Of course I hadn't, because they were the usual mix of people from within the state coming up for weekend getaways and those who'd come from much farther away, visiting Jerome because it was almost as much a place to see in Arizona as Sedona or even the Grand Canyon.

Not that I would know what the Grand Canyon looked like in person. That was Wilcox territory.

And all the while my great-aunt was watching me, I was studying her in return, looking for any signs that might indicate she was feeling weaker, or failing somehow. I couldn't see any; she looked as bright-eyed and sharp-minded as she ever had, and I told myself that maybe she'd simply wanted me to start preparing for the day when she would be gone, even if that might be somewhere far off in the future.

Wishful thinking, probably. But right then, wishes were about all I had.

CHAPTER SEVEN

Masquerade

A RARE RAINSTORM THREATENED THE DAY OF THE DANCE, but the weather-workers of the coven—including Adam—quietly got together and nudged those moisture-laden clouds a little farther to the west, so they might hold off for another twelve hours. Messing with the weather wasn't something we did lightly, but sometimes a little meddling was in order. A critical observer might have noticed that it never rained or snowed during any of Jerome's most important events: the Halloween dance, the holiday lighting ceremony…the Mardi Gras dance in February.

Even so, it was a gray sort of day, not the kind to inspire much enthusiasm. It helped a little that Sydney came up early, saying she wanted to give me a manicure, because I needed red nail polish to match the lipstick, and between that and watching her spend a good hour curling her hair while my nails dried, we managed to use up a large chunk of the afternoon. And after that Aunt Rachel fed us smoked chicken enchiladas and her famous Spanish rice, saying she knew we'd be drinking and so had better lay down a good base first. I noticed Sydney didn't make much protest, despite the tight-fitting dress she'd be wearing later; no one in their right mind turned down my aunt's enchiladas.

Then it was time to change, and the two of us headed up to my room to put on our dresses and makeup. That is, Sydney insisted on doing my makeup, too, since she was the expert. I didn't bother to protest, since deep down I had to acknowledge that I wanted to know what I'd look like with real makeup on and not some hastily applied lip gloss.

"I'd love to smoke up your eyes," she said as she worked away on my face, dabbing foundation on with a sponge, "but you're doing a red lip, and that would be too much. We don't want you looking like a streetwalker."

"Well, it would fit the neighborhood," I joked. Hull Avenue, where Spook Hall was located, had been the center of the red light district back when Jerome was a bustling mining town.

"But it wouldn't fit *you*," she said severely, then set down the sponge and picked up a brush, lightly applying blush in upward motions along my cheekbones.

"Probably not."

For the next few minutes she worked in silence, expertly tracing liner along my upper lids, brushing on mascara, using a pencil to define my brows before at last applying the red lipstick. Finally she said, "Okay, I think I'm done. It's pretty amazing... but don't peek until you have the dress on."

"Seriously?"

"Seriously."

I just shook my head, feeling the unfamiliar weight of my hair gathered into a low chignon. But I did as she requested, keeping my eyes cast downward at the Persian rug on the floor as I went behind the mirror and took off my shirt and jeans, then pulled on the unfamiliar and not very comfortable hose I had to wear under the gown.

"Goddess, people actually wear these horrible things every day?" I muttered as I wriggled into the pantyhose.

"Oh, stop grousing. I can only imagine what you'd say if you had to wear something historical with a corset."

"I would've put my foot down about that," I retorted.

"Quit bitching and get that dress on already. It's almost eight."

I didn't bother to point out that she'd just spent almost a half hour doing my makeup. Instead, I stepped into my gown and drew it up, then gave the zipper a quick mental yank. Then I sort of pushed and pulled until everything more or less felt as if it were in the right place. I'd left my borrowed shoes back here so I could step into them easily once I was dressed, and I did that now, then came out from behind the mirror.

"About time," Sydney began, and then she stopped, staring at me. "Wow."

"Really?" I asked.

"Oh, yeah. Look at yourself."

Almost fearfully, I turned and regarded myself in the mirror. Well, that is, I knew it was me, but it definitely didn't look like me. My usually unruly hair was sleek and shining, my mouth full under its coating of red lipstick. Long gold earrings danced against my neck, and the dress, with its built-in padding, was doing some spectacular things to my cleavage.

"It's...nice," I said finally.

"Nice? Give me a break. Adam's going to take one look at you in that and have a heart attack."

"Well, that's really not what I was going for." To put it mildly. Adam's infatuation was already enough of a problem...what was he going to do after he saw me looking like this?

Sydney grinned. "No worries. I'll run interference if I have to." She came over and stood about a foot behind me, regarding herself critically in the mirror. "No one's even going to notice *me* with you looking like that."

"I highly doubt that." Maybe at first glance my outfit was more eye-catching, but she looked like the perfect golden girl, with her hair curling over her shoulders and the gleaming fringe of her dress shimmering with every move she made. Also, that dress was *short*. Her legs looked about ten miles long in it. "Anyway," I added, "why do you want people noticing you? I thought you were with Anthony."

"I am. But that doesn't mean I don't still want guys looking at me."

"I really don't think that's going to be a problem."

She grinned, her blue eyes twinkling. "Yeah, probably not. But can we both agree that putting masks on top of all this is really a waste?"

My gaze flickered to the mirror. Sydney was a golden goddess, and I looked far more sultry and exotic than I'd ever thought I could. Wearing a mask did seem kind of silly. "You're right. No masks."

"Thank God." A quick once-over of her ensemble in the mirror, and she asked, "So are you ready?"

"As I'll ever be." I went over to the bed and picked up the black fringed shawl I was using as a wrap—another loan from my aunt.

We clattered down the stairs and heard voices coming from the living room, where apparently Adam had been waiting for us. He'd been chatting with my aunt, the cowboy hat he was wearing as part of his costume tipped back on his head, but when I entered, Sydney a few paces behind, he apparently lost all power of speech. His mouth dropped open, and his eyes widened. Great. Just what I'd been fervently hoping wouldn't happen.

My aunt, bless her, scoped out the situation immediately and rose from the couch, exclaiming, "You girls both look wonderful! Sydney, it was so good of your friend to loan out her dresses!"

"Oh, well, she wasn't going to wear them again, so she figured they might as well get some use," Sydney replied, her voice full of suppressed laughter. I could tell she was having a hard time not bursting into giggles at Adam's reaction to my appearance.

"You look great, too, Aunt Rachel," I said. And she did—she'd sort of piled together some of the choicest boho pieces from her wardrobe, making an awesome gypsy fortune-teller costume. Big gold hoops hung from her ears, and it looked as if she were possibly wearing every necklace she owned.

"Oh, well...." She waved a hand. "Tobias is running a little late, so you three should just go on ahead."

"What, no armed escort?"

That remark earned me a sour look. "There are several...guardians...at the hall already, and you'll have Adam with you."

"What am I, chopped liver?" asked Sydney.

"In this case, unfortunately, yes." My aunt softened her words with an accompanying smile. "But there is always strength in numbers, I suppose. Anyway, there are also a good many people on the street as well, so I think it should be safe enough."

"Then let's get going," I said. "I want to get a decent table to sit at."

That comment seemed to snap Adam out of his stupor. "Right. It's better to get there early, or you end up having to stand all night."

I had a feeling that really wouldn't be an issue, that because of the bodyguards and my status as *prima*-in-waiting I'd somehow magically I'd get a table no matter how crowded it might be already, but there really wasn't any reason to delay any longer. "Okay—we'll hold some seats for you and Tobias."

"No need for that. We'll manage. You go and have a good time."

That seemed to be our cue to leave, so the three of us left Aunt Rachel in the living room and trooped to the back door. The sun had been down for a few hours by then, and the night air that greeted us was already chilly. Sydney had decided against a shawl or coat and now looked as if she regretted it. Good thing we didn't have far to walk.

Because she was there, Adam kept silent, although I noticed how his gaze kept darting over at me. I pulled the shawl closer and pretended not to notice.

There was a line to get into the hall, but it looked as if we were early enough that we'd still be able to snag a table without having to resort to any magical intervention. We paid our ten dollars to get in—for a second I was worried that Adam would try to pay for my ticket, but one quelling look from me seemed to let him know I wasn't going along with that idea—and found a spot toward the back of the room but on the side closer to the bar.

"You two want some drinks?" Adam asked, hovering at the table without sitting down.

"Bacardi and Diet Coke," Sydney said promptly. One of her mottoes was definitely "never turn down a free drink."

Since arguing with him about buying me a drink seemed petty, I made myself smile and say, "Whatever red wine they have would be great."

"Got it." He smiled back at me, and I hoped he wasn't going to take my accepting his offer of a drink as a sign of encouragement. But then he headed off toward the bar, black frock coat flapping behind him. It was a nice-looking getup, I had to admit, although his boyish looks made it seem a little more *Young Guns* than *Tombstone*.

"Lose that shawl," Sydney commanded. "You're inside now, so stop covering up."

I'd forgotten I was still clutching the shawl around me. I did feel safer with it resting on my shoulders and hiding my chest, but I had a feeling Sydney would forcibly pull it off if I didn't ditch it. So I unwrapped it and draped it over the back of the chair, then made myself look around me instead of down at the alarming amount of cleavage I was currently displaying.

"Satisfied?" I asked.

"Much better." She shifted in her seat and tossed her hair back over her shoulders. I supposed if she were going for an authentic flapper look she would've pinned it up somehow to make it simulate a bob, but she was far more interested in looking sexy than being authentic.

She wasn't the only one, either. I saw women in saloon girl costumes and sexy vampire costumes and sexy nurse uniforms and just about every permutation of "sexy" that you could think of. There were scary ones, too, of course…zombies and ghouls and aliens, as well as people dressed as characters from all kinds of movies, including a group of four ghostbusters, not to mention Beetlejuice and Batman.

Behind the costumes and masks I recognized members of the coven, of course, but there were a lot of strangers, too, and I relaxed a little. My worries about the McAllisters taking over the whole dance appeared to be unfounded. It was an eclectic crowd, too, in terms of age—you had to be over twenty-one to get in, of course, but I saw everything from people my own age up to men and women who had to be in their sixties. Good for them, too. Who says you have to stop partying just because you're not in your twenties anymore?

Adam returned with the drinks. "Good thing I went early, too," he said, "because that line's just going to keep getting longer."

"Well, one of us will get the second round," Sydney said, taking her Bacardi and Diet Coke from him, then helping herself to a healthy swig.

He handed me mine before sitting down in the chair on my left. I would've preferred that he sit on the other side of Sydney, but I knew that wasn't going to happen, especially with Anthony supposedly showing up later that night.

What difference does it really make? I asked myself with a mental sigh. *It's not as if your soulmate is going to come waltzing through those doors.*

Which was depressing but probably true. I couldn't really accuse Adam of cock-blocking when there probably wouldn't be any cocks to block.

I drank some of my wine, and Adam took a swallow of his beer. Right then it was early enough that they were just playing canned music; the band wasn't supposed to start until eight-thirty. I could see some of their roadies finishing up with running wires and that sort of thing, so it probably wouldn't be too long before they got started.

Sydney's eyes roved over the crowd, obviously taking stock of the cute-guy quotient, and I wondered how serious she really was about being with Anthony. That was kind of her pattern, though— go after someone, get hot and heavy quickly, and then have the whole thing collapse a few weeks or a month later, depending on how fast their quirks got on her nerves. It wasn't as if she dated around, exactly…more like practiced serial monogamy on speed.

I'd been less than thrilled with my fate of having to wait for Mr. Perfect to show up on my doorstep, but I had to admit that it did have the benefit of keeping a lot of drama out of my life.

But not all, I thought then, trying to ignore Adam's attempt at not looking at my cleavage. It probably would've been easier if I could have just told him I didn't want him tagging along with us. I wasn't that cold-hearted, though. Maybe someone would show up tonight who would distract him from his obsession with me.

That didn't seem too likely, though; most of the girls our age in attendance seemed to be either with a date or hanging out in groups of four or five, which would make approaching them difficult for someone like Adam. He was easy enough with me, but we'd known each other all our lives. Going up to a strange girl and asking her to dance probably was not in his cards that night.

Although the band hadn't started yet, the music was still loud enough that it made talking difficult. I sipped my wine, noting how the table just behind ours was populated entirely with members of my "bodyguard" group: Wyatt McAllister, Margot Emory, Henry Lynch, my cousin Rosemary. There were two seats empty, and I wondered if they were saving those for Aunt Rachel and Tobias. I doubted that their position was accidental, either. Yes, I was supposedly in a safe place, but that didn't mean they weren't going to keep an eye on me.

"I hope Anthony will be able to get in," Sydney said loudly as she eyed the rapidly filling hall.

That could be a problem, because I'd heard they closed the doors after the building reached capacity. "Do you want me to go say something? That's my cousin Shelby at the door—I know she'll squeeze Anthony in if I ask."

"Would you? It would really suck if he drove up here and couldn't even get inside."

"No problem." I pushed out my chair and stood. At once Adam's eyes were on me, obviously curious, and I pointed at the front door. "Just want to tell Shelby something."

He nodded, seeming to relax a little. What did he think I was going to do, take off because I was already tired of him pretending to not stare at my chest?

On second thought….

I pushed back a smile and wove through the crowd to get to the door. Once there, I explained the situation to my cousin.

"Sure," she said, taking a twenty-dollar bill from a guy dressed as Gomez Addams. The Morticia with him was pretty amazing, and I wondered how much competition Gomez was going to have when it came to getting Morticia out on the dance floor. "People are always going in and out, so the building's never totally at capacity. I'll sneak him in. Where're you sitting?"

I pointed at the table where Adam and Sydney sat, my empty chair between them. "Send him over there."

"Will do."

"Thanks!"

After that I turned and walked a few steps, then had to pause as the group of ghostbusters cut in front of me, clearly heading for the bar. Once the way had cleared, I began to move forward again, only to freeze as I came face to face with a tall man all in black, his face partly shaded by the wide-brimmed black hat he wore. Even the mask covering the upper half of his face couldn't hide the lean, handsome features, the sensual mouth.

My brain sort of registered that he was dressed as Zorro, just as I also realized I was blocking his way.

"Sorry," I mumbled, moving to the side so he could continue on his path.

"I'm not," he said with a smile.

Right then I was glad Sydney had talked me into wearing that flashy dress, because from what I could see, the stranger's expression was more than a little admiring.

The moment passed, though, and he just sort of nodded and kept going, clearly headed toward a table that had several other guys and a few girls seated at it. They all looked to be around my age, maybe a few years older. I didn't recognize any of them, but that didn't surprise me much. The Jerome Halloween dance was advertised all over the state, and we had people driving in from Phoenix and even Tucson to attend. The town's B&Bs were generally booked on this weekend up to six months in advance.

Somehow I kept myself from staring at the stranger, though, and went on to sit back down at my own table. I plopped into my chair and reached for my glass of wine.

"Did you take care of it?" Sydney asked. It was a little quieter right then, as they'd turned off the canned music. I saw the band starting to walk onstage.

"Yes." Then I leaned in close to her and hoped Adam wasn't eavesdropping. "I just saw the hottest guy."

"You did? Where?"

I lowered my voice further. "A few tables over to the left...the Zorro."

At least she'd mastered the art of the casual over-the-shoulder glance. I doubted Adam could even tell what she was doing. She leaned in close to me immediately afterward and said, "Holy crap. You weren't kidding. Are you going to ask him to dance? You have to—your costumes are *perfect* together!"

"I-I don't know. Maybe." I didn't think I was brave enough for that. Yes, this wasn't the Victorian era, and there certainly was nothing wrong with going up to a guy and asking him to dance, but.... I risked a quick look of my own in the direction of the table where Zorro sat. It was hard to tell whether he was with any of the girls in particular or whether they were just a group of friends who'd come to the dance together.

"Something interesting over there?" Adam asked, craning his own neck.

"No—I was just looking to see whether Aunt Rachel had shown up yet."

Since that was a perfectly plausible explanation, he just said, "Oh," and returned to his beer. And whether my little lie had manifested her presence or she'd just shown up at that particular moment, I actually did see her walk in the door a few seconds later, followed by Tobias. At least, from his height I assumed it was Tobias. He was dressed in black hooded robes and carried a scythe. I hoped he didn't give her a heart attack when she opened the door and saw him in that getup.

She appeared to spy us and gave a little wave, and I grinned back. Behind her, the Grim Reaper lifted his scythe in greeting. Sydney saw where I was looking, noted Tobias's costume, and said, "Well, that's cheery."

"But comfortable."

"True. I doubt the Grim Reaper has his feet shoved into four-inch stilettos."

"You could've worn something lower."

"But these ones matched my dress."

I couldn't really argue with that. Besides, Lara, the lead singer for the band—not a McAllister, or a witch, but a longtime Jerome resident and someone who knew the score and wasn't fazed by it—had just stepped up to the mic.

"Hello, Jerome!" she called out, and the crowd started clapping and cheering. "Are you ready to get this party started?"

More cheers and whistles and clapping. I wondered if everyone stomped and pounded the floor hard enough whether it would start Spook Hall sliding down the hill the same way so many of the town's other buildings had done over the years.

"Then let's do it!" She turned toward the drummer, and he started in, the lead guitarist playing some twanging chords along with the beat.

I recognized it half a bar in and had to grin. "Bad Moon Rising," by Credence. Well, that was one way to kick things off.

Immediately couples started to crowd onto the dance floor. Adam turned to me. "You want to dance?"

Maybe I should have said no. But dancing was harmless enough, right? Especially a fast song like this one. No way was I going to slow dance with him. I wasn't that crazy.

"Sure," I said, as Sydney cocked an eyebrow at me. I stood up and followed Adam out to the dance floor, and squeezed past one of the ghostbusters, who had the sexy nurse as his partner.

Not that Sydney had much time to get judge-y, because one of the other ghostbusters came up to her and invited her out to the dance floor as well. He wasn't bad-looking, either...maybe a few years older than we were, with sandy hair and dark eyes. She sort of shrugged and then got to her feet, squeezing out there with the rest of us.

Adam turned out to be a decent enough dancer, and since it was a lively song I didn't have to worry about him reading much into it except that it was a dance, after all, and so it would have been kind of silly to go and then not, you know, dance. Even so, I couldn't help glancing past him and through the crowd of dancers to the table where I knew Zorro was sitting. He hadn't gotten up to dance, although several of the members of his group had. So maybe neither of the girls at his table were his girlfriend after all.

Like it really mattered one way or another. Yes, he was extremely good-looking, but so what? I doubted he could possibly be my soulmate. It was dark enough in the hall that I hadn't been able to tell what color his eyes were. Maybe if I got close enough....

I shook my head at myself and refocused on the dance, on the rhythm of the music and the guy in front of me. It wasn't really fair to Adam to be staring off at someone else while we were on the dance floor together.

The song ended, and we all headed back to the table. I was glad that my own borrowed shoes had sensible heels of around two inches, so my feet might actually last the night. Sydney already looked a little wobbly on her stilettos. I had a feeling by the end of the evening they were going to end up kicked under the table.

But that first song had gotten things going, and although I sat out the next one, I went ahead and danced to "Witchy Woman" with one of the ghost-busters—if he only knew how apropos that song was—and the one after that with Tobias, while Adam gallantly partnered with my aunt. In between dances I kept stealing surreptitious glances at Zorro, but he never seemed to look in my direction. Actually, he didn't seem to be dancing at all, but just watching his friends as they came and went. Like me, he was drinking red wine, but he seemed to be careful about it, and only took a sip every now and then. Well, if he had to drive back down the hill after this, I could see why he might be watching it.

A little after nine, Anthony appeared, flying solo this time. I guess he'd learned his lesson about bring-ing his friends along. Or maybe Sydney had told him we'd have Adam with us, so things would come out even on the whole guys/girls front. We'd saved a seat for Anthony but let a saloon girl and her gunslinger boyfriend take the remaining two chairs at the table. They weren't locals—it turned out they'd driven in from Winslow and were historical reenactors, which explained their costumes—but it seemed that sharing tables was the thing to do if your own party wasn't big enough to take up all the seats.

While the band was taking a break, Anthony and Sydney went to get a fresh round of drinks. I'd offered to get them, but Anthony wasn't hearing of it. He did seem like a nice guy, even if his friend Perry was an asshat, and I hoped Sydney might be able to make this one last longer than a month...or at least not completely break his heart once she got tired of him. Once again I stole a glance at Zorro's table, but he wasn't there. My heart sank a little. Maybe he'd gotten bored and left already. He didn't seem that into the party.

But then I saw him come in from outside as he slid a cell phone into his pants pocket. I didn't exactly allow myself a sigh of relief, although I felt the tension in the back of my neck ease up a little. So he'd just been making a phone call. It made sense, since even though the band was taking a break, the recorded music they were playing was loud enough that you'd have to scream into your phone to be heard.

I sipped my wine and attempted to return my attention to the people sitting around me, but it wasn't easy.

"...Fun?" Adam was saying.

"What?"

He raised his voice slightly. "Having fun?"

I was, more or less, even if I couldn't help being distracted by that gorgeous Zorro. "Oh, yeah," I replied, and lifted my wine glass in sort of a "cheers!" motion.

Adam lifted his beer bottle in return. That was his third, if I'd been counting correctly. Oh, well, he didn't have to drive home at least. His parents had a big Victorian on the same street as Aunt Ruby's house, but he'd moved out this past summer, getting himself an apartment over the ice cream store on Main. Like the rest of the McAllisters, he had his own stipend to live on, but he was also pretty handy and helped out with the various renovations and repairs that seemed to be going on around town at all times. He'd mentioned getting his contractor's license, but I didn't know if he was actively working toward it or not.

On my other side, Anthony and Sydney were sort of hanging all over each other...not kissing, but they might as well be. I didn't really appreciate the PDA, since I didn't want them giving Adam any ideas. However, I figured a "get a room" remark wouldn't go over very well, either, so I sighed and took another sip of wine, and hoped the band would start up again soon.

I didn't know if my wishing had anything to do with it, but Lara and her bandmates returned to the stage a few minutes later. "We thought we'd ease into this set," she said, her voice a teasing growl. When she sang, she sounded like she'd spent the last ten years smoking cigarettes and drinking whiskey in every back-road saloon within a hundred-mile radius...which was actually a good thing.

The bassist started, a slow succession of notes, and Lara snarled into the mic, *"I put a spell on you...."*

A voice said from somewhere over my right shoulder, "Do you want to dance?"

I looked up. Zorro stood there, smiling down at me. Dumbfounded, I could only gape up at him, until Sydney kicked me—sans stilettos, luckily—and I said, "Um...sure."

He held out a black-gloved hand and I took it, rising to my feet as Adam glowered from the seat next to me. I supposed I couldn't blame him too much, since I'd steadfastly refused to slow dance with him, yet here I was taking off with the first stranger who'd asked.

But he wasn't just any stranger....

His hand still holding mine, he led me out onto the dance floor and to a spot somewhere close to the middle. Feeling more than a little awkward, I put one hand on his shoulder and my right hand on his left. He pulled me close, but not too close. At least in that position I was able to look up into his face, to get a better glimpse of the eyes half-obscured by the mask.

Brown. Dark brown.

Disappointment stabbed through me, even as I told myself not to be an idiot and to just enjoy the fact that he'd asked me to dance out of all the girls here...especially since he hadn't danced with anyone else all night.

"So are you a local?" he asked.

"Oh, yeah. Born and bred. Well," I added, "not born, I guess. I was born in California."

He smiled. "That's cool."

"Not really. My mother brought me here when I was less than a month old."

A nod. "Have you ever gone back?"

There was a loaded question. At least, it was loaded to me; he probably thought it was innocent enough. Just making conversation. "No. I don't get out much. What about you?"

"Well, if you're a local, then you know I'm not."

"True. I'd definitely remember you." Oh, that was brilliant. If both my hands hadn't been occupied at the moment, I probably would have smacked myself on the forehead for making such a stupid comment. Hot blood rushed to my cheeks, and I hurried to ask, "So where are you from?"

Another grin, his teeth flashing in the dimly light room. "Scottsdale. Well, my family is. I'm going to ASU right now, so I live in Tempe."

It all sounded so refreshingly normal. "What's your major?"

"I'm working on my master's in studio art."

Hunky *and* artistic? I might as well have custom-ordered him. He was so close to me, too, his body only a few inches from mine. The only other times I'd ever been this close to a guy my age were when a candidate swooped in for his kiss. Then that made me think of what it might be like to kiss this stranger in the Zorro costume...and I knew my thoughts were veering in a very dangerous direction. Voice a little breathless, I said, "That's really cool. We have lots of artists here in Jerome."

"So I've heard. This is the first time I've made it up here, though." He sort of jerked his chin in the direction of the table where his friends were sitting. "My friend Dylan saw an ad for this party in a campus paper or something, and so a group of us decided to come up and check it out."

"Are you staying here?" I knew it was silly to ask, that he was a civilian and not the guy I'd spent the last five years dreaming about, but some part of me wanted to ignore all that, to pretend we could dance tonight and talk and maybe steal a kiss or two, and then meet for coffee in the morning like a couple of normal people.

He shook his head. "No. That is, not in Jerome. We got a room down in Cottonwood because everything here was already booked."

"Good. I mean, that's safer than driving a hundred miles back to Phoenix."

"That was the idea."

After that we both fell silent, but I didn't mind that, either. It felt good to be out on the dance floor, his arms around me. It felt right, which was stupid, I supposed. Probably it was just that he was tall and dark-haired and good-looking, and so close enough to the ideal I'd held in my head for so many years that I wanted this dance to be more than it really was. And I would've known if he were like me—a member of one of the witch clans, that is. We didn't exactly give each other the secret handshake or anything, but each of us has a little core of power within us that sort of gives off a glow others of our kind can detect. I didn't feel anything like that with the man holding me right now. Well, I'd be lying if I said I didn't feel *something*, but it wasn't that.

The song ended, but he didn't seem all that eager to leave the dance floor...at least, not until the band started in on "Werewolves of London." Then he drew me to the side and bent close.

My heart started to pound. Was he going to try to kiss me? And if he did, would I even try to stop him?

But then he said, "Can I get your number? I think I might like to come back to Jerome in the near future."

If Aunt Rachel had heard that, she probably would have shaken her head. No point in giving him any false hope. She wasn't anywhere near us, however, and he was already pulling his phone out of his pocket so he could enter my information.

Taking a breath, I said quickly, "Angela McAllister. It's 928—"

My name, echoed, interrupted me. I felt someone's hand on my arm, and I turned around to see about the last person I expected: my cousin Dora, her face pale and her eyes brimming with tears.

"It's—it's Ruby," she gasped. "She's going, and she needs to see you. You have to hurry!"

The warm afterglow of the dance abruptly disappeared. "Are you sure?"

"Yes, please, you have to come now!"

Helplessly, I looked up at Zorro. "I have to go. I'm sorry."

He looked more than a little confused, but he just nodded. "Sure. It sounds like an emergency." And, more softly, even as I was turning from him and beginning to follow Dora through the crowd, "I know where to find you."

CHAPTER EIGHT

Passing the Veil

I DIDN'T HAVE TIME TO THINK ABOUT MUCH ELSE. NOT THE man I'd just left behind me, or my friends sitting at the table and probably wondering what the hell was going on. I couldn't think about anything as I emerged into the biting night air, except, *She can't be dying. She can't.*

Out the front door of Spook Hall, then across the street and hurrying up the stairs through the park, the quickest route, even though my heels weren't doing me any favors on those steep steps. The cold hit my exposed neck and chest and shoulders almost immediately. Or maybe that was simply the chill of realizing what my great-aunt's passing would mean to me. To all of us McAllisters.

Dora a few paces ahead, the two of us hurried up to Paradise Lane, where Great-Aunt Ruby's house stood.

The light on the front porch shone forth serenely, as if nothing was wrong, but I knew better.

As soon as we entered the house, Dora paused in the entryway. "She's up in her room. She—she wanted to see you alone."

Mute with worry, I could only nod. Then I grasped the shining oak banister and more or less pulled myself up the stairs. Although I'd never been there before, I knew her room was on the left of the landing, in the location that would give her a panoramic view of the town and valley beyond. Not that there was much to see tonight. It was a dark night, heavy with clouds, the moon not yet risen.

Somehow I made myself cross the landing, knock on the door. "Aunt Ruby? It's Angela."

"Come in, child." The voice I knew so well, usually so imperious, now sounded fragile, brittle as the bones in the body it emanated from.

Swallowing, I opened the door and let myself in. The room was warm with candlelight, tapers flickering from the dresser and the delicate writing table under the window and the carved walnut mantel of the little marble-faced fireplace I'd always loved. Great-Aunt Ruby lay propped up against the pillows, pale hair let down from the hard little bun she usually wore it in. Something in her face seemed to have slackened, lost its usual wiry strength, but the blue eyes were clear enough as they met mine.

To my surprise, she smiled. "Well, just look at you. Like something out of a movie. Always thought you'd clean up good."

My face grew hot, and I made an off-hand gesture. "Oh, it's just for the Halloween dance. I—"

She shook her head. "Goodness, child, don't apologize for looking beautiful. Come here."

I couldn't disobey. Slowly I walked to her bedside, and she reached out and took my cold fingers in her bony ones. I had thought she'd be cold as well, but she felt strangely warm, as if some fire were burning within her, consuming the last of her long life.

"I haven't got long," she began, "so I need you to listen, and listen well."

"Oh, Aunt Ruby—"

"No time for that. I told you I made my peace with it, and the truth is I've held on far longer than I wanted to. But I needed you to be ready, and you are."

I wanted to protest that I wasn't, not at all. Arguing with someone on their deathbed didn't seem like a particularly wise thing to do, though, so I just nodded and waited for her to speak again.

"I'm not going to say you know everything, because you don't, and there are some things you can't plan for, however much you know. But you've got the strength in you, Angela, and the power to do the right thing. You'll protect this clan, and do a good job of it."

My fingers tightened around hers. "Can't you— can't you just stay a little longer. Just until—" I broke off, my throat tightening with tears I didn't want to shed in front of her. I didn't want her to see how weak I really was.

"It's hard, I know. You shouldn't have to face this alone. But I told you he's out there, and he'll come to you when the time is right. You won't be the first witch who's had to lead her clan without a consort. We all know everything happens because it's meant to, even if we can't see the reason right away." She shut her eyes for a moment, and I held my breath, wondering if this was it, the moment I'd been dreading for too long. But then the crepe-y eyelids fluttered, and she looked up at me once more. "Don't give up hope, child. It's the one thing that will always be there to guide you."

"I won't give up hope, Aunt Ruby. I promise." I wasn't sure if I really believed that; I just wanted to say something I thought she wanted to hear.

She smiled, gently, and her eyes went wide. Her focus was not on me, though, but on some point past me. An expression of incredible joy passed over her features, and for the briefest second I saw not the withered shell she'd become, but a vibrant, beautiful young woman. "I'm here, Pat!" she cried out, her voice strong and full. "I'm here!"

Then her head fell back against the pillows, and the fingers dropped away from mine. A warm rush, as if I could feel her life energy moving over me and through me, like the gentle winds of a summer long gone.

And deep inside me I felt a new stirring, a glow of power, of strength. As she'd gone, she'd passed her powers on to me. The powers of the *prima*.

Slowly I lifted her lifeless hand and pressed my lips against it. *Thank you, Ruby. I will be strong...for you.*

———

They were waiting when I descended the stairs— Dora, and Aunt Rachel, and Tobias, and Adam and so many others, including the clan elders, Margot Emory, and Allegra Moss, and Bryce McAllister. Not all, of course. To have every single member of the clan just up and leave the dance would attract far too much notice. But enough.

"She's gone," I said clearly, pausing on the bottom step. My eyes burned with unshed tears, but I didn't want to weep in front of them. I had to be strong. I was the *prima*. "It was a good passing. She called out to him, at the end. I think he was waiting for her."

Her two sons, Lionel and Joseph, stepped forward. "Can we go to her?" asked Lionel.

"Of course." I moved aside so they could go upstairs and make their own farewells. It was probably hard for them, to think that she'd asked for me at the end, and not her own sons, but allowances had to be made for the passage of power from *prima* to *prima*.

I hoped it would be enough that they could spend this small bit of time with her before we had to let the outside world in, call the funeral home in Cottonwood, make arrangements for her burial in the McAllister plot in the town cemetery. There'd once been a "Boot Hill" up in Jerome, but the hill was far too unstable; no one had been buried there for generations.

Aunt Rachel stepped forward, Tobias just a pace behind her. "How are you, sweetie?"

The endearment almost made my tears burst forth. Somehow I held them in check and managed a weak smile. "I'm okay. Tired. I just want to go home."

At the word "home," the clan elders exchanged a significant glance. Tradition held that this should be my home now. But I had no consort. True, as Aunt Ruby had said, there had been *primas* without consorts before me. None from the McAllister clan, however, and probably not many in as vulnerable a position as I currently was. And frankly, the thought of having to live in this big old house, with its antiques and portraits of former McAllisters, was not very enticing.

Rachel must have caught the unspoken dialogue amongst the elders, because she frowned slightly and said, "Nothing needs to be decided tonight. We all need our time to grieve. Let me take Angela home."

Margot Emory nodded. She was a striking woman with gray-streaked dark hair and clear gray eyes under strongly arched brows. Ruby had been her aunt as well, but her expression was serene and calm, with no evidence of the sorrow she must be feeling. "Yes, she needs her rest. There is much that will have to be done."

Those words were more than a little ominous, but my aunt just reached out and took me by the hand, led me through the watching crowd. As I passed him, I felt Adam's worried gaze on me, and wished I could stop to ask him what had happened with Sydney and Anthony, whether they knew why I'd had to leave so precipitously. But I couldn't think of a way to do so without making it seem as if my friends' concerns were more important than those of the clan, so I only shot him an uncertain smile as I passed by and then went on out the front door.

A cold wind washed over me, but of course Aunt Rachel had thought of everything. She pulled an embroidered wool shawl from where she'd had it draped over one arm and handed it to me so I could cover up my exposed chest and shoulders. I murmured a thank-you, and we went down the front steps and to the quiet street, then down the steeply sloping hill back to the store. Tobias followed us the whole way, not speaking, but keeping watch over the two of us. At least he'd left the scythe behind, and had dropped the hood of his black robes. Now he looked more like a burly bear of a friar, although he had a full head of hair and not one of those silly-looking tonsures.

Maybe it was foolish of me to even be thinking of such things, but it kept me from brooding on what had just happened. Great-Aunt Ruby was dead. I was the new *prima*.

I didn't want to believe it. There had always been this small part of me that had thought they must all be wrong, that there had been some sort of mistake. Yes, I could talk to ghosts, but I didn't possess any great power. Or so I had thought.

Now, though, with the gift that Ruby had passed on to me coiled like a glowing snake somewhere in my belly, I thought I began to understand. It wasn't simply the gifts one was born with, but whether a given person had the predisposition within them to accept the *prima* energy and make it their own. What precisely I was supposed to do with it, I didn't quite know, but I guessed the clan elders would have some insight on that.

The main thing, though, was that I be kept safe until my consort came to me. Until we were joined, I would not be able to fully use these powers. They were powers meant for a grown woman, not the girl I still was. The girl I would remain until I met the one who would take that girlhood from me.

We went inside, Rachel closing but not locking the door behind us. As we'd approached the building, I'd seen out of the corner of my eye the approaching forms of three of the "bodyguards," and I knew they would come in and secure the place once I was upstairs.

Never before had the stairs up to my room felt as steep, but eventually I got there, my aunt and Tobias pausing out in the hallway.

"If there's anything you need—" she began, and I shook my head.

"I just want to sleep," I told her. "There'll be— well, I know there'll be a lot that has to be done over the next few days, so I might as well get my rest now."

Her eyes glittered with tears. "That's right, sweetheart. You sleep, and we'll work everything out tomorrow."

I doubted everything would be worked out. However, I knew she was just trying to reassure me, to let me know this wasn't all as horrible and awful as I thought it was. So I nodded, murmured "good-night," and closed the door.

My room looked just as it always did, the embroidered bedspread cheerful with its primary colors and background of soft ecru, the walls painted a bold turquoise and covered with folk art and candle sconces and an assortment of symbols: crosses, a carved "om" symbol, the leafy face of the Green Man. That familiarity should have comforted me, but instead it sent a painful pang through my chest. Would this still be my room, my home? Or would I be forced to take my place as *prima* in the cluttered Victorian mansion on the hill?

I didn't want to think about that now. I didn't want to think about anything. I walked over to the bed, kicked off my borrowed shoes, and then collapsed, sobs finally wracking my body.

Even then I wasn't sure whether I wept for my great-aunt, or the life I knew was about to change forever.

"Of course you must go up to the house," Bryce McAllister said calmly. "It's yours now. You've seen the will."

My head ached. I'd cried most of the night, slept fitfully for a few hours just before dawn, then went downstairs and brewed myself a strong pot of tea.

It hadn't helped my head much, but at least now I didn't feel as if I were going to fall asleep standing up.

The other two elders, Margot Emory and Allegra Moss, nodded. We all sat at the long dining room table in the apartment, with Aunt Rachel on my right and the three of them facing us. Tobias had spent the night, I thought, but he was gone now. This was business between the *prima* and the elders, and he was not needed…or that seemed to be their view on things, anyway. Rachel they'd grudgingly allowed to stay, since I still lived under her roof.

And yes, I had seen the will; they'd brought it with them so I would know my rights and responsibilities going forward. The big house was mine, as well as a far larger share of the money that came to everyone in the clan every month. Ruby's individual wealth, as well as a number of personal items, was to be divided between her two sons, with them deciding which pieces should go on to their own children, who numbered five altogether.

Even so, I realized tiredly that my great-aunt's bequest had made me a very wealthy young woman. Too bad I really didn't care about that.

"I don't think it's safe," I argued. "Down here I'm surrounded by people. Aunt Ruby's house only has neighbors on one side." I didn't bother to mention that those neighbors were Adam's parents, which would only make things that much more awkward.

True, he'd moved out, but I got the feeling he'd find excuses to go visit if I were right there, too. "That is, I think we can all agree that I'm in sort of a precarious position right now."

An expression of dismay crossed Allegra's normally placid features. "Of course we would maintain the guard on you. That is not going to change."

Of course not. So I'd be stuck in that house with a bunch of bodyguards, and not even my aunt's leavening influence to make things a little more tolerable. I turned to her. "I don't really have to move out, do I?"

Her fingers knotted together on the brightly printed tablecloth from India. "I know it's hard, Angela, but that is the *prima's* residence. You knew you wouldn't be staying here forever."

Yes, but I'd thought that when I left this comfortable apartment, I'd be moving to my new home with my consort at my side. I hadn't thought I'd be camped out there with a bunch of babysitters making sure that dark specters or roving Wilcoxes or whatever peril might be lurking nearby didn't have a chance of getting close to me.

It hurt to think that Aunt Rachel was siding with the elders against me. "So you—you *want* me to leave?" I asked, my voice barely above a whisper.

Her face crumpled, and I could tell she was close to tears. "No, of course not. But what I want isn't a factor in all this. There are…traditions. I can't let my own feelings get in the way."

I wanted to say, *Fuck traditions!* That wouldn't be productive, though, and I knew I had to grow up and face reality…even though I really, really didn't want to. "All right," I said wearily. "But it doesn't have to happen right this minute, does it?"

"No, that was never our intention," Bryce said. "There's the funeral the day after tomorrow, and then Lionel and Joseph will have to take out the things Ruby left them. Next week, I think."

His reply calmed me a little. All right, so I was apparently stuck with that Victorian white elephant, but I would have a week to come to terms with everything, to say goodbye to my lively room and the view that had greeted me every morning since I was too young to remember. Would I be able to change anything in the house I'd inherited, or would I be expected to keep it in its current museum-like state, with all the furniture that dated back to the same time the house was built?

That was a question I knew I'd better leave for another day. In the meantime, there was still a great deal to do.

It was only when we were gathered together like this that I realized how many of us McAllisters there really were, even if we didn't all share the same last name. We clustered in a corner of the cemetery, more than two hundred of us. A casual passerby might have thought us a strange-looking crew to be attending a grave-side service, for very few of us wore black. It wasn't our custom to mourn in such a way. Of course we would all miss Ruby, miss her strength and her wisdom and her fierce loyalty to the clan, but we knew she had merely crossed over, not ceased to be. She was still living, only elsewhere. And I had seen for myself the expression of joy cross her face when it was time to walk over that threshold to the next world. I had no doubt that her husband Pat was there to welcome her. How could I be sad, when she had clearly been so happy to go?

As I stood by the grave, and watched the burnished mahogany casket with its beautiful crown of yellow roses—Ruby's favorite—and spider mums be lowered slowly into the ground, I wondered if I would ever love someone like that.

There were too many of us to fit into anyone's house, so we'd rented out Spook Hall for the reception afterward. More yellow roses greeted us there, and I thought of how I'd been here only a few days earlier, and danced with Zorro and worried—hoped?—that he might try to kiss me. That opportunity was long gone, and so was he, I supposed, back to Tempe and his master's program and the real world.

Sydney had called me, eschewing texts in her worry, and I'd explained what happened. Too many things going on for me to be able to talk with her for very long, but she did tell me that Adam had said it was a family emergency, and so she and Anthony had slipped away not too long after that.

"I could tell it was something important," she'd said, "since so many people began to leave, even though they hadn't gotten to the costume contest yet. And your Zorro came up and asked about you."

"He did?" I asked, cheered a little despite everything.

"He sounded worried, and I said it was a family thing, and then he told me you were just about to give him your number but had to leave, so…."

"So?"

"So I gave it to him. I figured it would be okay, since you were about to do it anyway." She hesitated. "Was it not okay?"

"No," I said wearily. "It's fine. I doubt he'll call. He lives in Tempe, and besides…."

"He's a civilian?"

"Yes."

A long pause. Then she said, sounding a little too cheerful, "Well, hey, you never know. I am sorry about your great-aunt."

I'd thanked her for that and hung up. I could tell that she wanted to talk more, to ask about me being *prima* now and all that, but I just didn't have the time…or the heart. Maybe after things had settled down somewhat I could have her come up and visit, but it would have to wait for a few days.

Now I stood off to the side and watched the clan members moving through the hall, or standing and talking in small groups. Toward the front was a table decked with flowers, and a large reproduction of a photo of Ruby when she was close to my age, her mouth painted with red lipstick, hair in perfect Rita Hayworth waves to her shoulders. She was smiling, but not directly at the camera. Maybe Pat had been standing behind the photographer, and she'd been smiling for him.

She really had been strikingly beautiful. I could see why there would've been plenty of young men vying for her attentions, and not just because she was the next McAllister *prima*. I wondered if her looks had factored into the Wilcoxes' desperate attempt to steal her for themselves, or whether her beauty was just a nice bonus.

A shiver went over me then. I didn't want to think about the Wilcoxes, or what they might be plotting…if anything. Ever since that long-ago kidnap attempt, they'd stayed on their turf, just as we'd stayed on ours, and they'd been quiescent enough for the most part. Even so, they weren't to be trusted.

"Are you okay?" came Adam's voice from over my shoulder.

I turned toward him. "Sure. Why?"

"You were frowning."

"Oh, just thinking."

"About nothing pleasant, I guess."

"The Wilcoxes."

"Definitely *not* pleasant, then."

Despite everything, I grinned. "Not really, no. I'm just borrowing trouble, I think. By the way, I never got a chance to thank you for letting Sydney know what was going on so she wouldn't think I'd totally bailed on her."

"No problem." He shifted from one foot to the other, looking vaguely uncomfortable.

Maybe it was the button-up shirt and loafers he was wearing, instead of his usual T-shirts and Converse high-tops. No, we weren't required to wear black dresses and black suits and all that, but it was a sign of respect to dress nicely at the funeral of a clan member. I had on a vaguely retro full-skirted dress I'd bought at one of the shops here in town, and had borrowed Aunt Rachel's pumps again. We all looked pretty respectable—probably more respectable than an outsider would've expected a gathering of witches to be. Just more of that whole staying inconspicuous thing. You tend to attract more attention when everyone in your group looks like a refugee from a Stevie Nicks concert.

"So," he went on, drawing out the syllable as if pondering what exactly to say next. "I guess you really are moving into Aunt Ruby's house."

"Yes," I said shortly. "Next Monday, I guess." A day I was really not looking forward to.

"Oh." Then he brightened a little. "You know, Saturday is that Day of the Dead thing over in Sedona. I was thinking it might be, I don't know, good to go to that. Say another goodbye to Great-Aunt Ruby."

I'd completely forgotten about the festival. Halloween was two days before that, although I knew this year there wouldn't be too much revelry amongst the McAllister clan. Of course there would be our usual Samhain observances on Halloween itself, another way of connecting with the dead, when the veil between the worlds was at its thinnest.

Now that I thought about it, though, going to the Day of the Dead celebration seemed like a good way to make my final farewells and honor my aunt before my life went through its own change. "We'll have to take the bodyguards," I warned Adam. "No way are they going to let me go to Sedona with just you."

"Oh, I figured that. Maybe your aunt and Tobias, too, if they're interested."

The offer touched me. Clearly he was doing this because he thought it would help me, and not to seize some opportunity, however artificial, to get me alone. I didn't know if Aunt Rachel would really be up to it, as the double shock of losing Ruby and me at roughly the same time had shaken her a good deal. There was still a sign on the front door of the shop that said "closed due to a death in the family." I hadn't yet gathered the courage to ask her if she intended to open up on Halloween, which tended to be a busy day even when it fell in the middle of the week.

"I'll ask," I said. "But Rachel's taking the whole thing pretty hard. I'll let you know."

"Okay." He reached out then and gave my hand a quick squeeze before heading off toward the refreshment table.

I wouldn't let myself sigh. I had to look as if I were in control, no matter what. But it was hard not to wish, just a little, that things had been different, that Adam was my one. No, he didn't set my heart on fire or anything, but he'd been supportive and friendly the past few days, and I knew I could trust him. It would have been a lot easier if he'd turned out to be the consort.

But of course nothing can ever be that easy.

CHAPTER NINE

Día de los Muertos

A FULL MOON DRIFTED OVERHEAD, SURROUNDED BY CLOUDS that reflected its light, only more diffuse, cloudy and yellow. The wind was from the northeast, cold and biting. I tried not to think about where it was coming from, blowing down the passes from Flagstaff.

An ill wind….

I shook my head and made myself concentrate on the group around me. We always held our Samhain observance late, almost at midnight, long after all the shops and and restaurants had closed. Yes, there were still some late-night partiers at the Spirit Room, but they would be otherwise occupied, and hopefully not noticing what we all were up to.

Well, not all. The McAllister contingent in Jerome numbered a little more than two hundred these days, and two hundred people gathering anywhere in a town that small was bound to get noticed. So a little more than half of us met in small groups in people's homes, sharing their own versions of the rituals, celebrating the Goddess as Crone and the Horned Hunter.

But because November was the dead time, a month and more of darkness before Yule arrived and the world began to tilt once again toward the light, we always had the strongest witches and warlocks come together in one place to invoke the spirits of our ancestors, to ask for their guidance and their strength in helping to protect us against the forces of the dark. We met on the grounds of the building that had been the miner's dormitory, once upon a time, mainly because it was enough out of the way that any tourists lingering at the Spirit Room wouldn't be able to stumble upon us. They might see the lights of our candles and torches as they made their way back to their cars, but they wouldn't be able to get to us. No visible barrier blocked the road that led to the dormitory, but anyone going that way would find their car's engine suddenly sputtering and dying, or would suddenly be overwhelmed by the feeling that they needed to get out of there *right now.*

That north wind cut bitterly through the thin cotton of my robes, even though I wore a long-sleeved T-shirt and long skirt underneath. In the spring and summer, some of the more abandoned among us went naked under their robes, but I'd never done that even in warm weather and certainly wasn't going to start now. Difficult enough to know that I was the one who would have to lead the coven in the ritual. The *prima* always presided at the great celebrations.

My throat was dry. I coughed, a dry little scratch that didn't do much to help relieve the tickle I felt, and stepped forward. "Let it be known that the Circle is about to be cast. All who enter the Circle may do so in perfect love and perfect trust."

The watching crowd nodded, and waited as I made my way around the huge circle, invoking the deities of the four quarters and lighting the ritual candles in their prescribed shades of green and yellow and red and blue. I had been to enough of these ceremonies over the years that the words came as naturally to me as if I'd written them myself. Each coven had its own liturgy, if you wanted to call it that, something codified through many, many years of use, and ours was no different.

There were far too many of us to have every individual come to me and affirm his or her ritual entry to the circle, and so I asked the question of all of them as a group: "How do you enter the circle?"

"In perfect love and perfect trust," they all responded, a low murmur, powerful as the mountain upon which we stood.

They all took up the circle, and the ceremony of Samhain began. Great-Aunt Ruby had varied it from year to year, sometimes focusing on the harvest, sometimes concentrating on invoking the spirits of our ancestors. Because we had so recently lost her, I'd thought that was what I had better do here tonight as well.

Rosemary is for remembrance,
and tonight we remember those who have
lived and died before us…

It was a longish ritual, or at least it had always seemed that way to me as a semi-bored teenager repeating the words, shivering and wishing I could be off at the Halloween dance at the high school (even though in general I wasn't much for socializing), or over at Sydney's house, eating popcorn and watching scary movies. Anything that a normal teenager was supposed to do on Halloween. But I guess I'd never really been normal, even when I pretended to be.

Now, though, the words seemed to spin out of me with strength and sureness, as if it really were Great-Aunt Ruby reaching from beyond the veil to lend me some of her wisdom. I didn't falter, and the flames of the candles burned bright and true, even with the wind blowing all around us.

After facing the four quarters and once again invoking the deities of each direction, I went to the altar Tobias and a few others had erected in the center of the circle. I picked up the black candle and called forth the flame with my mind, saying, *"The Wheel of the Year turns once more, and we cycle into darkness."*

As I did so, I halfway expected that black specter to appear once more, hand outstretched, cold whisper echoing in my mind. But nothing happened, and I hitched in a little breath and went on to light the white candle, signifying the light that would return after the solstice. From there I invoked the spirits of our ancestors, all the McAllisters who had gone before us, asking them to bless us with their strength and their love.

Although the night was cold, somehow it seemed to turn warm then, as if we were all surrounded by the good wishes of the loved ones we had lost. I almost thought I felt Great-Aunt Ruby's quick caress of my cheek, and a quick, "Well done, child."

Most people would say it was their imagination...but I knew better.

After that I closed the circle by dismissing the deities who had watched over us, and thanking them for their service. Once that was done, everyone broke off in little groups, heading back to their cars or, for the hardier ones, to the paths that would lead them up to their homes.

There hadn't been any question of my walking; I'd ridden down in Tobias's truck with him and

Rachel. In the moonlight, I thought I saw the glitter of tears on my aunt's cheeks, but she smiled and hugged me when I approached her.

"That was beautiful, Angela," she told me. "Ruby would be so proud of you."

"Thank you," I said awkwardly. I knew Ruby was proud, or at least I had a good notion that she was. I didn't mention what I had heard, though, as everyone had a different experience in the circle, and I didn't want to say anything that might change hers.

We were silent then as Tobias went and got the altar, and he and Lionel brought it over and wrapped it in the blankets that had been waiting in the bed of Tobias's pickup. After that we drove back up to the shop, where he led us inside, wished Aunt Rachel and me goodnight, and kissed her quickly on the cheek. Just in time, too, as that night's "bodyguards" showed up then, and we all trooped upstairs to the apartment.

They wouldn't sleep, of course, but instead settled themselves down on the sofa and easy chair in the living room. One would think that the ritual I'd just performed would be enough to ensure some protection for this night at least. Obviously not, though; they weren't about to take any chances. So I bade them goodnight, and went to the bathroom to wash my face and brush my teeth while I was still dressed. Even after a few weeks of this, I hadn't gotten to the point where I was willing to let them see me wandering around in my bathrobe.

After all that, though, I slipped back into my bedroom and closed the door behind me. I'd left a white candle burning on my own little altar there, one of those saints' candles you can buy at the supermarket, although this one had a guardian angel on it, not a saint. That kind of candle was safe to leave unattended, and I wanted that white light to fill my room so no evil could enter there.

And all the gods and goddesses knew that I could use a guardian angel about now.

I pulled off my robe and hung it from the hook on the back of my door, then kicked off my shoes and took off my long skirt and T-shirt as well. After shaking my hair loose from the rubber band I'd used to hold it out of the way while I washed my face and brushed my teeth, I went to the window and pushed the curtain aside slightly so I could look out on the sleeping town.

There was no sign that a large group had gathered earlier out on the promontory where the old dormitory was located. Neither could you tell just by looking that we'd invoked the spirits of the dead and cast yet another spell of protection around Cleopatra Hill and the town built on it. But I knew. I could still feel the power thrumming through my bones. No one who wished us any ill could come near here. I felt it.

The moon shone down on me, naked of clouds now. I gazed up at it, drinking in the white light. I had survived my first ritual, and hadn't botched anything or opened up the clan to dark influences.

Maybe this *prima* thing wouldn't be so difficult after all.

———

To my surprise, Aunt Rachel did open the store the next day. "Can't stay closed forever…and it's the weekend," she told me.

Or maybe she was just trying to take her mind off the reality of my moving out in a few days. When I'd gotten up that morning, I started packing some of my less essential items—summer clothes and flip-flops, books I knew I wouldn't be reading any time soon—but I hated doing even that much. It felt so… final.

She'd declined going to the Day of the Dead festivities but didn't forbid my going. That is, she really didn't have the option of telling me what to do anymore, and instead said, "Well, you'll need to discuss that with the elders."

None of them had been exactly thrilled at the prospect. Margot Emory had frowned and shared what sounded like a heated convo with the other two elders, and then Allegra Moss shrugged and said, "If you take five of our strongest with you, then I think it should be all right." Since she had some of the strongest precognition in the clan, generally when she said something like that, you were good to go.

Apparently Bryce had thought the same thing, because he didn't offer any other argument. "I'll choose them," he remarked, but that was about it.

Not that I really wanted five witches and warlocks trailing me the whole time. Still, it was better than being under house arrest, and it had been months since I'd gone into Sedona. It was neutral territory, an agreement having been made more than a hundred years earlier that the resort town had too much power on its own, what with the energy vortexes that surged up through the rocks there. Any clan living within its boundaries would have an unfair advantage. I was sort of surprised that the agreement was still honored to this day, considering you couldn't trust a Wilcox any farther than you could throw him (or her...although they skewed heavily toward warlocks and not witches). I'd asked Rachel about it once, and although her expression turned dark, the way it always did when the subject of the Wilcoxes came up, she said that the other clans, especially the de la Pazes, would have come up here and assisted us if the Wilcox clan had ever attempted such a thing. They were powerful, but even they weren't strong enough to face down all the other Arizona clans at the same time.

Anyway, we were all allowed to go into Sedona to eat and shop and go to the movies, as long as we didn't stay overnight and didn't attempt to cast any spells or perform any rituals there. The McAllisters probably went far more often than the Wilcoxes, simply because we were closer, only about fifteen miles away, and up in Flagstaff there was at least a movie theater and a mall, whereas we had to drive all the way to Prescott for those amenities.

I helped out in the shop part of the day that Saturday, but I couldn't stay until closing, since we'd be leaving a little after three. One of the warlocks in the bodyguard contingent was Lester Phillips, partly because he excelled at defensive spells, and partly because he had a big van that all of us could pile into. Adam met me at the shop, the van pulled up about five minutes later, and then we were off.

It was a clear, bright day, with just a few thin clouds overhead. The air was cold, though; the north wind had decided to hang around for a few days. I wore one of Rachel's wool shawls over my black sweater and spangly skirt, since somehow it hadn't felt respectful to go to a Day of the Dead festival in jeans and cowboy boots. Adam had traded his T-shirt for a hoodie, but otherwise his attire didn't look much different from what I saw him wear every other day of the year.

His eyes had lit up when he saw me, and I hoped I hadn't done the wrong thing by agreeing to come. No, he knew how things stood between us. I told myself he was probably just glad that I hadn't called everything off at the last minute.

He didn't seem that inclined to talk during the drive. I was glad of that, since it meant I could stare silently out the window and watch the golden fields pass by outside. We'd greened up with the monsoon rains during the summer, but things had dried out again and would stay that way through the winter.

The trip took a little more than a half hour. Sedona was crowded, as it generally was on the weekends. Cars had backed up onto the highway while trying to get into the parking lot at Tlaquepaque Village, where the Day of the Dead festivities were being held, but Lester had a handicapped placard because of his bad back, so once we actually got in, we were still able to find a place to park without too much trouble. Yes, I know a warlock with a bad back sounds incongruous, but we hadn't had a good healer among us since Dottie McAllister, my second cousin once removed (or something like that), passed away a few years ago. And, as Lester liked to point out, having that handicapped placard came in, well, handy.

As soon as I got out of the van I could hear the rippling sounds of flamenco music coming from one of the courtyards. The place was mobbed with people, and I experienced a small thrill of apprehension. I wasn't used to being out among that many people, especially strangers, on territory that wasn't mine.

Everyone else got out of the van, and Adam and I stood there, unsure as to which way we should go. The five bodyguards waited patiently; clearly they were just here to keep watch, and it was up to me to decide where we would go and what we would see.

I figured we might as well head toward the music. "Let's see what's going on over there," I said, and pointed more or less in the direction of the guitar player.

Adam nodded, and we set out, winding through the crowd, trying not to stare at all the sights around us. Tourists in fanny packs and sweatshirts, naturally, and boho Sedona types in long skirts and Navajo jewelry, and couples with babies in strollers and people walking their dogs. But I also saw people wearing Mexican costume, with their faces painted like *calaveras*, or skulls, and women in long skirts and shawls wrapped around their hips, clearly dressed for flamenco dancing. It was all fascinating, and I tried not to stare too hard at the sights around me.

We came out into a courtyard with a fountain in the center, and everywhere I looked I saw little glass containers with candles inside them, and labels stuck on the outside with short messages or the names of relatives who had passed away. Against one wall was a huge altar with more offerings and bouquets of flowers and fruit.

"Look," said Adam, who was taller than I and therefore could see better. "It looks like there's a place over there where you can buy the candles. Let's get one for Great-Aunt Ruby."

I agreed that sounded like a great idea, and we picked our way through the crowd, trailed by the bodyguards, until we got to a little pavilion on the far side of the courtyard where you could make a donation and get a candle. Since the donations went to benefit the local animal shelter, I pulled out a twenty and dropped it in the donation jar, then waited for the man handling the candles to fetch one for me, along with a sticker and a Sharpie so I could write down my message.

"What are you going to say?" Adam asked, once we'd shuffled over to one side to make room for the next people wanting to get their own candles.

Good question. I'd come here with the idea that we would be paying tribute to Ruby, but the carnival atmosphere had my brain a little muddled. Not that I didn't like it, but it wasn't what I'd been expecting. I'd thought it would be a little quieter, somehow, a little more introspective. But that was probably my own fault for not reading up on it before I came.

I was here now, though, so I tried to focus. I knew my great-aunt wouldn't want us to mourn. No, I wanted to write something that paid tribute to her without being all weepy about it. Finally, I bent over the table and wrote on my sticker, *Ruby, your strength inspires all of us, and you will live in our hearts forever.* There wasn't really room for anything more than that, so I showed it to Adam, who nodded his approval.

"I think she'd like that. Now, where do you want to put it?"

Hmm. Already candles covered almost every available level surface—crowding the altar I'd spied earlier, ringing the fountain in the center of the courtyard, even running along the edges of the stucco and concrete planters. But then I noticed off to the side a smaller altar with a few open spots in front of it.

"How about over there?"

He peered through the crowd. "That looks good. Better hurry before someone else fills it up."

No kidding. Everywhere I looked I saw people hunting for the perfect spot for their own candles. I put the sticker on the glass container—the man who'd given us the candle had prelit it for us—and then pushed through the crowd to set it down in one of the few remaining spaces. The flame flickered a little, but then stood up straight and tall, strong the way my great-aunt had been almost until the day she died.

"Okay, now what?" Adam asked, once I straightened and stood next to him.

Why he was asking me, when it had been his idea to come here, I didn't know. Maybe he just thought as *prima* I should be the one calling the shots. I decided it wasn't worth arguing about and pointed to the next courtyard over, which was where the flamenco music seemed to be coming from.

It wasn't quite as crowded in that spot, although there were still plenty of people milling around. Here I spied some tables with chairs around them, and a second or two later I saw the reason why: the restaurant at the far end of the courtyard had an outside stand where they were selling margaritas and sangria.

Now that we'd paid our respects to Great-Aunt Ruby, I didn't see why we couldn't have a little fun. She certainly hadn't been above having a drink or two, although her poison of choice was gin martinis.

"Buy you a drink?" I asked, and Adam grinned.

"Sure."

We went over to the stand and waited for the couple ahead of us to finish their transaction. I stepped up to the pretty Hispanic woman who was taking the orders and said, "A sangria and..." I trailed off, since I hadn't asked Adam what he wanted.

"Regular margarita—on the rocks, not blended, please."

She smiled and said, "Just a minute," then poured our drinks. "That'll be fifteen dollars."

I handed over a twenty and told her to keep the change. Her eyes widened a little, but she just thanked me before going on to assist the next set of customers who were waiting for drinks.

Truth be told, it was probably a little chilly to be drinking either sangria or a margarita, but I found I didn't mind too much. The sangria was good, too. I knew there was probably a lot more to go see. For some reason I wanted to linger here for a while and listen to the guitarist in the center of the courtyard playing intricate Spanish tunes that matched the architecture around me, the white stucco walls and the red tile roofs and the balconies and overhangs of dark wood. The bodyguards had paused a few yards off, pretending to be looking at a display of fine art photographs in a gallery window.

A half-familiar voice said from over my left shoulder, "Angela? Angela McAllister?"

I turned and saw him. All right, not *him* him, not the man of my dreams, but a close second— the Zorro from the Halloween dance a week ago. I blinked, certain I must be hallucinating. Or maybe that sangria was a lot stronger than I'd thought it was.

"Hi, um…." I managed, realizing that I'd given him my name, but I still didn't know his.

He grinned, even as I felt Adam shift irritably next to me. "Sorry about that. We didn't get to the formal introductions. I'm Chris Williams."

"Hi, Chris." Then, realizing that I really shouldn't neglect Adam, I added, "And this is my cousin Adam."

"Hi," Chris said, extending a gloved hand. Maybe it was my imagination, but I thought he looked almost relieved at the word "cousin," as though he'd been worried that Adam was my boyfriend or something. Or maybe I was just flattering myself.

Adam looked like he really didn't want to shake Chris's hand. After I slanted him a sideways glance through my eyelashes, though, he reached out and took his hand, saying, "Nice to meet you."

"So what brings you up here?" I asked Chris, figuring I'd better step in and keep the conversation going in more or less innocuous directions. From across the way I could see the guardians pause and give him their own inspection, relaxing visibly when they sensed that he was just a civilian, no one to worry about.

"I'm not stalking you, I swear," he replied with a small laugh. Seeing him like this, in the last of the afternoon light, I thought he was even better-looking than I remembered. I could see that his dark eyes were surrounded with a heavy fringe of lashes, now that they weren't hidden behind the Zorro mask, and he had nice strong brows that balanced the slightly long nose and high cheekbones. "A friend of mine is getting his master's in anthro, and he wanted to come up here and check out the festivities. I'd heard about it but hadn't been before."

"So where's your friend?" Adam asked, tone not quite brusque enough to be called rude...but close.

"Over in the next courtyard, taking pictures of one of the altars there."

I noticed that besides the gloves, Chris was wearing a heavy leather jacket over a sweater, and he had a wool scarf around his neck. "Planning to go up to Flagstaff or something?" I inquired, with a lift of my eyebrows toward the cold-weather gear.

He startled slightly, then grinned and shook his head. "I'm from Phoenix, remember? If it gets below sixty-five degrees, we break out the snowshoes."

Despite myself, I chuckled. I also found myself wishing I didn't have Adam there, glaring at me like a chaperone in one of those Victorian novels where the heroine can't even step out on the veranda without having her actions questioned.

"Have you been to this before?" Chris asked, and I shook my head.

"No, I—that is, we lost our great-aunt last week-end. That's actually why I had to run out of the dance like that. Family emergency."

"Oh, I'm so sorry," he said at once, the little smile he'd been wearing abruptly disappearing.

"It's okay," I told him. "That is, she lived a great life. It was sad to lose her, but not entirely unexpected. She was eighty-eight."

"A good round number."

"Exactly." I smiled up at him, wishing more than ever that we could be alone together. Then again, what good would that do me, except to frustrate me further?

If only he weren't so damn good-looking....

He seemed to notice my edginess and glanced over at Adam. "Mind if I borrow your cousin for a minute?"

Adam looked as if he wanted to say he minded very much, but he seemed to collect himself and shrugged. "Sure," he replied, and took a sip of his margarita before glancing over at the flamenco guitarist, as if scrutinizing his intricate fingerwork was the only thing on his mind right then.

Maybe I should've been relieved, but I couldn't help wondering what exactly Chris wanted. He moved off down the walkway that led from the courtyard out to an open area behind the buildings, then paused once we were more or less out of ear-shot, if not eyeshot.

"I am sorry to hear about your great-aunt," he said quietly, "but in a way I'm kind of glad."

"You are?" I couldn't quite figure out what he meant by that.

"Not that your family lost her. I mean, I'm glad you didn't disappear like that last Saturday because of something I did."

"Oh, no. Not at all."

He hesitated, looking down into my face. I was very glad that I'd taken a little more care with my hair than usual and had put on some lip gloss. Not that my current fresh-faced look wasn't a far cry from the diva I'd appeared to be at the Halloween dance. Even so, he didn't seem too fazed by the alteration in my appearance.

"Do you get down to Phoenix often?" he asked.

I shook my head. "I think I might have mentioned I don't get out much." An expression of disappointment passed over his features, and I quickly continued, "But we do go down in early December every year for holiday shopping and to stock up on some things that we have a hard time getting up here." Of course I had no idea whether we were going to uphold that tradition this year, what with everything that was going on, but if it was in my power to make it happen, then it would.

"Okay, that sounds a little more promising. I need to get back to my friend, though. And school's going to be kind of crazy between now and the end of the semester, so I don't think I'll be able to get back up here. But I'd really like it if you'd call me when you're in town."

"I don't have your number," I told him.

"Well, that's easy to fix. Can I borrow your phone?"

I dug it out of my purse and handed it to him. He went to the contacts screen and entered his information. I took another sip of my sangria while I waited, then took my phone back once he was done, slipping it into a pocket in my purse.

"I'm not sure when we'll be down," I said. "We usually go mid-week, though, to avoid the crowds."

"You don't work?"

"Of course we do. I mean, my aunt has a store up in Jerome and I help out there, and I also make jewelry."

"You do?" he inquired. The note of interest in his voice sounded genuine. "So you're kind of an artist, too, then."

"I guess so." For some reason my cheeks heated as he gazed down at me in admiration. "But anyway, it's not that big a deal for us to close down in the middle of the week if we need to." I didn't bother to add that a lot of the shops in Jerome had rather lackadaisical schedules. If you wanted to close up for the afternoon to go shopping or get your toes done, why not? No big deal when your storefront was more of a hobby rather than your bread and butter.

"Well, good." He sent me another one of those knee-melting smiles, then said, "I really have to get going before Tyler thinks I was kidnapped by aliens or something. But don't forget to call if you do make it down to Phoenix." With that he lifted a hand in a small wave, then turned and headed toward the next courtyard. Because it was so crowded, he disappeared from view pretty quickly. Even so, I stood there watching in the direction he'd gone for at least another minute, hoping to catch a glimpse of his dark head above the others in the crowd. But he was well and truly gone, and I sighed, knowing I needed to get back to Adam.

Don't forget to call. Like that was even a possibility.

Smiling suddenly, I drained the last of my sangria and tossed the empty cup in a nearby trash can.

Things were starting to look up.

CHAPTER TEN

Moving On

"Holy crap," Sydney said as she stood in the foyer of my new home and looked up at the brass and crystal hanging from the ceiling, two stories up. "What are you going to *do* with this place?"

"I have no idea," I said wearily. The day before, Tobias had come over with his truck and moved my meager belongings into Great-Aunt Ruby's house. Okay, my house. I was staying in one of the spare bedrooms at the moment, because no way was I sleeping in the bed she'd died in. Her spirit certainly wasn't hanging around the place, I could tell that already, but even so I had my limits.

"How big is it?" Sydney had moved from the foyer into the dining room and was gawking at the long table with its accompanying twelve chairs and matching sideboard.

"A little over three thousand square feet."

"That's kind of a lot of house for one person, don't you think?"

I couldn't agree more. Then again, I did have the "bodyguards" lurking around, so technically I supposed there would be at least four people there at all times. I didn't feel like explaining that to Sydney, especially since they'd made themselves scarce and were upstairs in the library-slash-study, ostensibly cataloguing the books there but really just trying to stay out from underfoot.

"Yes, but it's tradition for the *prima* to live here, so…." I shrugged. "And normally I would've been moving in with my consort, but since he has yet to materialize, it's just me."

"Maybe you should get a dog."

There was an idea. I was horribly allergic to cats—not a good allergy for a witch to have, I know—and Aunt Rachel hadn't wanted the responsibility of a dog in a house with no yard, so I'd been pet-less my entire life. But this house had a small yard off the side, where there was an even tinier plot of grass and a few flowerbeds. It wasn't big enough to keep a German shepherd happy, but maybe a smaller dog, one I could adopt from the Humane Society or something.

"Maybe," I said. "Although I've probably got enough on my plate right now without adding a dog to the mix."

"I suppose." Sydney had walked back into the foyer and crossed over into what Great-Aunt Ruby had always called the parlor, although really it was just the living room. It had a massive fireplace with a mahogany mantel and furniture that looked as if it should be in a museum. The floral wallpaper was positively eye-crossing. "So can you...I don't know...change it at all?"

"Um, I'm not sure." Actually, I hadn't even stopped to consider that. I'd gotten the impression that when Ruby inherited the house, she and Patrick basically moved in and didn't alter much of anything, except to update the kitchen appliances. Of course, now those "updates" looked like museum pieces themselves. "I guess so...I mean, it's mine now, right?"

"You should." Planting her hands on her hips, she looked up at the ten-foot ceilings with their crown moldings. "I bet you could do a lot with it. That is...." She trailed off, looking hesitant...for her. "It would probably be kind of expensive."

"That really isn't an issue." I'd already had a fairly substantial chunk in the bank, just because living at Aunt Rachel's hadn't cost me anything (well, besides chipping in for groceries, which I'd insisted on after I turned eighteen). So my monthly McAllister dividend and the money I earned from my jewelry mostly went into my savings account, since I wasn't spending it on clothes or cars or going out to clubs, or any of the other things a girl my age might conceivably spend her money on.

"So you inherited more than just the house?" Her tone sounded envious. If only she knew that being *prima* wasn't just living in a big house and having apparently unlimited funds.

"Some," I said cautiously. "Enough that I could do a few things to this place if I wanted to."

"Good. Because that wallpaper has got to go."

I laughed at that, and we went on from room to room as I gave her the grand tour of the place. By then Lionel and Joseph had already removed all of Great-Aunt Ruby's personal effects, so her clothes and jewelry and family photos and all that were gone. It didn't feel quite so intrusive to walk through the house with those personal touches taken away, but even so I couldn't help feeling like a trespasser. I hoped that sooner or later I'd be able to wrap my head around the fact that this was now my home.

Even so, I had a feeling Sydney was right. I really should be doing something to make it feel like mine, and not just a place where I was camping out.

"Change it?" Aunt Rachel said blankly at dinner that night. She'd insisted that I come back to the apartment to eat, and I wasn't about to argue. The transition didn't feel so abrupt when I could still indulge in the familiar ritual of sitting down to eat at her dining room table. "I guess I never thought about it."

"Place could do with an update," Tobias said around a bite of cornbread. My aunt had made chili verde that night.

"That's what I was thinking," I said, shooting him a grateful smile. "I mean, I'm not going to make it totally modern or anything, but all that floral wallpaper and all those fussy antiques are just not my style."

She was silent for a moment, pushing the chili around in her bowl. "Well, I *suppose* you could. You probably should speak to the elders first, just to make certain."

"I will," I said, although I wasn't looking forward to that discussion. What was I supposed to do if they said no? All those florals and chintz would probably make my head explode.

To my surprise, though, they seemed mostly uninterested in the subject. "It's your house now— all we ask is that you not alter the exterior," Margot Emory informed me, and that seemed to be the end of the matter.

Well, almost. I was walking back up to the house when Jocelyn Riggs, the clan's strongest medium, came hurrying after me. I turned to her, surprised, wondering if she was going to tell me that the elders had changed their minds and that I was going to drown in chintz to the end of my days.

But she only fixed me with a steady gaze and said, "I have a message for you from Great-Aunt Ruby."

"You do?" I wasn't sure whether this was a good thing or not.

Normally Jocelyn was a rather pinch-faced woman. She was a few years older than my Aunt Rachel, but she looked more like a decade separated them. Now, though, she shot me an incongruous smile and said, "Yes. She wants me to let you know that you can do whatever you want with that house. Her exact words were, 'Tell Angela that I've no more use for that house now than I do those old bones they buried in the Cottonwood cemetery. So tell her to stop fretting and get on with it.'" Jocelyn's pale gray eyes glinted. "I get the impression that she's rather curious to see what you do with the place. Good afternoon."

And she turned and went back down the hill, heading for the far more modest cottage she called home. I stared after her for a minute, then grinned and shook my head.

I of all people was not someone to disregard messages from beyond the grave.

———

The distraction of redoing the house was a welcome one. Still no sign of that mysterious dark being, no more assaults in my dreams…no nothing. I hadn't even dreamed of him lately, which I wasn't sure was entirely a good thing. Better that, though, than another visitation from the unwelcome shade that had visited my aunt's store.

I hired a decorator from Sedona and told her that I wanted to keep something of an antique feel but with less fussy furniture…and no wallpaper. She swept through the house with swatches and paint chips, made suggestions, and generally took over. I was okay with that, though. She was a professional, and I was just a girl who up until that point had never had to decorate anything bigger than a ten by twelve room. She used her own crew, for which I was grateful. Having Adam there every day to help with steaming off wallpaper or sanding the floors could have been awkward.

Through all this, I was adamant that the other family members have first pick of the furniture I didn't want to keep. Even so, there were a few pieces that hadn't found a home, but Leila, the decorator, assured me she would be able to sell them with no problem, including the huge Eastlake-style bed from Great-Aunt Ruby's room.

"I know a couple in Prescott who're doing over a Victorian who'll take that, no problem," she told me, and the next day some movers came to haul it away.

The bed went for so much that I was able to buy a whole new set of bedroom furniture to replace it. That was good, because I did want that room to be mine—it had the same view as my old bedroom at Aunt Rachel's place, albeit a few hundred feet higher up the hill. I was once again able to look out over the Verde Valley, and see the red rocks of Sedona. By then, only a week before Thanksgiving, all the fall color was in full swing, and the blaze of the trees was somehow a comfort to me, telling me that even though everything else in my life had changed, the world would still follow its familiar old cycles.

The room still smelled of fresh paint. I'd chosen a warm terra-cotta color for the walls, and the ceiling was a soft parchment hue. My new furniture was dark-stained oak, more Spanish hacienda than Victorian mansion, but it worked with the new color scheme. I settled down on the bed after pushing back the heavy turquoise and warm red patterned duvet cover, and took in a deep breath.

Really, if I hadn't known I was sitting in Great-Aunt Ruby's old room, I would never have guessed I was in the same place. The colors were warm and rich, the furniture simple and sturdy. Leila had put up a lot of the old wall decorations from my former bedroom, and added more in the same style, along with Mexican mirrors and heavy wrought-iron sconces on the walls. The place was intimate, welcoming. The only thing missing was someone to share that big bed with me.

I didn't quite let myself sigh, although I wanted to. Somewhere in the daydreams I'd had about the man who'd be my consort, I'd thought about making a home together and doing all the things I'd had to do on my own: buying furniture, deciding on paint colors, figuring out what went where. Not that I'd imagined it happening in this house, necessarily. Moving here had always felt like something that would happen far in the future. But there were always places coming available when needed—a bungalow farther down the hill, a loft apartment over a store. Those were the places I'd imagined making a home with my consort, not this huge echoing relic.

Even so, it felt good to have a lot of the house done already—I'd put off the kitchen and bathrooms until next year, since those were massive projects and I didn't feel like having the place that torn up over the holidays. Despite all that, there was something missing…the man who should be lying here next to me. That king-size bed felt awfully empty, especially since I'd spent my whole life sleeping on a twin bed.

Through the whole process, I'd also had a hard time keeping myself from thinking about Chris. I knew I shouldn't, that it was a lost cause, but attraction was a harder thing to control than I'd thought it would be, mainly because I'd never really experienced it like this before. Of course there were guys in high school I had thought were cute, although even then I'd known all I could do was look, but that was not the same as this almost aching need I felt for him. We'd exchanged maybe a hundred words, so I knew I was being silly. How could I miss someone I'd barely spent ten minutes with?

I didn't know, and there wasn't really anyone I could talk to about it, either. Aunt Rachel would give me hell for even thinking about a civilian like that, and Sydney would only encourage me and tell me to call. Yes, he'd asked me to call him, but only if I was down in Phoenix. That seemed a little strange to me, since I didn't see the harm in talking beforehand. Then again, he'd said he would be really busy for the next month. Maybe he didn't want the frustration of talking if he wasn't sure he would even see me again.

Frowning, I gave the lamp on the nightstand one of those quick mental flicks, and the room went dark at once. And it was really dark, too. It was a new moon tonight, and clouds hung over the town, making it seem as if I were adrift in a well of blackness. Normally that sort of thing wouldn't bother me, but in that moment I felt more alone than I ever had, even though that night's bodyguards were sitting down in the living room, watching movies on the shiny new flat-screen in the sitting room. Well, it used to be the sitting room. Now it was the family room, I supposed, although whether this house would ever be filled with a family, I wasn't sure.

Probably I should stop torturing myself. True, it was less than a month until my twenty-second birthday, and the window of opportunity was rapidly closing, but stressing about it wasn't going to do me—or anyone else—any good. And there was a new candidate coming in the next day, so that was something. Not that I was expecting much. Somehow the thought of kissing a stranger was even less appealing than usual.

Because it won't be Chris Wilson, my mind whispered at me.

I shut that thought down right away. Truthfully, I didn't really know what would happen when/if I went down to Phoenix, or, even if we did go, whether I'd have the courage to call him. He'd seemed interested in me, so I didn't think I'd be impinging. Goddess knows I was interested in him, but that didn't matter in the long haul. He was off-limits.

That time I did let out a sigh. Telling my brain to shut up and leave me alone, I turned over on my side, closed my eyes, and tried to convince myself that the bed didn't feel quite as cold and empty as I thought it did.

———

None of my failed attempts at finding a consort had been exactly pleasant, but this one was definitely the worst. For one thing, I didn't have the buffer of Aunt Rachel there to take the edge off, only the dubious comfort of that day's bodyguards, who pretended to be immersed in a discussion of the upcoming "lighting up the mountain" festivities next weekend, but who I could tell were trying to eavesdrop on everything the new candidate and I were saying to one another.

He'd come loping up the front steps, looking at the house with what I thought was an avaricious gleam in his eye. I knew this because I was peeking through a clear spot in one of the stained-glass panels that flanked the door. All right, maybe I was already predisposed to expect the worst, but his expression was decidedly different from that of the candidates I'd met at Aunt Rachel's far more modest apartment.

The doorbell rang. I weighed the possibility of pretending I wasn't home, then decided against it, since I knew one of the bodyguards would just come answer the doorbell if I didn't. So I grasped the handle and turned it, then opened the door.

Like most of the candidates, he wasn't bad-looking. A little above average height, short brown hair, brown eyes. I gave a mental shrug. Really, it would be so much easier if I could just look at their eye color, say "nope," and move on to the next one. But although everyone more or less thought there must be something important about my dreams, they weren't willing to give them enough weight that they could rule out every candidate who didn't have green eyes.

Although I'd been dressing a little more nicely these days, mostly because it didn't seem right for the *prima* of the McAllisters to be slouching around in jeans with holes in them and pilly sweaters, I hadn't gone to a lot of effort today. My hair was pulled back in a loose ponytail, and I wore one of my Jerome sweatshirts over a pair of faded jeans. No, they didn't have holes in them, but they were starting to get a little threadbare.

I could tell by his disappointed expression that this new candidate wasn't overly impressed with the McAllisters' *prima*.

Good.

"Hi," I said, and stuck out my hand. "I'm Angela."

"I know," he replied. Then he shrugged and extended his own hand. "Griffin Dutton."

I knew that as well. I also knew that he came from Wickenburg, worked at one of the guest ranches there, and was my fifth or sixth cousin lord knows how many times removed. Back in the twenties one of the McAllister girls had married a rancher in those parts, and Griffin was her great-great-grandson. Or so Aunt Rachel had explained.

After a lackluster hand shake, I said, "The parlor is over here. Do you want me to get you anything first? Water? A Coke?" I didn't drink soda, but a couple of the bodyguards were caffeine fiends, so I kept it around for them.

"A Coke would be good."

Fetching it would give me a small reprieve. I pointed to the parlor, which opened on the foyer. "Why don't you go on in and sit down? I'll be back in a minute."

He nodded and headed into the parlor, and I went the other direction to fetch his Coke from the kitchen. I found my cousin Kirby with his head in the fridge, eyeing a pizza box from Grapes.

"Don't you dare," I told him. "That's my dinner tonight."

Looking over his shoulder, he shot me a grin. He was a few years older than I and had a loft apartment down on Main Street that he shared with his boyfriend. Even ten years ago there probably would've been a hell of a ruckus over that, but these days no one even batted an eye. I wished my love life were that uncomplicated.

"What, you don't think you're going to have a celebratory dinner with Rachel after this candidate proves he's the One?"

I shot Kirby a very sour look. "I'd say the odds of that are roughly the same as me getting elected President."

"Hey, you never know." With a visible show of reluctance, he put the pizza box back in the ancient Frigidaire. "Did you need something?"

"He wants a Coke."

Another grin. "Well, at least he didn't ask for a beer."

"I didn't offer." I took the cold can of Coke from Kirby. "And hands off that pizza. I'm serious."

"But I'm hungry."

"Then have some cheese and crackers or something. There's some white cheddar in there, and I have crackers in the pantry."

"If I must." He heaved an exaggerated sigh, then extracted the package of cheese and shut the refrigerator door.

Any longer, and Griffin Dutton would know I was stalling for time. So I left the kitchen and headed back to the parlor, where I found him looking around at all the new furniture and the art on the walls, most of which was from local artists and was all original. I could practically see the dollar signs in his eyes as he mentally added up what it all must have cost.

"Your Coke," I said, and extended the hand holding it.

"Thanks." He took it and popped the tab, then took a few large swallows. "That's better. It was kind of a long drive."

I only nodded. Yes, it was, but I'd had candidates come a lot farther than that, so I feared my expression wasn't entirely sympathetic.

If he noticed, he didn't give any indication. Instead he gazed up at the ceiling, which had been painted a soft cream color, and then around at the deeper toast hue on the walls. "Been doing some work on the house?"

"Some," I admitted. "It was very retro, and not in a good way. I'm not big on florals."

"Hmm." He drank some more Coke, then set the can down on the coffee table.

I immediately swooped in and relocated it to a coaster.

"Oh, sorry," he said, although he didn't sound all that sorry...more amused by my anal-retentive protecting of the table.

Once again I thought this would be a whole hell of a lot easier if I could have a few drinks before forcing myself to go through with this ridiculous ritual. On the other hand, I didn't think there were thick enough beer goggles in the world that would make me believe kissing Griffin was a good idea.

"So..." I said. I really didn't want to kiss him, but I did want to get this over with.

"So..." He moved closer to me.

I sighed. "Just go ahead and do it."

A lot of guys probably would have been put off by my tone. I'd already taken the measure of this one, though, and he wasn't seeing *me*. He was just seeing the *prima* of the McAllisters and her big house and the position he'd have as her consort. Boy, was he in for a disappointment.

He leaned in and pressed his mouth against mine. That was it—no reaching up to caress my cheek, no finesse at all. Just lips against lips. I suppose he thought he didn't need to do anything else, because if he turned out to be the one, the spark would start on its own.

Of course it didn't. *Thank the Goddess,* I thought. Bad enough that I should have to kiss him at all, when I'd been spending my days mooning over Chris Wilson. But it hadn't worked, so I started to pull away immediately.

"Sorry—"

I didn't get out anything else other than that, because he'd grabbed me by the shoulders and pulled me back toward him, forcing my mouth open with his tongue. He tasted of Coke, and I gagged. This time I didn't even have to invoke the Goddess. Even as my mind cried out a "no!", an invisible force grabbed hold of him and pushed him away from me with enough force that he tripped over a footstool and went tumbling to the floor. In the process he knocked over the fireplace tools, which hit the slate hearth surround with a clatter.

Almost at once, Kirby and the other two body-guards, Tom and Alison, came running. They took in the scene before them and then hurried over to me.

"What happened?" Kirby asked, as Griffin shook his head, as if to clear it, then began to push himself up to his feet.

"That crazy bitch attacked me, that's what happened."

At their *prima* being called the big "B," all three of them frowned. Tom, a heavy-set man in his middle forties, said, "You might want to reconsider what you just called Ms. McAllister."

Griffin matched their scowls with one of his. "Well, it's the truth."

"I was defending myself. We did the kiss, it didn't work, and I guess he didn't like it, because he decided to stick his tongue down my throat. So I…did something about it."

"I think you'd better leave," Alison said grimly.

Griffin glanced from her to Tom to Kirby, who was looking angrier than I thought I'd ever seen him. Actually, before that moment I wasn't even sure Kirby could get angry.

"Fine," Griffin said. "Like I want to be part of this freak show anyway. She's not even good-looking."

After delivering that parting shot, he stalked out of the room and into the foyer. The front door banged a few seconds later.

The three bodyguards just stared at me. I hesitated, then went over to the footstool and righted it, putting it back in its proper position. "I'm going upstairs," I told them, and walked with as much dignity as I could muster to the staircase in the foyer. I went upstairs, closed my bedroom door behind me, and threw myself down on my bed, where I wept stormily and wished this would all be over.

CHAPTER ELEVEN

A Wind From the North

ON THANKSGIVING MOST OF US CONVERGED ON SPOOK HALL for a huge, rowdy McAllister feast. They'd been doing this ever since I could remember; Aunt Rachel had once told me it was Great-Aunt Ruby's idea, that after spending Thanksgiving going from house to house so she could try to see everyone, she put her foot down and said we should all gather in one place and save her some work. So we shopped like we were buying food for a soup kitchen or something, making the run to Prescott so we could go to Costco and the Trader Joe's there, and then set up the long tables in the hall with warm russet tablecloths and centerpieces of autumn flowers.

The kitchen was large, but even so we did a good deal of tripping over one another. My aunt supervised, more or less, since she was an amazing cook. Some turkeys went in the oven, and others were smoked in the smokers across the street at the English Kitchen restaurant. My specialty was homemade spiced cranberry sauce, so I handled that and tried to stay out of the way as best I could.

We really hadn't discussed my disastrous encounter with Griffin Dutton, but I noticed that she hadn't sent any more candidates my way after that. Thanksgiving was late this year, so there were only three weeks until my birthday at that point. Both she and I—and the entire clan—were aware of the rapidly approaching deadline. We couldn't not be. But either she'd decided to let the universe handle it from here on out, or she thought she might as well leave it alone until after Thanksgiving. I wasn't going to question her actions, mostly because I was just relieved to not have another candidate shoved down my throat. Literally.

It was mainly women in the kitchen, but that didn't mean the men got off scot-free. From the hall came scraping sounds as they brought out the long racks of chairs and started setting them up. There was another group congregating across the street, ostensibly in order to keep watch on the turkeys in the smoker, but I had a feeling there was more beer drinking than turkey-watching going on there.

All around me was the chatter of cheerful voices and the warm, rich smells of turkey roasting and pies baking. Everyone looked happy, glad to be surrounded by family, glad of the opportunity to share in the world's bounty. I knew I should be feeling the same way, but I didn't.

Suddenly the kitchen felt stifling. My cranberry sauce had more or less gelled by then, so I turned off the gas and moved the pot to the back burner. "I need to get some air," I told Aunt Rachel, and then hurried out of the kitchen and threaded my way through the tables to the front door.

It was one of those beautiful late autumn days, the air cold but the sun warm, the sky deep sapphire punctuated by downy white clouds. I took in a deep breath, raising my face to the sun and the wind, and headed down the side street in an attempt to get away from the hustle and bustle.

"That's quite the shindig you're putting together in there," came Maisie's voice from a few feet away.

She hadn't been there a second earlier, but that was sort of how she did things. Just appeared out of nowhere. Once I'd tried to ask her where she was when she wasn't here. She'd shaken her head and said vaguely, "Around." Which of course wasn't illuminating in the slightest.

Right now she sounded more wistful than anything else. "Didn't you have big Thanksgiving dinners?" I asked.

"Maybe when I was really little, before Papa died." Her expression hardened. "But that no-good dog my mother married afterward didn't hold with Thanksgiving. Said turkey was too expensive and it was silly to go to all that fuss."

I didn't press the matter further. From our previous conversations, I'd gotten the impression that her stepfather had gotten a little too friendly as she got older, and she ran away. How precisely she'd ended up in Jerome, I wasn't sure. I could tell she didn't want to talk about it.

So I only replied, "Yes, I think it's even bigger this year. Of course, part of it is that everyone wants to be here for Thanksgiving with the new *prima*." I shrugged.

Her expression turned sly. "Yes, I seen that you did all that work on your great-auntie's house. Can't say for sure that I think it's an improvement, but then, I'm not much of one for all these new-fangled styles."

I wondered what my interior decorator would think if I told her that a ghost had criticized her work. Leila was pretty no-nonsense for someone who lived in Sedona, woo-woo capital of the world, so I had a feeling she wouldn't take it all that well.

All I said was, "I like it, though. It feels more like me now."

Maisie appeared to consider that, then nodded. "Well, I s'pose that's the important thing, as you're the one living in it."

I nodded, and looked past her out across the valley, past Sedona...all the way to Flagstaff, where Humphries Peak brooded amongst a crown of dark clouds. It didn't look like the version from the movies, but it still reminded me of Mordor, especially on days like this, where it was sunny here but broody and dark all those miles away. Kind of silly, I supposed, because although the Wilcoxes were not exactly what you would call nice people, they were far outnumbered by all the ordinary folks who lived in Flagstaff and worked and shopped and went to school without having any idea that a coven of evil witches and warlocks lived amongst them.

"What do you know about the Wilcoxes?" I asked abruptly, after turning back to Maisie.

She looked surprised by the question. "No more than you, I guess. They aren't very nice, are they? And of course all that hullaballoo when they tried to grab Ruby when she was your age. But that was a long time ago."

"Not very nice" was a hell of an understatement. But Maisie was a ghost. There wasn't much they could do to her at this point.

I didn't even know why I was thinking about the Wilcoxes, except for seeing the mountain, standing dark and tall a hundred miles away. Did they have their own Thanksgiving observance, or did they consider that sort of thing hopelessly plebeian?

It was kind of silly to wonder about such a thing, I supposed. I wasn't likely to find out any time soon.

Rachel's head popped out of the side door of the building, startling me and causing Maisie to dissolve immediately. "Oh, there you are. We're about to start pulling the turkeys out of the ovens, and I need you on gravy duty."

I reflected that sometimes being a witch wasn't exactly what it was cracked up to be. Yes, we all had our individual powers and abilities, but that didn't mean we could wiggle our noses like Belinda from *Bewitched* and have a feast magically appear. There was still a lot of grunt work involved.

"Coming," I told my aunt, and started to walk up to meet her. Yes, I was the new *prima*, but that didn't absolve me of kitchen duty. Just as well, probably. At least that way I'd be busy inside, instead of standing out in the middle of the street and brooding about the Wilcoxes.

After that it was sort of a frenzied bustle of getting all the last-minute things—the gravy and the rolls and the mashed potatoes—ready at the same time. Aunt Rachel supervised with the practiced skill of a field marshal, so everything made its entrance into the hall and onto the long tables set up buffet-style on the far wall at the anointed hour. Then it was time to eat.

I sat at the head of one table, which I hadn't expected but probably should have, if I'd stopped to think about it. Rachel was on one side of me, once she finally sat down, and Tobias was on the other, so I didn't have to worry about Adam trying to keep me company all during dinner. He was at the same table, but farther down, sitting with his parents and his younger sister, who was a senior at Cottonwood High. I didn't see Jenny, his older sister. Maybe she had to work—the lowest person on the totem pole usually got the crap shifts on holidays and weekends. Once or twice during the meal he tried to catch my eye, and while I smiled at him, I didn't have time for much else.

At last, though, after everyone had had seconds or even thirds, it was time for pie. I'd been sort of selective in my eating, skipping the stuffing altogether, since I didn't like it that much to begin with. It would be a crime to be so full that I didn't have room for any of Aunt Rachel's pumpkin pie, which was divine.

I was just putting a piece on my plate and giving it a healthy dollop of freshly whipped cream—none of that canned stuff around here—when Adam came up to me. Well, it looked more like he was just there for pie, too, but I had the feeling he'd timed his approach so he'd be there when I was.

"Everything okay?" he said in an undertone.

"Of course it is," I replied, even though I didn't know if it actually was. "Why do you ask?"

"You just looked sort of...cranky...during dinner."

"Well, I'm not," I snapped. Then, as a hurt expression crossed his face, I added, "That is, I'm fine. It was just busy getting everything ready, and I've been kind of stressed out with my birthday coming up, and...." I decided to stop myself there. He knew what the problem was...mostly. No way would I admit to him that I'd spent more time than was probably healthy brooding over Chris Wilson. That match was even less viable than one with Adam. At least Adam was a McAllister, and a warlock.

"I've been thinking about that."

Why does that not surprise me? But we were blocking the pies, so I sidled a few feet away. "Everybody's probably been thinking about it. But I don't think there's much we can do except hope that the consort shows up damn soon."

"There might be another solution."

Since he was the one volunteering it, I had a pretty good idea what that might be, or at least what he *thought* it might be. Affecting unconcern, I took a bite of pie, then asked, "There is?"

A light flush appeared along his cheekbones. "Well, I've been doing some reading, trying to see what the precedents were. I mean, we all know that it's not a good thing for a *prima* to be without a consort when her twenty-second birthday rolls around. But I found an instance where that happened, and a warlock from her clan married her even though he wasn't the consort, and it actually worked out just fine. So maybe that's what we should do here."

It took a few seconds for his words to sink in. Lowering my voice, I said, "Are you asking me to marry you?"

The previous flush was swallowed up in a wave of bright red that went over his face from forehead to chin. "Well, yeah. Wouldn't it be better than what happened to Great-Aunt Ruby?"

"Nothing happened to her. I mean, the Wilcoxes tried, but they weren't successful. And it turns out she was right all along for waiting, because then she met Great-Uncle Pat a few weeks later. All's well and all that."

"Yeah, but—"

I realized then how hard this must have been for him. He had to know I wouldn't agree, but because he was worried and because he cared, he'd gone out on a limb anyway. "It'll be all right. You'll see."

He hesitated. "Maybe. But can you promise me something?"

"What?" I asked, my tone guarded. I knew better than to make a promise without knowing what it was about.

"If we get to your birthday, and there's still no one else, can you please think about it? I want you to be safe."

I looked up into his pleading blue-gray eyes. If the man of my dreams never materialized, did it really matter? I didn't want to be alone for the rest of my life, and no matter how much I might yearn for him, I knew Chris Wilson was not an option. Witches and warlocks married civilians from time to time—heck, Adam's own mother was one—but a *prima* didn't have that option.

"Okay," I said slowly. "If we get to that point, then...okay."

His face lit up then, and for a second I was worried he was going to pull me into a hug and smash my plate of pie right against me. Somehow he managed to keep a grip on himself, though. "Great. I mean, I doubt it'll happen, but if it does..."

"...you know where to find me," I said wearily. I gestured with my free hand back toward the table where I'd been sitting. "And now I'm going to sit down and eat the rest of this pie."

"Sure." He grinned at me. Since I didn't want to show him how unexcited I was by the prospect of having to marry him because there was no one else,

I summoned a smile in return before heading back to my empty chair.

In that moment, I wondered how much I really had to be thankful for after all.

———

Clean-up seemed to take forever, but finally around nine o'clock I headed home with that night's bodyguards in tow. No one spoke, probably because we were all feeling sleepy and stuffed after the enormous meal we'd eaten earlier. By that point pretty much everyone had done a rotation watching over me, so I didn't see the need to show anyone where the snacks and sodas were. Or the coffeemaker; more than once I'd awoken in the middle of the night and smelled the rich scent of coffee drifting up the stairs, beating out the lingering paint fumes.

I just said goodnight to them and went upstairs, thinking I'd read in bed for a while or watch a show on my laptop. Something normal, prosaic. It felt way too early to go to bed, even though I was wiped out from the long day and all the heavy food I'd eaten.

But after I'd washed my face and brushed my teeth and climbed into the flannel pajama bottoms and long-sleeved thermal shirt I wore to bed—it was a magnificent house, but drafty—I found that the book I was partway through really didn't interest me, and neither did any of the shows I had queued up on

Netflix. So I shut my laptop and wandered down the hall to the library to see if I could find anything more enticing there.

I say "library" because that was what everyone called it, but it was really more of a combination study and library. A big rolltop desk stood against one wall, and two of the other walls were covered in bookshelves. This was a room I hadn't touched yet, mainly because I hadn't decided what I wanted to do with it. Sydney thought I should turn it into a media room, sort of a home theater, but I thought it felt sacriligious to tear out those lovely dark oak bookshelves.

Not that what they contained looked all that intriguing. An old out-of-date set of World Book encyclopedias, probably from when Great-Aunt Ruby's sons were young. Books of fairytales. Some tattered paperbacks looking out of place amongst the more dignified hard-bound books, mysteries and some science fiction and a few more sensational titles like *Peyton Place* and *Valley of the Dolls.*

Wow, Ruby...who knew?

Fighting back a smile, I pulled out what looked like a first edition *Wizard of Oz* and shook my head. How much must that be worth? It still wasn't really what I was looking for, though, so I put it back. As I did so, my gaze fell on a slim book bound in dark red leather. It had no lettering on the spine, but I didn't know whether that was because it never did or because it had worn off over the years.

Intrigued, I opened it up and saw that, instead of being filled with type, it was hand-written. I flipped over to the flyleaf and saw inscribed on the yellowed paper there, *Ruby Lee McAllister, 1947*. I did some quick mental math. This was her diary, and from her twenty-first year.

My heart started to beat a little faster. Now, maybe I shouldn't read her diary at all, since it was private. Then again, how private could it be if she'd just left it out on the shelf in plain view of everyone? And there could be things she'd written down that would help me now. A lot had happened to her that year. If there was anything in that diary that could be of use, it would be silly of me to ignore it. For all I knew, she'd put it there precisely so I would find it once the house came to me.

With that rationalization to buoy me, I tucked the book under my arm, and slipped out of the library and down the hall to my room. After closing the door behind me, I climbed back into bed, plumped up my pillows so they'd give me good support while reading, then opened the book to its first page.

Mama took me into Cottonwood today to go shopping as part of my birthday treat. Yesterday was my real birthday, and everyone came over for cake and ice cream. How nice to have a birthday in June when ice cream is appropriate. While we were in Cottonwood, she bought me this book. She said twenty-one is special for any girl, but especially for the next clan prima. *It's in this year that I'll meet my consort, and everything will change.*

I stopped for a moment, thinking of pretty young Ruby with the Rita Hayworth waves and the red lipstick. She hadn't been afraid of her future—she'd had no reason to be. She had her parents and the members of her clan, and seemed to look forward to being *prima*. Of course, back then she couldn't have had any idea how long she would have to hold that post. The *prima* of her youth, Abigail McAllister, had died early. Rheumatic fever, I thought, but I couldn't remember for sure. What I did recall was that Ruby had barely a year after meeting her consort before she had to take over as *prima*. There was no comfortable overlap period for her, either.

Frowning, I looked back down at the book and began to read again. A lot of what I saw really was just commonplaces—descriptions of some new dresses she'd bought, comments about the weather, write-ups of various clan parties and gatherings. Here and there she'd mention working magic, but it wasn't something she particularly dwelled on, as if it was taken far more for granted than a pretty new pair of shoes.

Then, *The first candidate came today. I didn't like his looks much, but I knew I had to kiss him, just in case he turned out to be the consort. To my relief, he wasn't. It's funny to think that if any other girl were discovered to have kissed so many boys, people would think she was fast, but in my case it's expected.*

That entry was dated July 12, 1947. I flipped through a few more entries, until I came to a page dated a few weeks later where she wrote of meeting another candidate. *This one didn't work out, either, and I was disappointed, because he was handsome enough to be a movie star. My mother warned me that sometimes it can take a while to find the right one. I hope not, because right now I can't decide which is worse, having to kiss someone you don't like, or kissing someone you think you might like, only to find out he's not the one, either.*

I could definitely relate to that. But at least she didn't have one of her cousins bugging her to marry him if the whole consort thing didn't work out.

There was a gap of a week or so after that. She didn't make any mention of why she'd skipped so much time, but I supposed she had decided to write an entry only when something really notable occurred. I could relate—I'd started a diary when I was around eleven, thinking I should get down all the fabulous details about my life. Only most of the details weren't that fabulous, except for the whole talking to ghosts thing, and after a few weeks I'd given up and shoved the diary into a drawer, never to be looked at again.

Then, in late August, *There were three candidates this week. None of them suited me, not one bit. I complained to Mother that this was turning out to be no fun at all. She only smiled at me and said the fun would begin once I found my consort. Maybe so, but whoever he is, I wish he would show up soon.*

On the twenty-first of September, there was an entry about the town's celebration of the autumn equinox, the second harvest. We still had these observances as well, and it didn't sound as if they'd changed much in the last sixty-odd years—everyone gathered for large feasts, although back then it seemed those were spread out among individual households. These days we use Spook Hall for that, and of course back then wine-growing hadn't yet taken hold in the area. She described drinking beer as if it were a delicious, semi-forbidden thing, with no mention of wine at all.

All this was an interesting slice of local history, I supposed, but I'd been hoping to find something more. All during October there were entries about more candidates, more kisses that went nowhere. I could commiserate with her predicament, but at least I knew her story had a happy ending—fifty years of marriage, two children, five grandchildren.

There was an entry on October thirtieth about her looking forward to the Samhain celebration, but she didn't write anything again until November fifth.

And on that one, her handwriting looked shaky and almost messy, whereas before it had been clean and neat. That was back when they cared about penmanship, I supposed, feeling slightly ashamed. My own handwriting was so bad that I block-printed anything that someone else would have to read.

I am safe.

I am safe.

I am safe.

There's an old saying Mother told me once: "What I tell you three times is true." So I imagine I wrote that down three times so I could give the notion a power of its own. Everyone is watching over me, and I know such a thing couldn't possibly happen again. But I imagine I am getting ahead of myself.

I was so happy on Samhain eve. I put on a pretty dress, even though I knew my robes would cover it up. It was a warm day, almost too warm for late October, but I was determined to enjoy it, since I knew it would get cold soon enough.

I decided to walk down to Hull Avenue and look at the view from the little park there, since I was done with my chores for the day and didn't have much else to occupy me. And it seemed fitting to go enjoy the sunshine on this last day before we went into the dark time between Samhain and Yule.

No one took much note of my going. I walked along in the sunshine and enjoyed the feel of the wind in my hair, even though I knew I'd have to give it a good brushing again once I got home. When I got to the park, it was deserted. Well, almost, anyway. A man I'd never seen before stood over by one of the stacked stone walls, smoking a cigarette and looking out at the view. A shiny black Cadillac was parked a few yards away from him.

I tried not to stare, but it was hard. We didn't get a lot of strangers here in Jerome. Well, we got people driving through, as it was only one of two routes you could use to get from Prescott to Flagstaff, but they didn't stop here much, except to get gas. And of those who did stop here, I'd never seen one who looked like this man. His hair was jet black and gleamed in the sunlight, and he had a profile that wouldn't have looked out of place on a movie screen.

I looked away quickly, but he must have noticed me. He smiled, and dropped his cigarette and ground it out on the dirt with the heel of his shiny black shoe, then said to me, "That's a heck of a view, miss."

"Yes," I said cautiously, although talking about the view seemed safe enough.

He took a few steps toward me. "Are you from around here, miss?"

I nodded, not quite trusting myself to reply. Something about his dark eyes was mesmerizing. I tried to tell myself that I'd seen handsome men before, so it was silly for me to stand here and look at him like a mouse staring at a snake.

His smile widened. "You have a name, miss?"

Something was telling me not to answer, but the word popped out as if I couldn't bear to keep it in any longer. "Ruby."

"That's a pretty name for a pretty girl."

"Thank you, sir." I decided to tack on the "sir" because he was some years older than I, maybe as old as thirty.

He moved a little closer, although he was still a few feet away. "You like looking at the view, Ruby?"

"Ye-es," I said.

A nod, but it wasn't directed at me. Suddenly two more men, also tall and black-haired, and wearing dark suits, got out of the car. My heart began to pound, and I realized something was very wrong here.

"I-I have to go," I told him, my voice sounding weak and stammering, not like the voice of the McAllisters' future prima.

"Yes, you do," he agreed. "Although probably not where you were thinking." Those coal-black eyes fastened on me, and it was as if the world began to spin around me, sky and trees and buildings all swirling like a kaleidoscope. My knees began to give way, and then he was reaching for me, grabbing me. His touch was cold, so cold, and I realized then who he must be.

Jasper Wilcox, primus *of the Wilcox clan.*

I didn't know which spell he had cast, or what he had done to me, but I retained enough presence of mind to call out from within, my cry echoing to all the McAllisters. The enemy is here!

Right away people started to converge on the park. Mr. Song came out of the English Kitchen, cleaver in hand, and next to him were my cousins Leonard and Stephen.

I could feel Jasper Wilcox's hand tighten on my arm. "What did you do?" he demanded.

"I called to them," I said. "Bet you didn't know I could do that, did you?"

He scowled at me, and began dragging me to the car.

"There are only two ways out of here," I told him. "If you let me go and leave now, you might get away. Maybe."

He cursed, horrible, foul language no one had ever spoken in my hearing before, but I could see that he realized his dilemma. He let go of me, said, "This isn't the end of it," and hurried back to his car, his two clan members jumping in, one of them getting the engine started. They sped off with a squeal of their tires, going the wrong way on the one-way street.

No one was coming the other way, and so they made their escape just as I heard the sirens from the town's one and only police car blaring away up on Main Street. It wasn't my gift to see the future, but somehow I knew Jasper Wilcox would get away.

Everyone began to crowd around me, asking what had happened. I told them I was fine, which I supposed I was. Nothing had happened, not really. Then my parents came, my mother weeping in fright, and I went with them back home, where they set up a guard to make sure no one else could get to me. Although Jasper Wilcox had said this *wasn't the end, he didn't reappear the next day, or the day after. No one let down their guard, but people did seem to relax, just a little.*

What I couldn't tell any of them was that I still felt his hands on my arms, still saw his face when I laid myself down in bed at night. So handsome...so evil.

I want my consort to appear. I want that kiss, the one that will bind me to him.

I hope that then I can forget what it was like to look into Jasper Wilcox's black eyes.

———

I shut the diary, my hands shaking. No one had ever told me what exactly had transpired when the Wilcoxes tried to kidnap Great-Aunt Ruby, only that the attempt had been made, and had failed. I'd never really understood why they'd bothered, since I'd always been told that a *prima's* true power only manifested when she was matched with her consort. For some reason, though, this Jasper Wilcox had believed differently.

I needed to find out why.

CHAPTER TWELVE

Secrets and Lies

Margot Emory didn't look exactly happy to have been summoned to see me, but she knew it wasn't good to refuse a request from the clan's *prima*, even a young and inexperienced one such as myself. She sat in one of the new arm chairs in the living room, looking around at the alterations I'd made. Maybe her sour expression came from disapproval at my remodeling efforts. Since I hadn't asked her here for input on my design choices, I really didn't care one way or another.

A fire crackled in the hearth; it was a cold day, with a promise of snow overnight. We were both drinking coffee from my new Keurig coffeemaker. Aunt Rachel had turned up her nose at pre-fab coffee, but I found myself having a great time drinking a different flavor every day.

I set down my mug of hazelnut roast. "I wanted to ask you about the Wilcoxes' kidnap attempt of Aunt Ruby."

That did seem to surprise Margot; she lowered her own cup of French roast and shot me a quizzical look. "Why?"

"I found her diary," I said frankly. I'd decided I might as well be up front about reading it. "She described the whole thing in some detail."

"Interesting." She tilted her head to one side, as if considering. "She never mentioned that she kept a diary."

"I don't know if she did, except for this one that she started around her twenty-first birthday. After the kidnap attempt, she didn't write it in very much, except for writing about the day she met Great-Uncle Pat, and then a few entries about ordering her wedding gown, that kind of thing." I wrapped my hands around the mug I held. It still felt cold in here, even with the fire blazing away. "I tried to ask Aunt Rachel about it once, and she just sort of blew me off. But I'm getting the feeling I haven't been told the whole story."

For a few seconds Margot didn't say anything, only watched me carefully. She was a coldly beautiful woman who always reminded me of a retired ballerina, with her graceful neck and fine, sharp features. "I suppose Rachel thought she was trying to protect you. But you are *prima* now, and because you are in such a…vulnerable…position at the moment, it's only right that you should know." A pause, and she set her coffee mug down on a coaster on the side table next to her chair. "How much do you actually know of the Wilcoxes?"

"The usual," I replied. "They came out here after losing some sort of clan war back in the 1800s—"

"The 1870s, to be precise. Yes, they'd been caught doing some of the blackest kind of magic, and the other clans in New York united to drive them out. It wasn't just the magic itself they feared, but that it would be discovered by the non-magical population. So Jeremiah Wilcox and about fifty of his followers headed west, and ended up in Flagstaff, which was very much a wild frontier town back then. My guess is that they thought their goings-on wouldn't draw as much attention there. But Jeremiah's wife died on the journey out here—"

"And he took a wife from among the Navajo," I finished for her.

She gave me a very thin smile. "'Took' being the operative word. He stole her from her tribe because she was supposed to be a very powerful witch, and he wanted to join her magic to his. This didn't go over very well with her own people, as you can imagine, but they feared his magic, his ruthlessness, so there was no retaliation. She gave birth to a son, then took her own life—but before she did that, she laid down a curse on the Wilcox men so that no girl child should be born to them, and that the wives of Jeremiah's line should never live to see their children grow up."

This was all news to me. I sat up, eyes widening. "And no one thought to mention this to me?"

"It's not common knowledge. The clan elders know the particulars, and the *prima,* but otherwise we see no need for it to be spread around. It's enough for most people to know that Flagstaff is Wilcox territory, and Jerome is ours, and we must all stay away from one another."

"And when precisely were you going to get around to telling me?"

A thin smile. "I'm telling you now."

"So that's why the Wilcoxes always have a *primus*, never a *prima.*" As far as I knew, the McAllister clan had always had a *prima* as its head.

"Exactly. They also tend to marry outside their clan more than we do, since their genetic pool was smaller to begin with. That hasn't diluted their power, though, and their *primuses*—the men of Jeremiah's line, and his stolen Navajo wife—are very strong."

That I could believe. Of course I'd only known Great-Aunt Ruby as an old woman, used to a lifetime of ruling the McAllister clan, and not the young, unworldly girl she must have been, but from her diary entry it was clear that she'd almost been overpowered by Jasper Wilcox. It took a lot of strength to best even a *prima*-in-waiting.

"And so they tried to kidnap Ruby so they could bind her power to theirs, the way they'd done with the Navajo witch?"

"Yes."

Here was where I came to the crux of the conundrum. "I don't understand that, though. I mean, I've always been told that a *prima*'s powers will only fully develop if she's with her consort. Obviously, Jasper Wilcox wasn't Ruby's consort. So why did he think he could force her?"

For the first time during our conversation, Margot looked uncomfortable. She picked up her coffee and drank, but didn't set the mug back down, instead cradling it in her hands the same way I was doing with my own mug. Maybe her hands were cold, too. "The energy of a *prima* is a receptive energy, what some refer to as a female energy. A *prima* cannot force her energy on another. But the energy of a *primus* is something different—it can be aggressive, outward-seeking. Dangerous, which is also why all the clans have a *prima* rather than a *primus*...well, except the Wilcoxes. We learned over the years what was the safer, wiser way and selected for it."

Like breeding dogs, I thought with some irony, although I knew better than to say something like that to Margot Emory. "So this Jasper Wilcox thought he could just snatch up Great-Aunt Ruby and produce a line of super-warlocks or something?"

Her mouth tightened. I got the impression that she would have liked to call out my remark for being irreverent but wasn't quite willing to confront her *prima* in such a way. "Or something. But it's why we've watched over you so carefully, even before this latest incident."

I assumed she was referring to the dark wraith-like figure I'd seen in the store. No one yet had quite been able to figure out that one, although it did seem as if the smartest thing to do was what the clan elders had been doing—never let me out of their sight. "And what if my consort never shows?"

"It's best not to borrow trouble, Angela—you'll find you may end up paying heavy interest on it."

As may be. Abruptly, I said, "Adam wants me to marry him if my birthday rolls around and I'm still unattached."

"That would solve a few things." Surprisingly, she seemed unfazed by the prospect.

I couldn't say the same for myself. "It would? But I was always told that it was bad for a *prima* to be with someone who wasn't her consort, almost as bad as making it to twenty-two without a partner."

"It's not optimal, of course, but given the alternative…." She let the words trail off, and flicked a significant gaze northward. "If you're not a virgin, you can't be bound to a *primus*. Just reaching your twenty-second birthday would not be enough to protect you. Of course you carry your greatest potential for power now, but don't think that you will be safe as long as you are on your own."

This just kept getting better and better. "So why shouldn't I just go with someone I choose, if my consort bails on me? Why not a civilian?" Obviously, this was not an idle question. Laying aside the problem of not even being able to contemplate going to bed with Adam, no matter what I might have promised him, I didn't see why I couldn't make a serious try for Chris Wilson if things went sideways. There was someone I wouldn't mind losing my virginity to.

Now Margot did look annoyed. The sweeping dark brows drew together, and she gave an impatient wave of one hand. "Because even a warlock who is not your consort can bring some power to the relationship. A civilian? Never. Not with a *prima*. At least Adam is a McAllister, and a warlock with some talents, even if of course they're not equal to your own."

It seemed she had me boxed in fairly neatly there. My mother had escaped the trap, but then again, she'd never bonded with a consort, had bolted before that could happen. I'd never been given that opportunity, and I wondered how she'd managed it. Just gotten in her car and told everyone she was going out for groceries, then took off with only the clothes on her back and the money in her purse? I'd never been brave enough to ask Aunt Rachel, as I could tell the subject was too painful, even now, and somehow I guessed Margot Emory wouldn't exactly be forth-coming if I tried to probe too deeply.

So I sipped at my rapidly cooling coffee, then said, "Thanks, Margot. That does answer some of my questions." I didn't add, *That will be all,* but she seemed to take the cue, setting down her mug a final time before getting to her feet.

"I'm glad I could help out. And if you have any other questions, I'll do my best to answer them." She smiled at me, although the expression seemed stiff, as if she were forcing it.

Since it was the sort of thing I really couldn't call her on, I smiled at her in return and then saw her to the door. A blast of cold air came in as I opened it, but she didn't seem to notice, only sailed serenely down the steps and in the direction of the restored Victorian where she lived on the next street over.

I closed the door, and shivered. Maybe it was the cold.

Maybe not.

Despite everything, the decision was made to go ahead with the shopping trip to Phoenix the week after that. That decision was made without my input; I had a feeling Aunt Rachel had to go plead her case to the elders to get them to agree, but finally they did acquisce. We wouldn't be driving ourselves, but would be going in Lester Phillips' van, along with five bodyguards. Adam wasn't coming along—not because he didn't want to, but because the elders decreed he wasn't a strong enough warlock to make much of a difference, should push come to shove.

As with any expedition into a neighboring clan's territory, certain overtures had to be made. Since I was now *prima,* I was the one who had to call Maya de la Paz—apparently she didn't do email—and explain that some of us would like to come to town to do our holiday shopping, and would that be all right?

I'd halfway been expecting her to give me some kind of grief for not latching on to her grandson as my consort, but she only gave a chuckle and said, "Of course you are welcome here. Where will you be going?"

That hadn't been set in stone yet, but I told her we'd be focusing mainly in the Biltmore District, the mall itself and some of the satellite shopping areas, like the ones with Nordstrom Rack and Best Buy, and possibly going over to Scottsdale if there were time.

She said, "That is good. Thank you for asking, but the McAllisters are always welcome in Phoenix."

Right then I wondered why I'd been worried about making the call. She seemed very gracious. "You're very welcome, Mrs. de la Paz."

A laugh, and then she said, "No need for that. You are *prima*, as am I. Have a good night, Angela."

I hung up then and gave my Aunt Rachel, who'd been watching, a thumbs-up. She shot me a relieved smile, and then we both headed down to her place, since she'd heard about me eating leftover pizza for dinner and wanted to make sure I got at least one decent meal in me that week.

Even as we went, I knew I had one more call to make that night.

———

I sat on my bed and stared at the number in my contacts list. It should have been easy—just dial those ten digits, and….

But it wasn't. I'd never cold-called a guy like this before. Yes, Chris had given me his number and told me to let him know when I was coming down to Phoenix. Even so, I found I was having a heck of a time working up the nerve to do it.

For Goddess' sake, I told myself. *You're the* prima *of the McAllisters, and you don't even have enough of a spine to call a guy?*

Not just any guy. Chris Wilson, who was the best-looking guy I'd ever seen. And friendly. And nice.

And a civilian, so all this angst really isn't getting you anywhere.

I scowled down at my phone. It was probably stupid to call, since I knew anything with him would of necessity be a dead end. But maybe it would be fun just to see him again, meet somewhere for a drink (although how that would go off, with five bodyguards and my Aunt Rachel following my every movement, I wasn't sure).

You said you'd call him if you were coming to town. So call him. Stop making this into a federal case.

Fine. I hit "call" before I could back out. His phone rang once, twice, three times. Then it went into voicemail. Great. Then again, maybe it was simpler that way.

I spoke quickly, as if that would somehow make this easier. "Hi, Chris, it's Angela McAllister. I know it's kind of late notice, but it turns out we will be in Phoenix tomorrow to do some shopping. We'll be over in the Biltmore District mostly—I know that's kind of far from Tempe, but maybe we can figure something out. Anyway, I just wanted to call and let you know. We should be down there sometime in the late morning." Providing any more details would just make me sound desperate…if I didn't already… so I thought I'd better leave it at that. "Talk to you soon. 'Bye."

I hung up then, hoping I'd done the right thing. But I did want to see him, even if it was for the last time. After all, my birthday was only two weeks away.

———

By the time we hit the road the next morning, I still hadn't heard anything from Chris. Well, he had said he was going to be really busy. I didn't know exactly what that entailed for someone getting a master's degree. Did he have finals? If I'd been thinking straight, maybe I would have remembered to look up the academic schedule at ASU online and see when finals even were, but it didn't really matter now, one way or another. He should at least have time to check his voicemail, and if our schedules didn't mesh, well, I wouldn't be happy about it, but I'd understand. Or so I told myself.

Aunt Rachel kept up a fairly steady stream of chatter on the drive south, asking me if I'd decided how I wanted to redo the kitchen, or whether I was going to tackle the bathrooms first. All of that felt distant and vaguely unreal, as I'd decided to wait until after the holidays to do any of it. By then my life should be very different. Either my long-lost consort would have shown up, or I'd be living in domestic bliss with Adam. Now, with the possibility of seeing Chris Wilson again dancing in my mind, I was beginning to wonder why on earth I'd made Adam that promise. Temporary insanity was my best guess.

If Rachel noticed that I wasn't all that engaged in the conversation, she didn't show it. I did keep wondering why Chris didn't call, then tried to console myself with the realization that cell service was pretty spotty for long stretches on I-17, and even if he were calling, it would just go to voicemail since it wouldn't be able to punch through.

That helped a little, although once we came down into the outskirts of Phoenix and the bars on my phone abruptly shot up, I felt deflated all over again when I looked at the display on my cell and realized I didn't have any missed calls.

"...first?" Aunt Rachel was asking, and I blinked.

"What?"

She gave me a patient smile. "I was asking where you wanted to go first. I thought maybe we should stop at Nordstrom Rack first, since it's on the way, and then we can have lunch somewhere at the Biltmore shopping center."

"That sounds fine," I said. It didn't matter much to me which order we shopped in, although it did make more sense to make the Rack our first stop, since there were more places to eat at the shopping center.

We cut east on the 101 Loop and then onto a smaller highway that brought close to Camelback Road, which was crowded with shopping centers and strip malls. This wasn't my first trip to Phoenix, of course, but since it was at least six months and sometimes a year between visits, I always forgot about the vast urban sprawl, the amazing variety of shops...the aggressive drivers. I was glad it was Phil behind the wheel and not me.

But since we were smart and had come down on a weekday, trying to navigate the roads and get a parking spot at the shopping center wasn't as difficult as it would have been on a weekend. Also, Phil's handicapped placard got us a choice spot up toward the front.

I took one last look at my phone, tried not to sigh, and climbed out of the van, glad of the chance to stretch my legs a little bit. The drive took about two and a half hours, and it was now a few minutes after eleven. Down here it was much warmer than in Jerome, and I pushed up the sleeves of my shirt. I'd thought I was dressing for Phoenix by not wearing a sweater the way I had for the last few weeks back home, but it had to be in the upper 70s here.

Previously we'd agreed that it would be all right to split up once we were inside the store, as it was not so big that the bodyguards couldn't be back at my side within a minute if something strange happened. I'd argued that I didn't want onlookers watching me buy underwear, and neither did I want to be selecting holiday gifts while everyone could see exactly what

I was doing. Sort of took the fun out of the whole thing.

So we all did go our separate ways once we were in the store, with Phil, Boyd Willis, and Henry Lynch heading toward the men's section, while Aunt Rachel and Allegra Moss and I went straight to the shoes. I wanted a new pair of winter boots, which I found almost right away, nice leather riding-style boots with rubber soles. I loved my cowboy boots, but they were hell on ice.

I slipped the boots into the heavy net shopping bag I had with me, then said, "I'm heading over to lingerie."

They nodded, apparently entranced by the amazing selection around them. Good thing I wasn't much of a "shoe" girl, or maybe I would've felt the same way. As it was, I knew I needed some new underwear, so I figured I'd get that out of the way before heading over to accessories, where I hoped I could find some fun pieces for Sydney and maybe Rachel. Yes, I could've made them something, and had in the past, but my jewelry-making had been sort of disrupted the past few weeks, and now I wasn't sure if I would even have time to get anything put together. Besides, it never hurt to have something different every once in a while.

After picking up some new pairs of underwear and a bra, I got sidetracked on the way to the accessories section and ended up adding a pair of jeans and a couple of sweaters to the growing pile in my shopping bag. Eventually, though, I wandered over there and started sifting through the earrings and necklaces, wondering if maybe Aunt Rachel would rather have a new watch, or possibly a purse.

I had just turned away from the jewelry rack after finding a pair of long, sparkly earrings I knew Sydney would love when I noticed the man standing a yard or so away, over by a table full of sunglasses. His gaze was intent on me, and I looked away immediately. True, I'd tried to dress up a little bit, just in case I did get to see Chris, and was wearing the dark green top Sydney had bought me and my favorite pieces of turquoise jewelry, but I didn't think I warranted that kind of inspection. There were plenty of other girls in the store better-dressed...and prettier...than I was.

The stranger said, "Hello, Angela."

Immediately my hackles went up. "Do I know you?"

He smiled. Even though he looked as if he were a good deal older than I—maybe as old as thirty-five—he was very handsome. His gaze intent on me, he replied, "My name is Damon Wilcox."

Ice flooded my veins, and I immediately took a step back. "How did you know I would be here?"

"Does it matter?" The smile widened, and I couldn't mistake the predatory gleam in his dark eyes. "I thought we should talk."

"We have nothing to talk about. Except," I added, "that I'm here with five members of my clan, so—"

"Five? I suppose I should be honored that you think I merit that kind of a response."

I opened my mouth to reply, but almost out of nowhere my Aunt Rachel appeared, flanked by those five bodyguards we'd just been discussing.

"You should not be here, Mr. Wilcox," my aunt said coldly.

"I needed to do some shopping," he returned, smile never fading.

"You can do that in Flagstaff. You have your own mall there, don't you?"

"But not this store. They have such a good shoe selection, and I happen to have very large feet." This last was said with a wink sent in my direction, and I felt heat flood my cheeks. Even I knew what that "large feet" comment was supposed to imply.

"That doesn't matter," Phil put in, voice harsh and quite unlike his usual jovial self. "We had permission to be here. You don't."

"And what makes you think that?"

"Because Maya de la Paz would have told us, that's why," Rachel said. Her normally pretty, rounded features were set in a mask of loathing.

"Interesting." He slanted another one of those sly glances in my direction. "It seems we have a stalemate, then."

"I don't see how," Allegra Moss said in acid tones, "considering there are seven of us and only one of you."

"About that...." he drawled, and from the clothing racks in the center of the store came five men and two women, all of them black-haired like their *primus*.

Shit. My mind raced, wondering how on earth we were going to get out of this without having a magical showdown right in the middle of Nordstrom Rack. Everyone in my group edged closer to me, clearly ready to do whatever it took to protect me from the clutches of the Wilcoxes.

"Ah, but you forget that you are all in *my* territory," a new voice chimed in, and I looked past Damon Wilcox and his clanmembers to see a small woman with gray-streaked black hair and olive skin stop in the aisle just past us, her arms crossed over her chest. Behind her was a group of seven men, one of whom I realized I recognized. Alex Trujillo, Maya de la Paz's grandson.

I'd never met her, but I knew at once she was the woman who now stared up at Damon Wilcox with the expression of someone who'd found a particularly disgusting species of cockroach infesting her pantry.

"You do not have my permission to be here," she said clearly. "The McAllisters, they know how to follow the rules of propriety. I have allowed you and members of your clan here before, out of courtesy, but I see you do not give me that same courtesy. Leave, and do not expect to come back any time soon."

His gaze shifted from her to the watching de la Paz men, then over to us McAllisters before coming to rest on me for a brief second. Another smile, and he said, "If I have offended, I do apologize." He made the briefest of gestures toward his own clans people, then turned and moved past us, heading toward the front door. The other Wilcoxes fell in behind him. A minute later, they were gone.

I let out the breath I'd been holding. Maya de la Paz approached me and said, *"Prima,* I apologize for this intrusion. We were keeping watch, just in case, and it seems our caution was merited."

"No need to apologize," I said quickly. "Really, thank you for coming to help. That could've gotten… nasty."

Her mouth twitched. "That one has been nasty for many years, I am afraid. I hope this will not deter you from your shopping. I will have the people from my clan stay with you and watch over you. I do not think the Wilcoxes will try anything again."

More thanks bubbled to my lips, but she waved them off.

"It is the least I can do, when your visit has been trespassed upon. Please, finish your shopping."

I turned back to Rachel and the others. "I was almost done, but—"

"I think we're all finished here," she told me. "But we do appreciate the assistance during the rest of our trip."

The sparkly earrings I'd chosen for Sydney had been dangling, unnoticed, from my hand this whole time, but when I turned around to retrieve the shopping bag full of the other items I'd selected, it was missing. I knew I'd set it down on the floor while I was going through the rack of earrings. But where had it gone?

I telegraphed my dismay to Aunt Rachel, but although she hunted around on the floor behind the other jewelry racks, she couldn't find anything, either.

"Do you think the Wilcoxes took it?" I asked.

"I don't see why they'd have a use for it—and I didn't see any of them carrying any bags." Her brow puckered in worry. "What are they up to?"

Goddess only knew, but I decided it wasn't worth worrying about. Maybe it wasn't the Wilcoxes at all. It was entirely possible that one of the store's employees had seen the bag sitting there and thought it had been abandoned, and so picked it up in order to put away the items inside. No, I hadn't seen anyone actually do that, but then again I'd been a little busy with Damon Wilcox and his goon squad.

Alex Trujillo fell into step beside me after I'd paid for Sydney's earrings and headed toward the front door. "I see you're still without a consort."

"Obviously," I snapped, "or none of this would have been necessary."

His eyebrow lifted, and I hurried to apologize.

"Sorry...it's been kind of tense lately, and that didn't help." I jerked the thumb of my free hand back toward the store.

"I understand." The sun glinted off his dark hair as he shot a sympathetic look at me. "So where to next?"

"The Biltmore shopping center." I paused and waited for Aunt Rachel to catch up to us. "Were we going to eat or shop first?"

Her expression was still grim. "I don't feel much like either after that, but...a little shopping first, I suppose."

"We can do the Apple store first and then decide if we're ready to eat," I said, and looked from her to Alex. "Sound like a plan?"

He nodded. "We'll follow you." A lift of his chin toward a large black Suburban parked a few spaces away. "That's ours. Make sure you stick with us, and when you get to the parking garage, wait until we can get two spots next to each other, even if you have to go up a couple of levels."

"Okay," I replied, and despite everything, I had to smother a grin. Those tall, capable-looking warlocks in their black Suburban. They reminded me of the de la Paz version of the Secret Service or something. All they needed was some business suits and those little earpieces with the wires running into their collars.

The rest of our group was waiting at the van, just a few feet away. I relayed Alex's instructions to Phil, and he said "okay" as we all piled in. Then we backed out of our parking space, waited a few seconds for the Suburban to do the same, and headed east toward our destination.

I had to hope the Wilcoxes wouldn't have that staked out, too.

CHAPTER THIRTEEN

Settling

As WE DROVE, THOUGH, INSTEAD OF BEING WORRIED OR frightened, I found myself getting angry. Aunt Rachel had recognized Damon Wilcox at once, which meant she knew what he looked like. How that was possible, I didn't know for sure. I'd heard his name, of course, but when I'd tried to do a little surreptitious Googling of him, I couldn't find anything about him. Which didn't make much sense, because one time when I was eavesdropping on a conversation between Tobias and my aunt, I overheard that he was a professor of some sort at Northern Pines University. Of what, I hadn't been able to catch, but still, a professor generally has some sort of public profile. Maybe he'd done a magical scrub of Google to keep his information off it. If that were the case, he'd accomplished a lot more than any computer hacker I'd ever heard of.

While I ruminated on that and watched the sprawling shopping centers with their chain stores and restaurants pass by, I only felt my irritation increase. It wasn't just that Aunt Rachel had never bothered to describe Damon Wilcox to me so that I could give him a wide berth if I ever met him. No, it was the way she hadn't told me that marrying a warlock who wasn't my consort would still be enough to protect me, even if such a union would forever bar me from developing my full powers. Or how she hadn't bothered to mention the curse of the Wilcox clan and the true reason why I'd had my entire existence bounded by the relative safety of Jerome.

Margot Emory had said Rachel was trying to protect me, but I couldn't see how not knowing the whole truth was of any benefit. All right, some of it might have been too frightening to tell a young girl, and waiting possibly served some purpose. But I was almost twenty-two now, and although I was sheltered in a lot of ways, I wasn't completely innocent. Plenty of information to be had on the Internet if you needed to have your curiosity satisfied.

The bright sun and the palm trees blowing in the warm wind and the gleaming high-rises around us seemed incongruous when balanced against my brooding thoughts. It wasn't the sort of place you expected to see a group of dark warlocks descend, that was for sure. Had they left, or were they still watching us, waiting to see if the de la Paz crew might leave us undefended at some point?

A chill went over me as I recalled Damon Wilcoxes hungry dark eyes, the way he had smiled so knowingly at me. Even the Verde Valley's oldest virgin could figure out exactly what he wanted.

I didn't know if I made a sound, or a sudden movement, but Aunt Rachel asked in worried tones, "Angela, are you all right?"

Of course I wasn't. Not really. But I was angry at her, for all the things she'd hidden and hadn't said. Angry as I was, though, this was not the place for me to blow up. True, everyone in the van was family, more or less. Even so, there was family, and then there was *family*. The things I wanted to say to her would have to wait until the two of us were alone together.

So I only shook my head and told her, "I'm fine. That was just…not something I was expecting. But I'm okay."

Her expression was still dubious, but she appeared unwilling to press the issue. Instead, she gave a little nod and then turned to look back out the window. We were turning now down the side street that led to the parking garage. I glanced behind us. The black Suburban was still there.

Since it was now past noon and people from the surrounding high-rise office buildings had apparently converged on the place for lunch, we did have to drive to the upper level of the parking structure to get two spots next to one another. Phil waited for the de la Paz men to get out of their SUV, and then he unlocked the doors of the van so we could all climb out as well.

"You know where the Apple store is?" Alex asked me.

"I think so."

He smiled even as he shook his head. "I'll guide you in. Come on."

Once we got to the ground level, we entered the shopping center proper. Most of the people around us were well-dressed and glossy, and I wondered what they thought of our contingent. Bad enough that we were now such a large group that we'd attract attention merely from our sheer numbers. Add to that Rachel's swirling India-print skirt and Phil's ponytail and dark brown tunic, which looked like he'd stolen it off someone in an ashram somewhere, and we didn't exactly fit in.

I generally didn't buy a huge number of holiday presents, mainly because once I went outside my own little circle, I felt as if I should be getting something for each and every McAllister in Jerome, and that would break the bank pretty fast. Sydney was already taken care of, and after I saw Aunt Rachel pick up an iPad mini, look it over, then set it back down with a regretful look on her face, I decided to get one for her. Yes, I was angry with her, but she'd done so much for me. I had more money now than I'd ever had before to spend on gifts, and I might as well get her something she wanted.

So I went over to one of the blue-shirted store employees and made my request in an undertone as Aunt Rachel turned away to inspect a display of laptop bags, then added a fun weather station you operated with your iPhone to my order. Adam would love that...and since it seemed we were probably going to be shacked up together in the near future, I figured I should buy him something good for Yule. And he did love his iPhone.

Most of the rest of my group was what you'd call technologically impaired, so they didn't get much. The whole time I was aware of the watching eyes of the de la Pazes on me, especially Alex. He was still as attractive as ever, but I didn't think he was *quite* as good-looking as Chris Wilson.

Who had never returned my call. After I finished paying for my items, I fished out my phone...trying not to feel self-conscious about using an Android device in an Apple store...and checked it for any missed calls. Nada.

By then it was almost one. "Everyone hungry?" I asked, after we'd regrouped in the courtyard outside.

Head nods and various yeses.

"Zinburger is good," Alex offered. "I'll show you."

We all trooped after him, following along like ducklings following the momma duck. I wondered if any of the people watching us go by thought we were on some kind of tour. There were far too many of us to be seated at one table, so we had to settle for adjacent spots toward the back of the restaurant. And although Alex looked as though he would rather have sat by me, we all ended up more or less segregated by clan, with my aunt on one side of me and Henry Lynch on the other.

I would rather have sat by Alex, too, especially now that Chris seemed to have blown me off, but it wasn't worth making a fuss over. So I perused the menu, eyed the wine listings wistfully, and decided against anything stronger than a milkshake. That and a burger should hold me through whatever other shopping we decided to do. I still needed to get something for Tobias, and probably small things for the clan elders, as that was sort of expected. For them, though, I could gift some of my talismans, which would certainly be more appreciated than anything store-bought.

"...should head home before dark," Henry was saying to Phil.

Setting down the menu, I sent Henry a quizzical look. He lifted his shoulders and said, "I know we'd discussed going more places, maybe staying down here for dinner, too, if it shook out that way. But after what happened back there"—a significant jerk of his chin in the direction of Nordstrom Rack—"I think it's safest to do what we can here and then get on the road. Too many isolated spots on the highway once you get out of Phoenix."

That was true enough. Yes, you could always count on there being traffic, but even so, there were long, dark stretches with no off-ramps, no towns... no nothing. It was easy enough to imagine the Wilcoxes lying in wait there, maybe with a spell ready that would blow out one of the van's tires, or kill the engine, or....

Quickly banishing that thought from my mind, I nodded. "You're probably right." Once we got off the highway at 260 and were heading to Cottonwood and then Jerome, we'd be safe enough. But there was a lot of open road before that, and night came early at this time of year.

The waitress showed up to take our orders then, so we cut the discussion off until she left. Henry repeated his suggestion, and although both Aunt Rachel and Allegra Moss looked a little disappointed, once he added, "And Angela agrees with me," there was no further discussion.

So apparently my word as *prima* had some weight, even with my aunt.

———

After lunch we told the de la Paz crew of our plans. Alex protested, saying that they'd follow us all the way home if necessary, but I said, "No, we couldn't ask you to do that. You've done enough already. There's plenty to keep us occupied here for the next hour or so, and then we'll get on the road. Besides, leaving so we can get home before dark will also get us out of Phoenix before the worst of the rush hour, right?"

He gave a reluctant nod. "All right. But I had to offer, or my *abuela* would have my hide."

I grinned at that. "I'll make sure she knows."

It was silly for all fourteen of us to be marching around the place in lock-step. There was no sign of the Wilcoxes, and we each had our own shops that we wanted to visit. Groups of three seemed safe enough, especially since one of the de la Paz crew's particular gift was being able to sniff out dark warlocks, which was why their *prima* had included him as part of the group. He informed us that he couldn't sense the Wilcoxes anywhere near. So I had him and Alex accompany me while the rest of the Jerome contingent went their separate ways, with a de la Paz in tow, of course.

At Pottery Barn I found a fun leaf-shaped candle bowl for Tobias, who always had some kind of interesting lighting going on. As the sales clerk was wrapping it up for me, Alex said, "You seem pretty calm about the whole thing."

"Well, I am now," I replied. "That was a pretty good show of the cavalry coming in to save the day back there."

I'd kept my tone light on purpose, but his expression was serious. The dark eyes scanned my face. "You took a risk coming down here, you know."

"We thought we'd taken the necessary precautions." Was Alex Trujillo trying to tell me we'd been foolish for coming to Phoenix? "What, are we supposed to just cower in Jerome indefinitely?"

"Not indefinitely, but...you know...." He let the words trail off, then appeared to be holding his tongue as the clerk came back with my package.

"Are you saying I shouldn't be out and about in my delicate condition?"

He didn't rise to the bait. "It was risky. My *abuela*, she thought the same thing, which is why she sent us to watch over you. I wonder if you know exactly what the Wilcoxes are capable of."

"Probably more than you, since it was my great-aunt they tried to kidnap back in the day," I retorted. Then I let out a sigh. "Wow, I really am cranky today."

This time he smiled. "I think you've had reason."

He pulled his phone out of his pocket and looked
at the time. "Almost three. I'd better get you back.
Everyone should be meeting up in the courtyard
now."

Sure enough, the rest of the Jerome party was
already there, all of them clutching a variety of
shopping bags. So at least they'd managed to salvage
something from the trip. We headed back to the
parking structure, the de la Pazes waiting while we
got in the van. As I fastened my seatbelt, Alex said,
"We won't follow you all the way, if that's your wish,
but we'll at least see you back to the highway."

"Thank you," I said, and meant it.

He nodded, then slid the heavy van door shut. I
settled back in my seat, watching his tall form as he
walked around the Suburban and got in the front pas-
senger seat. As I did so, I wondered if maybe part of
Aunt Rachel's reasoning for keeping certain truths
from me was to prevent me from settling for a handsome candidate like Alex instead of holding out for my
actual consort. If I were going to be perfectly honest
with myself, then I should admit that maybe I would
have been less inclined to wait, knowing that having
any warlock as my partner would still protect me
from the Wilcoxes, even if entering such a relationship would prevent me from gaining all my powers.

Who knew? *Coulda, woulda, shoulda,* I thought,
repeating one of Sydney's favorite fall-back phrases.

At this point it really didn't matter one way or another. Either my consort would show up in the next few weeks, or I'd be marrying Adam just to keep myself...and the clan...safe. More or less.

At least now I had a face to put to my enemy. Maybe it had been risky to come here. But Damon Wilcox had taken a risk, too. Before he was a stranger. Now he'd revealed himself. What was it Great-Aunt Ruby had written?

So handsome...so evil.

Obviously those traits had been carried down to the current generation. I shivered, and told myself it was just that Phil had the A/C turned up too high. Phoenix felt shockingly warm after the chilly early December winds up in our part of the world. Above Jerome, Mingus Mountain still had a faint dusting of snow from the last storm that had passed through.

As we turned onto Camelback Road and headed toward the freeway, my phone rang. Puzzled, I dug it out of my purse. Maybe Sydney was calling in a last-minute shopping request. Too bad, since we were already on the road.

But the number on the screen was from the 602 area code, not 928. I frowned at it for a second, then guessed who it must be. "Hello?" I said.

"Angela." Chris's voice. "I am so sorry—I let my phone run down last night while I was in the studio working on my latest painting, and I was up so late that I just crashed without even checking it. So are you in Phoenix?"

He hadn't blown me off, or forgotten about me. The warmth that flooded me was short-lived, though. "We're here, but we're already on the way home."

"You are?" he asked, sounding confused. "I thought you said you'd be spending most of the day here. It's only a little after three."

"I know." I really hated that my aunt was sitting next to me in the back seat. Not exactly the best conditions for a private conversation. "Something came up."

His tone sharpened a little. "Everything okay?"

Not really, I thought. "It's sort of a family thing." I didn't trust myself to say anything more than that.

A pause, maybe while he tried to decide what would be appropriate to ask and what wouldn't. "I'm sorry to hear that. Things are busy right now, since all my projects are due at the end of this week."

"No finals?" I asked.

"Not in the studio art program. Just projects. Lots and lots of projects."

There was such a rueful note in his voice that I had to chuckle a little, even though I was not all that happy about missing this one chance to see him. I had a feeling there wouldn't be any more.

"Well, maybe we can try again once you're out for the semester."

The slightest of hesitations, one I probably wouldn't have even noticed in person but which seemed more obvious over the phone. "Sounds like a plan. I'll give you a call when I unearth myself from these piles of paint and canvas."

"Sounds great," I said. "I'll talk to you later."

"'Bye."

The call ended, and I frowned as I shoved my phone back in my purse. I might not have been the most experienced girl around, but even I knew what "I'll give you a call" meant, i.e, "it might have been fun, but you're not really worth the effort."

I stared out the window at the endless succession of cookie-cutter housing tracts and shopping malls and industrial parks that flashed by as we cruised down the freeway. Maybe once I would have been fascinated, or wondered what it was like to live in such a vast sprawl, to have everything you needed right at your fingertips instead of having to drive miles to get it or order it by mail.

Right then, though, I just wanted to get home. Back to Jerome, where it was more or less safe.

Back home, where my Aunt Rachel and I had some unfinished business.

She seemed to sense that I wanted to talk to her…and was trying to do whatever she could to put off the confrontation for as long as possible.

"Tobias and I had discussed going to the Vaquero Grill for dinner, since I don't really have time to put anything together," she said as she got out of the van. "Do you want to come?"

Obviously I was not going to start a blowout in a restaurant, especially in front of Tobias. I shook my head. "I'm kind of tired. I think I'll stop in at Grapes and get a pizza, then go on home." I said this last bit with my voice slightly raised, so the bodyguards could know what I was planning.

They all looked worn-out and like they wanted nothing more to go home and crash. Amazing how tiring driving could be when all you did was sit for hours. "I'll send word to tonight's watchers and let them know," Allegra said.

Well, at least the day crew was getting a break. "Thanks," I told her, then waved to everyone and headed across the street to Grapes, which was busy but not heinously so. I waited at the bar until my pizza was ready, then went on up the hill to the house, juggling the pizza box in one hand and my shopping bags in the other. *My house,* I reminded myself, although it still didn't feel exactly like mine.

I shoved the bags under one arm and put my hand on the knob, sending out the little feelers with my mind to have the tumblers fall where they needed to. The lock clicked, and I began to open the door.

"Hey, Angela."

Adam's voice. I half turned to see him standing on the garden path, in front of the bottom step. Pushing back my irritation—I really just wanted to sit down and eat my pizza in peace—I said, "Hi, Adam."

"I heard about what happened today."

Great. So this wasn't merely a social call. Still balancing the pizza box in one hand, I told him, "You'd better come on inside. Have you eaten yet?"

He shook his head. There went my plan for leftovers tomorrow night. But since it would be rude to do anything else, I added, "Then you can help me with this pizza."

Face brightening, he hurried up the steps and then finished opening the door for me. I was happy to be inside; a cold wind was blowing, and I still had on only a light top and no jacket.

I went into the dining room and set the pizza down on the table, then dropped my shopping bags on one of the chairs. The house was mostly dark, with only a light on in the hall, so I hoped Adam couldn't really see where the bags were from. I wanted his present to be a surprise.

It seemed a little silly to be eating pizza in that grand space, with seating for ten and the heavy wrought-iron chandelier I'd picked out hanging overhead, so I turned to him and asked, "Do you mind if we go into the family room instead? It's a little cozier."

"Sure," he said, and came over and picked up the pizza before I could retrieve it. He didn't appear to notice the shopping bags at all, and I let out a little mental sigh of relief.

We needed napkins and plates, so I went in the kitchen and fetched some. Then my gaze fell on the wine rack sitting on the chipped tile counter. It had been a hell of a day. Maybe sitting down and drinking with Adam wasn't the greatest idea, but he was seeming more and more...inevitable. It might be time to stop fighting the whole idea.

"Wine?" I asked, and moved toward the wine rack. "I think I've got some chianti in here."

"Sure," he said, trying to act nonchalant, but I could see how he perked up at the suggestion.

Nothing for it, then. I extracted the bottle of chianti and fetched some glasses from the cabinet, then got out the corkscrew.

"Can you manage this?" I asked. "I never was very good at it."

"Some witch you are," he returned with a grin, then came over to pick up the bottle and the corkscrew.

"I did unlock the door without a key, you know."

"I guess that's handy, too."

He struggled a little with the wine as well, but I didn't offer to help. I had a feeling he spent more time opening beer bottles than wine bottles. At least he got the cork out, though, and I took the plates and napkins and pizza box while he brought the wine and our glasses to the family room.

It had been the sitting room when this was Ruby's house, but a family room seemed a lot more practical. There was another fireplace here, on the wall opposite the flat-screen TV. Logs had already been piled there, awaiting a cold evening.

Well, it was cold now. Adam must have noticed my glance toward the hearth as I set the pizza and plates down on the heavy coffee table, which was one large piece of polished juniper with glass on top. "Want a fire?" he asked.

"That would be great."

He grinned. "Watch this—I've been practicing." And he turned and focused his attention on the pile of logs, muttering something I couldn't quite catch under his breath.

Almost at once, I saw a lick of flame start at the end of one log, and then quickly spread along its length. Soon the whole pile was crackling away happily, warming the room.

"Hey, Angela!" I heard Kirby's voice echo down the hall. "The night crew is here."

"We're in the sitting room," I called back.

A minute later, Kirby's tousled brown head was peering around the doorframe. His eyebrows lifted a little when he saw me sitting there with Adam. "Oh, hey, didn't know you had company."

"Just grabbing some dinner," I told him, although between the bottle of wine and the fire and the low light from the sconces on the walls, it probably looked like more than simply dinner.

"Got it," he replied. "Well, we'll be over in the living room if you need anything."

"Okay," I said, not sure whether I should be relieved or annoyed by my built-in chaperones.

During that exchange with Kirby, Adam had been busying himself with setting out the plates and napkins, and pouring a healthy measure of chianti into each glass. He'd kept the pizza box closed, though, probably to make sure it didn't get cold before we even had a chance to eat it.

He handed a full wine glass to me. "Here's to surviving an encounter with Damon Wilcox."

I wouldn't let myself shudder. No point in asking how he knew; news like that traveled fast in the McAllister clan. I just took the glass from him and said, "Cheers."

We clanked glasses, and both drank. It hadn't been that long since lunch, but even so I could feel the warmth of the wine as it traced its way down my throat, relieving some of the tension in my neck and back. In silence we helped ourselves to some pizza. Adam had eaten most of his piece before he asked, "Do you want to talk about it?"

"Not really."

"Why not?"

"Because...." I let the word trail off, then shook my head. "Nothing really happened. The de la Pazes made sure of that. And I just...." Another swallow of wine heartened me somewhat. "Because I'm home now. I'm safe here. And I don't want to bring something that dark under this roof, I guess."

Expression sober, Adam nodded. Energy was something we all understood, since magic was energy. Invoking the name of something was giving it a chance to worm its way into your life. I wanted the energy in this house to be pure and strong.

"Okay," he said. He lifted his glass again. "Here's to the de la Paz clan, then."

I definitely could drink to that, and swallowed some more chianti. With each drink of wine and bite of pizza I was beginning to feel more relaxed. I was home, and the bodyguards were out in the living room, and the space where I sat now was warm and cozy, with the fire crackling away in its simple hearth of travertine and dark-stained oak, and the walls in a deep parchment shade reflecting the glow from the wrought iron and alabaster sconces.

In this light Adam's mid-brown hair looked darker, and I couldn't see his eye color at all. No, he wasn't exactly a Chris Wilson, or even an Adam Trujillo, but he was nice-looking. I'd spent a lot of time trying to ignore that fact since he wasn't my consort and therefore not someone I should be thinking of like that.

You'd better start thinking that way now, I thought with some resignation. *Sure, maybe there's the slightest chance of a Hail Mary pass this late in the game, but I wouldn't put any money on it.*

"You're looking very serious," Adam said, setting down his wine glass. After being raised by Aunt Rachel, I had the instinctive impulse to reach for a coaster, but then I realized that was silly. I'd put a glass-topped table in here precisely so I wouldn't have to worry about that sort of thing while I was trying to relax.

"Am I? Long day." That wasn't even a lie. I just didn't know if I was ready to admit to him what I'd really been thinking about.

Silently he reached in the pizza box and set another slice on my plate, then poured me some more wine. I wondered if he were trying to get me tipsy. Actually, that didn't sound like a bad idea. I was safe here, after all, and I thought after the confrontation with Damon Wilcox and the disappointment at not getting to see Chris Wilson, a slight wine buzz might be just what I needed.

So I ate some more pizza and drank some more wine, and watched the flames dancing in the hearth. Adam seemed to understand that I didn't feel like talking, and ate and drank along with me.

This wasn't so bad. Maybe it didn't have to all be blazing sunsets and grand passions and shooting stars. I'd dreamed of someone, but he'd never materialized, and I could tell the whole Chris Wilson thing was a total dead end. It was probably foolish to have thought otherwise.

And after what Margot Emory had told me about any warlock being enough to ensure my safety, even if it meant sacrificing the true strength of my powers....

I figured I could live with that.

A large drink of chianti, to give me courage. Then I set down my glass and looked across the table at Adam. I was sitting on the couch, and he on one of the two armchairs that faced it. "I want you to kiss me."

He'd been in the middle of lifting his own glass to his mouth. "What?"

"You heard me."

Instead of setting down the glass, he drained it—which sounds worse than it was, since he only had a few swallows left in it anyway. Once it was empty, he did place it carefully on the tabletop. "What's this about, Ange?"

"What do you think it's about? You're the one who said we should be together if my consort continues to be a no-show." I crossed my arms and met his gaze straight on...or as straight on as I could manage after two large glasses of wine. A heavyweight with alcohol I was not.

"Right, I did, but...."

"But nothing. All these years you've been on my case about this, and now when I'm actually inviting you to kiss me, you're going to act all weird about it?"

Something crossed his face then. Annoyance? Worry? In the dim light it was hard for me to tell. I could see him clench his fist on his knee, as if fighting some inner conflict. Then he got up from his chair and came over to me. Standing above me like that, he seemed very tall.

"Stand up," he said.

"Why?"

"Because if this is the decision you're making, if by asking me to kiss you, you're saying we're going to be together, then I want you to stand up and kiss me like the *prima* of the McAllisters. I don't want to be a couple of kids making out on a couch."

He meant it, I could tell. There was a note of authority in his voice that I'd never heard before, as if somehow this kiss would push us past a threshold, carry us from the last edges of childhood into our adult lives. Did I want to take that step? I'd asked him to kiss me, but....

It would have happened anyway, if your consort had come to you. But he hasn't, and you need to kiss Adam, to get used to the idea. It's not as if you haven't kissed a bunch of random guys over the past year anyway.

That seemed to clinch it. I looked up at him steadily, at the firm chin and friendly mouth, at the brown hair that had just enough of a wave that he couldn't get it to do much of anything.

I reached out and took his hands in mine. To my surprise, they were cold, despite the warmth of the room. So he was more nervous than he wanted to let on.

"Yes, Adam," I said. "I want you to kiss me."

The briefest moment of hesitation, and then he bent down and placed his mouth on mine. I hadn't been expecting a shower of sparks, and I didn't get one, but once I got past that I realized that his lips were warm and strong, and he tasted of wine as I opened my mouth a little and let him taste me as well. This wasn't so bad. I could get used to it, even if it wasn't thunder and lightning and choirs of angels singing.

After a minute, he pulled away and gazed down at me. His eyes were shining, so although I wasn't experiencing anything earth-shattering, I could tell he felt differently. "Okay?" he asked, his voice husky, rougher than usual.

"More than okay," I replied. "It was good. I liked it."

He smiled, his fingers tightening around mine. "Good. I mean, I thought it was good, too."

"Just good?" I teased.

"Okay, more than good. Great. It was—"

"Hey, Angela, the Coke's gone. Can I have—" Kirby again, this time stopping abruptly as he seemed to notice how close Adam and I were standing to one another, how we were still holding each other's hands. "Er...sorry."

"It's okay," I said quickly, releasing Adam's fingers as I turned toward the doorway to the kitchen. "What did you need?"

"Well, you're out of Coke, so I was going to ask if it was okay if I fired up the Keurig for the watch-dogs. Things start to drag around 3 a.m. if there's no caffeine to be had." He was studiously not staring at Adam, although I could see his eyes dancing with amusement.

"Sure. Let me show you where I keep all the packets." I sent Adam an apologetic glance. "Sorry— this'll just take a minute —"

"It's okay," he broke in. "Like you said, you've had a long day. I should just let you relax for a while.

We can talk tomorrow." He bent down and kissed me quickly on the cheek. Then, without looking over at Kirby, he headed out to the hallway. A few seconds later, I heard the front door open and shut.

Kirby quirked a questioning brow at me.

"Every girl needs a back-up plan," I protested.

At once he raised both his hands. "Hey, man, I don't judge."

I couldn't help grinning. "Let me show you where everything is."

The next few minutes were spent giving Kirby a rundown on how the coffeemaker worked, and where I kept all the supplies in the pantry. As I handed him some mugs, I had to stifle a yawn.

"You look like you're the one who needs some coffee."

I realized then how tired I really was. The wine, although great at the time, might not have been such a good idea after all. "I think I'm going to head upstairs and read in bed for a while. I'm too tired to even deal with watching TV. So you guys can have the family room. I'll just clear up the plates and glasses and stuff."

"No need. I'll do it," Kirby offered.

"You guys are here as my bodyguards, not my maid service."

"It's cool. I can tell you're wiped out. Just go to bed."

I shot him a grateful smile. "Thanks, Kirby."

And so I dragged myself up the stairs, wondering if I'd even be able to keep my eyes open long enough to read a chapter. It wasn't all that late, but it felt as if a century had passed since we set out in the van that morning. Well, a lot had changed in those intervening hours. But I stopped there. I didn't want to dwell on what had passed between Adam and me. Maybe I'd have the energy to sort that out in the morning.

For now, I only wanted to put this day behind me.

CHAPTER FOURTEEN

The Space Between

AFTER A GAP OF WEEKS, *HE* ENTERED MY DREAMS AGAIN THAT night. It was different this time, though; I lay in my own bed, but he was there next to me, his arms warm around me, my back against his chest. I leaned into him and breathed in the warm scent of his skin and felt his heavy hair brush against my cheek as he held me, even as I ached for him to turn around so he could kiss me.

Or should I kiss him? But I'd just kissed Adam earlier, told *him* we would be together. Now that I'd made that commitment, my dream man had suddenly decided to return? Was my unconscious trying to tell me that I'd made a huge mistake?

My dream mind was just as muddled as my waking one, apparently. In the darkness the stranger reached up and pushed my hair away from my face.

His voice was a whisper against my skin. "You need to wait for me."

"I have been," I told him, trying not to sound accusatory. How much longer could he possibly expect me to wait? Time was running out.

"Soon," he said, still in that whisper which revealed nothing of what his true speaking voice must sound like. Then he took me by the shoulders and gently turned me to face him. It was still too dark to see anything, but I knew he was there, knew he was scant inches away.

Would a dream-kiss mean the same thing as a real one?

I held my breath, waiting for the touch of mouth to mouth that I'd anticipated for so long. Finally his lips brushed against mine. They weren't warm, though, but cold, and the eyes staring at me were not deep green, but black, black as jet, glittering and cruel. He forced my mouth open with his tongue, made me taste him, and though I struggled, I couldn't seem to summon one spell to defend myself, do one thing to keep him from taking me as he'd planned to all along. Then he was pushing me down against the pillows, icy fingers digging into my flesh as I writhed beneath him, desperately trying to free myself.

The room blared with light. "Angela!"

Kirby's voice. I blinked and saw him standing in the door to my room, with Efraim Willendale and my cousin Rosemary crowding behind him.

"You were screaming," Kirby said. His tone was matter-of-fact enough, but he was frowning. "Are you all right?"

"Just a nightmare," I told him. Of course that's all it was. Not surprising, I supposed, after my run-in with Damon Wilcox earlier that day. Even so, I couldn't help reaching out and running a hand over the bedclothes next to me. They were relatively flat and unrumpled, my paperback still lying where I'd dropped it when I couldn't keep my eyes open any longer. No one had been there.

"You're sure?" Efraim asked in his deep voice.

I nodded. I didn't want to have to tell them what I'd dreamed. I didn't even want to think about it. "Too much pizza too close to bedtime. That's all."

The three of them shot worried glances at one another, my cousin Rosemary's mouth pursing in... what? Worry? Disapproval?

A quick look at the clock on my nightstand told me it was only eleven-thirty. Still a lot of night left for those kinds of dreams to invade my slumber once again. But I knew I had to try to sleep.

"It's fine," I said. *"I'm* fine."

They hesitated, but then Kirby said, "All right. But remember that we're just downstairs if you need us."

How could I forget? I thought, but I only replied, "Thanks. That makes it better."

Apparently they were willing to go with that. Kirby closed my door partway, leaving it open about six inches, and I heard the stairs creak as they headed back down to the family room.

The light coming in from the upstairs hallway helped a little. I lay in bed and looked at the long rectangle of pale yellow created by the sconces in the hall, and heard the faraway sounds of the TV cranking up again. Not too loud, of course, but just enough that I could catch snippets of laughter. Maybe they were watching *Letterman* or something.

Despite everything, my mouth curved in a smile at the thought of two warlocks and a witch sitting around and watching *Letterman*, but really, most of our lives were pretty prosaic. It wasn't all casting spells and flying around on broomsticks. Not that any of us could actually fly. Our talents tended to be a little more down to earth than that, if you'll pardon the pun.

I could feel myself begin to relax again. Kirby and Efraim and Rosemary were downstairs, and Damon Wilcox was a hundred miles away in Flagstaff. The town was protected; I was protected. My own thoughts were the enemy here, churning away, roiling up dark fears that should have stayed buried. Nothing was going to happen. The next two weeks would pass, and my consort would either show up or he wouldn't. And if he didn't, I had Adam to make sure I was of no use to the Wilcoxes.

That seemed to do the trick. I shut my eyes, and this time I slipped into a calm, dark sleep, with no nightmares to trouble my mind.

—————

A new crew had shown up while I was still sleeping. They generally switched out around eight in the morning, and I was startled to see that I'd slept until almost nine. That day in Phoenix really had done a number on me.

This time it was Tobias and Henry and Allegra. I shot Tobias a surprised look as I shuffled down to get coffee. The three of them were in the family room, with the TV tuned to some morning news out of Phoenix. The newscasters were currently discussing the weather, which meant nothing to us up here in Jerome. Phoenix might as well have been in another state, its weather was so different from ours.

"I thought you and Aunt Rachel had a hot date last night," I told Tobias as I slipped a hazelnut cream pack into the coffeemaker. "How'd you end up on duty this morning?"

He shrugged, and set aside the copy of the *Verde Valley News* he'd been holding. "My turn in the rotation. She was a little tired last night."

Well, I could relate to that. And if he were here, then I'd have an opening to talk to my aunt. True, the shop would be open, and there wasn't much I could do about that. But it was a Thursday and shouldn't be too busy. Technically I should be working at the store, but my status had been a little hazy since my elevation to *prima*, especially after I'd moved into the house. Rachel had said it wasn't that busy right now and that I should take my time getting adjusted.

Just the day before yesterday she'd told me she was thinking about having my cousin Riley come in and help out so I wouldn't have to do it anymore, would be free to work on my jewelry and finish up my degree, if that was what I wanted. It seemed a strange attitude for her to take, since she was the one who'd been gung-ho about me taking the online coursework in the first place. I hadn't really seen the point—it wasn't as if I'd ever have to go out and find a "real" job—but she said education was important, so I'd sort of dragged myself through the coursework, taking my time.

Although working at the store had certainly never been my *raison d'être*, the defection still bothered me. It was as if now that I was *prima*, my aunt was trying to distance herself from me.

All the more reason for us to have a talk.

Since I wasn't that hungry, I made myself some toast and finished my coffee, then headed upstairs to get myself together. It was a bright, clear day, but cold, with a brisk wind coming from the east. After I showered I put on a thick mohair pullover I'd found in a thrift shop down in Cottonwood—"it's so retro!" Sydney had exclaimed—along with my favorite jeans and boots. As a concession to Aunt Rachel's sensibilities, I finished off the outfit with some lip gloss and my favorite silver hoop earrings, then headed down to the store.

Of course I told Tobias and the other bodyguards where I was going, and they dutifully trailed after me, then parked themselves in the donut shop across the street. I really didn't see what possible trouble I could get into in the distance between the house and Aunt Rachel's shop, but I did have to admire their efficiency.

She gave me a surprised look when I entered the shop. "Hi, hon, but I told you that you didn't have to come in today."

"I know." The place was empty except for the two of us; midweek like this, most tourists wouldn't come by to shop until after lunch. "I wanted to talk."

"Talk?" Suddenly her hands were busy, rearranging a display of small tumbled semiprecious stones. "What did you want to talk about?"

"Yesterday…and a few things Margot Emory told me."

"You talked to Margot?"

So apparently I was able to keep a few things secret in this town. Then again, Margot had never been the type to share confidences…unless they were being dragged out of her. "Yes. She told me stuff I'd never heard about the Wilcoxes. Also a few things about this whole consort business. Things it might have been nice to know."

My aunt's expression grew guarded. "Such as?"

"The reason why the Wilcoxes wanted to grab Aunt Ruby in the first place…wanted to grab *me*. And how I don't *have* to be holding out for a consort. Yes, it's preferable, but it's not exactly a do-or-die situation like the way you'd always explained it to me."

She wouldn't meet my eyes, instead got out from behind the counter and began, quite unnecessarily, to make sure all the books in the rack on the far wall were lined up properly. "You know it's important for a *prima* to have her consort. Not just for her, but for all of us."

"Important, yes, but it's not the *only* way." On the walk down here I'd told myself I needed to stay calm, to not fling accusations at her, but now I could feel yesterday's anger bubbling up again. "Here you were standing on the sidelines, being all rah-rah every time a candidate came up to see me, but never *once* in the past year did you tell me that we would manage without a consort, that just settling for one of those candidates would be enough to protect me from the Wilcoxes."

At that she did finally turn to face me. Her hazel eyes glittered—not with tears, but her own particular brand of anger. Hands on her hips, she retorted, "Settle? *Settle?* The *prima* of the McAllisters should not have to settle! All right, it might have protected *you* from the Wilcoxes, but what about the rest of us? A *prima* without a consort isn't strong enough to protect her whole clan, or didn't Margot tell you that?"

"She said it wasn't optimal, but she also didn't make it sound as if the world was going to cave in, either." Since that particular remark didn't get a response, only a continuing irritated glare, I added, "And since she's a clan elder, I figure she must know what she's talking about."

"And I don't, I suppose."

"I didn't say that."

"So what are you saying, Angela?" She moved away from the bookcase and went back to her fussy tidying-up, as if those few minutes of angry eye contact were about all she could handle.

"I'm saying that you were so busy protecting me that you didn't give me a chance to make any decisions for myself! Maybe it would've helped me to know that Damon Wilcox wanted me because he knew as *primus* he could force me to be his whether or not he was my consort." The horrifying dream-memory of his mouth on mine, his hands grasping my arms, swam up behind my eyes, and I blinked it away. I couldn't let myself think about that right now. "Shit, you *knew* what he looked like—you recognized him back in Phoenix. And yet I had no clue. He could've walked up to me in Wal-Mart down in Cottonwood, and I would've thought he was just some random guy trying to hit on me in the freezer section."

Her mouth tightened. "That would never have happened. Even he wouldn't be so bold as to come into our territory like that."

"He didn't seem to have any problem in Phoenix."

"Because it's not our territory—it's the de la Pazes'."

"Oh, whatever!" I crossed my arms. "You know what I mean. It was that whole protecting me thing again. For some reason you didn't want to give me even that little piece of information. How can I make the right choices and do the right thing if I'm working in the dark? I'm the *prima* of this clan now, not some girl you can keep bundled up in bubble wrap for the rest of my life."

The bells on the front door jingled, and Tobias entered, holding two go-cups of coffee. Only a very stupid person could have overlooked the tension in the air, and Tobias was definitely not stupid. He glanced from Rachel to me and back again. "Everything okay in here, ladies?"

"Fine," my aunt and I both snapped simultaneously.

He looked supremely unconvinced, but only went over the counter and set the two cups of coffee down on it. "I'll just leave these here for you, then."

"Thanks," the two of us said, and he sent Aunt Rachel a searching glance before giving the smallest lift of his shoulders and heading back outside.

We both ignored the coffee, although it smelled good, its heavy, rich scent mingling with the spicy smell of the potpourri sitting in a basket on a high shelf.

"Anyway," I added, since it seemed clear she was keeping herself from saying anything else...saying something she'd regret, possibly, "Adam and I have talked it over, and if a consort doesn't materialize before a week from tomorrow, then we're going to...well, you know. Be together."

That did shock her. She set down the rag she'd been using to wipe off a display of wood carvings. "You *what?*"

"You heard me."

"So you're just going to throw everything away to be with someone I distinctly remember you saying you had absolutely no interest in?"

"What exactly would I be throwing away?" I could not understand her reasoning. "At that point the only thing I'll be throwing away is a virginity that's not such a great asset, considering it's the one thing Damon Wilcox seems to want. Get rid of that, get rid of him. It seems pretty simple to me."

She went very still, staring at me as if she'd never seen me before. "Do you love Adam?"

"Of course I don't," I said in some impatience. "But I like him, and he's a McAllister, and being with him certainly seems a better alternative than spending the rest of my life looking over my shoulder."

"You might think that now," she replied. Now her tone was sad, the anger somehow ebbing away. For the first time ever I thought she looked old, the lines around her eyes etched a little deeper than they'd been only moments earlier. "But you don't know what you'd be giving up."

"And what would I be giving up?"

"The life you should have had."

Watching her, I thought then that she was talking of something far beyond me. I didn't know if I should prod her any further. This confrontation had already hurt enough…probably because we so seldom quarreled. But the scab had already been peeled off the wound; walking away now would only let it heal halfway, if that.

"Are you telling me that because you really believe it…or because you think that's what happened to you?"

A stony silence. She went back to wiping off the wooden figurines, head down. Her eyes would not meet mine. Our roles might have been reversed—she the silent child, I the scolding adult. That wasn't how I'd intended things to progress, but I didn't see a way to back down now.

"Look, I get it. You would never talk about what was going on in your personal life when my mother showed up with me, and I suppose that's your business. But it was a huge disruption. You think I don't know that?" My throat was tightening now, but I gave a little cough and forced my way onward. "I'm pretty sure that getting a baby dumped on you wasn't something you planned, and I know you've said over and over that having a family of your own was never in the cards, but I'm not sure I believe that anymore. You don't want me to make a foolish decision now because you feel as if you've thrown away your own life, and that would just negate the sacrifices you've already made."

"I do not—" she began, but I cut her off.

"Yes, what you've done to raise me was incredible, and you've done an amazing job, but it was always focused on me. Maybe there were others who would've taken me in, but you wouldn't allow that, since you were my aunt, my closest relation."

She said nothing.

"I'm not marrying Adam because I want to throw my life away. I'm choosing to be with him because fate apparently doesn't want me to have my consort, and I am concerned about the safety of this clan. At least he cares about me…and I'll learn to care for him as a husband. He's already a friend, so I think we're halfway there." I paused, thinking she might finally want to say something, but she only stood there in front of the shelf with the carved deer and horses and javelinas on it, shoulders slumped. "And you can ignore this, but you know what I think? I think you and Tobias should get married. I'm out of the house. I'm *prima*. You don't need to watch over me anymore. Take care of yourself, and let yourself be happy. That's all. Because that's what I'm going to try to do. Be happy, even if things haven't turned out the way I expected."

Since there didn't seem to be anything else to say, and she clearly did not intend to respond, I went and got one of the coffees Tobias had brought in, then went outside. Luckily, the stretch of sidewalk in front of the shop was deserted. I really didn't feel like seeing or talking to anyone right then; I just wanted a chance to clear my head. That whole time my combination backpack/purse had been slung over one shoulder, and with my free hand I reached in and pulled out my sunglasses. I didn't want the world to see the tears that filled my eyes but refused to fall.

For some reason my feet wanted to carry me down Main Street, toward the overlook that afforded an amazing view of the valley beyond. Here there were a few tourists clustered around, taking pictures and chattering with one another, but they ignored me. I was glad of the barrier my sunglasses provided, though, glad they couldn't see the torment in my face.

I stood at the overlook for a long time, gazing out at the straw-colored, rolling hills of Clarkdale and Cottonwood. Maybe I should have stopped there, but it seemed impossible to keep myself from gazing beyond, to the looming conical shape of Mount Doom—that is, Humphreys Peak. I wondered if Damon Wilcox was looking this way, watching to see what I was doing. Which was silly, because I'd heard you couldn't just reverse the view…something to do with the differences in elevation and topography. We could see the mountains in Flagstaff, but people there couldn't really see Jerome very well, not with the unaided eye, that is. Even so, I knew he was there. Waiting. He'd made his play, but was it his final one?

Minutes passed. I don't know how long I stood there, but eventually I felt someone come up behind me. I turned and saw Tobias standing a few feet way, his normally jovial expression serious.

"Are you going to give me crap for talking to my aunt like that?"

He shook his head and came a little closer. The wind ruffled his overlong hair; in the bright sun I could see how much silver threaded its way through the brown. "That's not my place. She didn't want to hear what you said to her…but after she had some time to think about it, she admitted you might have been right. Well, partially right," he added.

I couldn't help smiling at that, although the smile faded abruptly. "And do you think I'm being stupid?"

"No." The reply was immediate, and firm. "I think you're doing what you think is best. None of us thought things would get to this point, but…."

"And you knew, too, I suppose," I said wearily. I was so tired of the secrets.

"Some of it, not all. But it wasn't my place to have that talk with you." He crossed his arms and gazed past me to the blue-purple bulk of Humphreys Peak, so many miles away. But even if it had been twice as far, I still wouldn't have felt safe. "Don't be too mad at Rachel. I get the impression she thought Ruby would have told you some of these things, not that you'd have to pry them out of Margot Emory, of all people."

I wondered about that, too. Maybe Great-Aunt Ruby had clung to the belief that my knight in shining armor would show up eventually. After all, hers had. There had never been a McAllister *prima* without a consort. That was something that happened to other clans, not us.

"Yeah, that was a little awkward," I admitted. "But at least she didn't clam up on me."

"And Adam? He's okay with this?"

"Why wouldn't he be? He claims to have been in love with me since he was seventeen."

Tobias made a wry grimace. "Even so, no one wants to think of themselves as second best."

"He's not. He's...." I trailed off, then shrugged. What was he? Third best, after Chris Wilson and Alex Trujillo, in terms of the good-looking guys in my life? That wasn't fair. I shouldn't be comparing them. I'd never had a shadow of a chance with Chris, not really, and Alex hadn't exactly shown any signs of pining for me. "He's just Adam. We know each other. We get along. It'll be fine."

"Now you sound like you're trying to convince yourself."

Irritation flared. "Look, Tobias, I appreciate the input, but shouldn't you be worrying about your own love life?"

An improbable grin lifted his mouth. "Well, it turns out I might not have that much to worry about after all. Rachel told me what you said...and so I asked her again. This time she said she'd think about it."

Whereas every other time before that I was pretty
sure he'd been shot down summarily. "That's great
news. Next time you might actually get a 'maybe.'"

"A man can hope." His gaze shifted to the coffee
I still held. "Did you end up actually drinking any of
that?"

I started, then gave a guilty shrug. "Sorry, guess
I was too busy brooding. It did make a good hand
warmer, though."

"Then it wasn't wasted." He looked around, at
the people walking to and fro, at the cars searching
for parking spaces. It was closer to noon now, and the
crowds would start to get thicker, even though the
real influx of tourists wouldn't start until tomorrow.
"Why don't you go on home? I think you and Rachel
need your space right now, and if it gets busy she can
call Riley to come in and help." A quick glance over
his shoulder to the sidewalk across the street, where
I realized the other two bodyguards were loitering,
pretending to look in a shop window. "Besides, I'm
pretty sure Henry and Allegra are getting tired of
looking at the same display over and over again."

A pang of guilt went through me. "You're right,
of course. I should have thought about that. Let's go
back up to the house, and I'll order some sandwiches
from the deli for lunch for everyone."

"I think they'd like that." He sort of waved at
them, and then jerked his thumb upward, appearing

to indicate that we were heading up the hill and back to the house. They nodded and began walking when we did, although they stayed on their side of the street. Didn't want to be too conspicuous, I supposed.

And actually, hibernating inside for a while seemed like a good idea. Maybe then I'd have a chance to figure out if I really was doing the smart thing…or making the biggest mistake of my life.

CHAPTER FIFTEEN

Ebb Tide

"You're what?" Sydney exclaimed, looking as if she were about to keel over. "You're going to marry *Adam?* The guy you've been avoiding for the past five years?"

"Well, I wouldn't call it *avoiding,*" I protested. "I'm starting to run out of options. And he's worlds better than the last candidate I had to deal with."

"That doesn't sound like much of a recommendation." She flipped her hair over her shoulder and frowned. "Okay, I'll admit that I've always thought he was kind of cute, so I could never really figure out what exactly you had against him, except that you told me he wasn't your consort and he couldn't get it through his head that he wasn't...." A look of puzzlement slipped over her features. "But he isn't, right? So how does that work? I thought you said—"

"I did say." Just when I thought I'd gotten things more or less figured out, Sydney's questions were only serving to make me confused all over again. "That is, it doesn't happen very often, but a *prima* can marry someone who isn't her consort. It's better this way." No way was I going into the whole Wilcox thing with her. Obviously she'd figured out that there was something about Flagstaff the McAllisters avoided, since I'd always turned down her offers to drive up there in the summer to avoid the heat. But I'd never elaborated, and Sydney was generally pretty good about not prying.

She wrinkled her nose and lifted her glass of chardonnay, but didn't take a drink. The day after my blowout with Rachel, Sydney had called, saying plaintively that we hadn't talked at all, and she wasn't working today but Anthony was, and could she come up?

I didn't have the heart to turn her down. Besides, after all the tumult of the past few days, there'd been something very appealing about the thought of sitting down with a friend and just talking things over. Anyway, she would've killed me if she'd discovered my plans before I had a chance to tell her myself.

"So...you're going to wait until the last minute, and if no Prince Charming shows up, then you'll just marry Adam? With no planning? No flowers, cake?"

An expression of comic alarm twisted her features. "No *dress?*"

Oh, boy. "Well, that will come later. I mean, we don't have to get married right away. We just have to, you know…." I couldn't quite complete the sentence.

"…have sex," she finished for me.

I winced.

"Jesus, Angela, don't be such a prude." At last she took a swallow of her chardonnay. "It's just sex."

Easy for you to say, I thought. She'd lost her virginity at sixteen. Sleeping with guys was old hat for her. For me it was frightening, unexplored territory. Especially since I'd been told that being with your consort was supposed to be this amazing, life-changing, ecstatic experience. Going to bed with Adam? Probably not.

I took a deep breath. "We haven't really talked about it, but sure, I know we'll have some kind of ceremony. We'll figure it out. Don't worry—there'll be a dress. And you can help me shop for it."

"Awesome." Relieved that she wouldn't be completely deprived of the fun of dress shopping, she went full force into a discussion of the various bridal shops in Prescott, and whether they'd be worthy of the occasion, or whether we should go to Scottsdale and find something really special, and how she hoped I wasn't just going to do something in Spook Hall, and maybe we could have a reception at the

Asylum restaurant up at the Grand Hotel at the top of Cleopatra Hill, and....

Listening to all that was enough to tire me out all over again, but I let her rattle on. A wedding didn't appear to be in her future anytime soon, although she and Anthony seemed to be holding on for the moment. Maybe she'd finally make it past the two-month barrier. And although I hadn't even stopped to think about dresses or flowers or any of that, Sydney discussing it made the situation seem somehow normal. All I'd been thinking about was how atypical my position was, and so different from what I had imagined my life would be. To someone on the outside looking in, it must not look that strange. Just two young people who'd known each other all their lives suddenly realizing they were supposed to be together.

Only I knew that we weren't meant to be together. This was a solution to a problem, nothing more. Of course I wasn't indifferent to Adam—I cared about him, just not in that way.

Maybe someday I'd figure out how to change that.

Sydney and I hung out for a while, but she didn't stay for dinner—she was meeting Anthony down in Cottonwood after he got off work. "You and Adam could come down," she suggested, as we stopped in the foyer. From the family room came the faint sound of the TV as the afternoon's bodyguards watched a football game, but I'd gotten so used to the background noise that I hardly paid it any attention anymore. "The four of us could go out to eat together."

I shook my head. "Maybe some other time. I'm not really feeling the whole 'going out on the town' thing."

She made an exasperated noise. "Having dinner at Nic's isn't exactly going out on the town. Besides, maybe you'd feel more...normal...about things if you two did some regular stuff together."

She did have a point there, but I still wasn't that interested. For one thing, I was in a sloppy sweater and ratty jeans, and I'd have to change and put on some makeup. It seemed like too much of an effort. Anyway, there would be plenty of time later for all of us to do the whole double-date thing.

I told her as much, and she shrugged. "Have it your way. Just don't go into hibernation, okay? I know you have your reasons for doing what you're doing, but don't hide out just because you're going to be with Adam."

"I won't."

"I mean it."

"I swear," I said.

For a second or two she didn't say anything. Then, out of nowhere, she reached over and gave me a quick hug. We were never that demonstrative with one another, so I blinked in surprise, wondering what had brought that on.

"It's going to be okay," she told me, then squeezed my hand a final time before letting herself out the front door.

I hoped she was right. But I didn't have time to think about it for much more, since when I turned around I saw Maisie standing in front of me. I gave a little gasp. This was the first time I'd seen her anyplace except wandering around Hull Avenue. I could never be sure whether this was because she couldn't leave her usual haunts, so to speak, or whether she simply preferred to stay someplace she was familiar with.

"Hi, Maisie," I said cautiously, keeping my voice down...not that the bodyguards probably could have heard anything over the sound of the football game they were watching.

She didn't reply at once, but moved in her soundless way into the living room. Once there, she looked around, as if absorbing the decor. I had no idea whether she'd ever visited the place while Great-Aunt Ruby was alive...or the *prima* before her, for that matter.

I followed Maisie and stopped in front of the fireplace, which was dark at the moment; Sydney had said she didn't want a fire while we hung out, so I'd left it alone. "Um…did you want something?" I asked.

Maisie halted her inspection of the room. "It looks better than I thought it would."

"Gee, thanks."

Either she didn't hear the sarcasm in my voice, or she chose to ignore it. "I've heard you're getting hitched to someone who isn't your consort."

"And you're here to tell me not to?"

"'Course not." She shook her head, and the curls gathered up at the back of her head danced with the movement. "He seems like a nice young gentleman. Sorta reminds me of my Seth."

"Seth?" I asked. This was the first time she'd ever mentioned anyone in particular. Considering her previous occupation, I'd sort of assumed she didn't have anyone.

Her expression grew wistful. "Seth Carlson. He was a miner—came here from somewhere east, Minnesota or Michigan or one of those places. He was saving up his money, wanted to buy a ranch over Prescott way. Wanted to marry me. But then this happened." She gestured toward herself, and for a few seconds I thought I saw livid black bruises appear on her neck before they disappeared again. "Anyway, your Adam calls Seth to mind, for some reason."

"So that's the general consensus of…everyone?" I asked. By "everyone" I meant the dearly departed population of Jerome. To be honest, up until this moment I hadn't really stopped to think what their input might be. They coexisted with us witches, but aside from me, there wasn't a lot of interaction. The ghosts were not clan members. McAllisters generally seemed happy enough to move on to the next plane with a minimum of fuss, from what I could tell.

"More or less." A shadow seemed to pass over her face, and she seemed to go slightly transparent before she gathered herself again. "There's something…something we can't see, can't feel. It's not one of us. It's always at the edge of our vision. But something about it doesn't seem right."

"Like…" I swallowed. "Like when that apparition showed up in my aunt's store?"

A small lift of her shoulders under the white pin-tucked blouse, so prim and proper, so opposite what she'd been when she lived here in Jerome. "Sort of. Not exactly the same…but still cold. It feels like it's watching." She shivered, as if recalling a chill she shouldn't be able to feel at all.

I was cold as well. Time for that fire. I made a small flick of my fingers, and the logs crackled to life, bringing some much-needed warmth to the room. Somehow that wasn't enough to dispel the ice that seemed to be running through my veins.

"What should I do?" I asked. The words came out in barely a whisper.

She took a step toward me and raised her hand, as if she wanted to pat my shoulder in comfort and then realized that would do no good at all, that her fingers would only move through my body as if it weren't there. Yes, she looked solid, but she was no more corporeal than a drift of river mist.

"What you are doing," she replied, sounding a little too cheery. I didn't know who she was trying to convince...me, or herself. "You have your own watchers, and that's good. And you have Adam. That's good, too. He'll help to keep you safe."

She seemed certain of that. I could only hope she was right.

Three days later, and only four days to go until my birthday. I could feel time running down, just as the year ebbed to the darkest night, the solstice. In the past I'd always sort of enjoyed having my birthday on that day, of feeling the power of the day I'd come into this world combining with that pivot point when the world shifted back toward the light. Now, though, I could only think that it was an unfortunate combination. It was on the solstice when some of the darkest magic was cast. If I were still vulnerable on that night....

You won't be, I told myself. *Because Adam and you will be...together...a few hours before. Well, unless this one works out.*

Talk about your Hail Mary passes. Things were still delicate and uncertain between Aunt Rachel and me, but she'd called late on Saturday afternoon to say she had another candidate for me and that he was coming over on Sunday. It hadn't been phrased as a question, and I hadn't bothered to argue. None of the other candidates had worked out, and I had no reason to think this one would be any different. But I figured I might as well humor her.

Adam, of course, hadn't taken it very well. "Like it's going to make a difference at this point!" he fumed.

I didn't bother to point out that he had a vested interest in my not seeing any candidates during this final week before my birthday. "She thinks it might," I said gently. "I don't think it will, either, but since she and I are still walking on eggshells around each other, I figure it might make things a little better." Adam and I were sitting in the nook off the kitchen and drinking coffee; it was a cold, blustery morning, and although the skies threatened, no rain had fallen yet.

"I don't like it."

"Neither do I, but it's just one more thing to get through. Okay?" I'd reached out and laid my hand

on his where it rested on the tabletop, and after a second or two he'd knotted his fingers around mine and
given them a squeeze. So, not perfect, but at least he
wasn't angry at me. I thought it best not to dwell on
his attitude toward Rachel at the moment.

He'd gone back to his apartment, since I thought
having him around would only make matters worse.
There wasn't much I could do about the bodyguards,
but they'd wisely remained in the sitting room, TV
tuned to yet another interminable football game.
Allegra was one of the bodyguards today, and she'd
seemed less than thrilled about that choice of view-
ing material, but Boyd and Henry had outvoted her.

The doorbell rang. I drew in a deep breath and
went to open the door.

Alex Trujillo stared down at me. I blinked.

No, wait, it wasn't Alex, but someone who
looked so much like him that they had to be closely
related. After a quick second glance, I realized this
man was older, maybe even as old as thirty. "Another
Trujillo?"

"You got me." He extended a hand, and I took it,
hoping I didn't look as surprised as I felt. Very rarely
did two candidates come from the same immediate
family. "Diego Trujillo."

"I'm Angela McAllister."

"Yeah, I kind of got that," he said with a grin.

"Come in," I said quickly, to cover my confusion and embarrassment. "This way." I shut the door behind him and then led him to the living room. This time I already had a fire going in the hearth, since it was hovering in the mid-40s outside. "Coffee?"

He shook his head. "Just some water would be fine."

I nodded and hurried off to the kitchen, where I poured a couple of glasses of water and added a slice of lemon to each. The lemon slices had been left behind in the refrigerator by Kirby at some point; he liked to add them to his Coke, apparently. As I put together the drinks, I tried to figure out what Diego Trujillo's presence meant. He was older than any of the other candidates; everyone else had been under twenty-five. But Aunt Rachel knew I'd found Alex attractive, so maybe she thought she'd try again from the same gene pool. I doubted it would make any difference, although I had to applaud her ingenuity in coming up with this possibility.

Diego was still standing up when I came back to the living room, although he'd moved to one wall where a painting of billowing monsoon clouds over a desert mountain hung. I'd admired the artist's work when I saw some of his smaller pieces hanging in one of the local wine tasting rooms, and it had been kind of wonderful to be able to purchase the sort of large painting I'd never thought I could afford.

"This is amazing," Diego said as I handed him a glass of water.

"I really love it, too." Then I realized maybe saying "love" hadn't been the wisest thing in this particular situation, so I drank some of my own water to cover up my awkwardness.

If he noticed, Diego didn't give any indication. He drank as well, seeming to study me. Although I didn't have any hope of this encounter turning out any differently from the others, I'd made a little more of an effort today, wearing some new jeans and a dark green cardigan with a lace-trimmed camisole under it, along with my ballet flats instead of boots.

Since he didn't seem inclined to say anything, I asked, "So how did my aunt manage to rope you into this?"

Another of those eye-catching grins. Like his brother, he had a very good smile. "Oh, she didn't. I volunteered, and my *abuela* called your aunt."

"You…volunteered?"

"You sound surprised."

"Well…I guess I am. I mean, after Alex didn't work out…."

"We're not the same person. Just because he wasn't your consort doesn't mean I can't be. And he had very good things to say about you, so I thought I should give it a try."

Well, how was I supposed to reply to that? I gave an embarrassed little nod, not meeting his eyes, and he went to the coffee table and set down his glass… properly using a coaster, I noted.

"Does it bother you that I'm a little older?"

"No," I said, finding my voice. "Not really." *You're still younger than Damon Wilcox,* I thought then, although I knew better than to say such a thing out loud.

"Good." He came over to me and laced his fingers through mine. His hands were strong, as his brother's had been. "Let's try this, then, okay?"

I couldn't do anything except nod.

His mouth came closer to me, then touched, and….

I didn't know what I wanted to happen. Part of me felt as if I were betraying Adam, and the other part argued that I needed to be doing this, that I needed to try. Too much pushing and pulling inside my mind.

It turned out that none of it mattered, because again I felt nothing. Oh, his technique was very good—I could tell he'd had a lot of practice—but there were no more sparks or fireworks than when I kissed Adam.

Diego pulled away. His expression seemed neutral enough, although by the way his jaw tensed slightly I could tell he wasn't thrilled by my lack of reaction. Probably he wasn't used to having girls just stand there like department store mannequins when he kissed them.

"Oh, well, it was worth a try," he said.

"I'm sorry."

"Don't be. I knew the chances weren't good."

I nodded, feeling an odd sense of relief. At least now I knew what would happen. There wouldn't be any more attempts. Maybe I wasn't meant to have a consort in the true sense of the word.

He went and retrieved his glass of water, then drank about half of what remained. "I'll be on my way."

No protests came from my lips. What would be the point? He wasn't the one, either.

I saw him to the door, then went up to my room and retrieved my phone from where it sat charging on the nightstand. After I went to the Contacts screen, I sat there for a long moment, staring down at Adam's number. Although I knew my Aunt Rachel had said there would be no more candidates after Diego, some part of my mind didn't quite believe it. There were still three days left. But no, she'd said there was no one else. No one unattached and in the right age group, of the right family. I'd run through them all.

After taking a deep breath, I pushed the phone icon next to Adam's entry. It rang twice, and he picked up. Without waiting for him to speak, I said, "We're on for Friday." Then I hung up before he could reply. I didn't want to talk about it anymore. I just wanted to get the whole thing over with.

———

We'd tried to act normal, but of course there wasn't anything normal about the situation. Everyone in the clan knew what was going on, too, which didn't make things any easier. Usually I would have been leading the clan's solstice celebrations this night, but there was an unspoken agreement that my being with Adam for the evening took precedence.

After some ruminating on the upcoming evening, I'd decided we should go out—dinner at Grapes, and wine, then off to the Spirit Room to hear that night's band play, and more wine. I figured if I were seriously tipsy, if not outright drunk, then the whole thing might be easier to handle.

Adam hadn't bothered to argue with me about all that. I guessed he was probably just relieved that no more obstacles had presented themselves. If I wanted to delay things as long as possible on the night itself, he could handle that. Technically, I wouldn't be twenty-two until almost midnight the following day—my time of birth was eleven-thirty. The solstice itself wouldn't happen until almost three in the morning. So partying late tonight shouldn't create any problems.

Once again Sydney had suggested that she and Anthony should come to meet us and hang out for the evening, but I thought that would just be too weird. "I appreciate it, but...no," I told her.

"Suit yourself," she replied. "And I won't even ask for the gory details tomorrow." She'd let out a mock-sigh and added, "My little girl is finally going to be a woman!"

"You are so weird," I replied, even though I couldn't help smiling a little. Then I'd hung up.

Dinner was all right. We talked about common-place things, about how he was helping with the conversion of a triplex into a single-family home, and how I couldn't decide whether to go with black appliances or stainless steel ones for the upcoming kitchen remodel. Just your ordinary date-night con-versation, I supposed.

Lara's band was playing at the Spirit Room, which meant the place was packed. We ended up having to hover at one end of the bar, but I didn't mind too much. The raucous atmosphere helped to deflect my thoughts from what was coming at the end of the night.

Jesus, you're acting as if you're going to your exe-cution, I thought. *It's just Adam. He knows what he's doing.*

At least, I assumed he did. I'd never heard of him seeing anyone in Jerome, but he went into Cottonwood a good deal, just like the rest of us did, and I know a few of those girls back in high school who'd thought he was cute would've been more than happy to have him pop their cherries, so to speak. He'd wanted to be with me, but I kind of doubted that meant he'd been depriving himself all these years just in case I changed my mind.

He bought me a glass of wine, and then another. By that point the room was more than a little swimmy, faces and sound and the dim lights over the bar seeming to swirl around and around one another. Most of the people I didn't recognize; a lot of bikers came to the Spirit Room, although it was always a more or less friendly crowd, locals and tourists and people from several motorcycle clubs mingling without much of a problem.

Adam and I danced. I wanted the contact with him. I wanted the music to draw us closer, to have our bodies moving together so that when the moment came, I'd already feel in sync with him, would think it a natural progression. That was what I hoped in my semi-drunken state, anyway.

Even there we weren't without our escort, although they'd taken up a table in a corner, staying out of our way. I had to thank the Goddess that Tobias wasn't among them. It would've been too awkward to have him watch me act like a tipsy fool as I psyched myself up into sleeping with Adam so I wouldn't have to worry about Damon Wilcox ever getting his hands on me.

Eventually midnight came and went, and Adam squeezed my hand, bending his head close to my ear. "I think it's time to go home now."

I wanted to protest, but I knew that was silly. It was already late; waiting another hour wasn't going to make any difference. So I nodded and let him lead me out of the bar, and up the street to the house. The trio followed a few paces behind, trying to be discreet but failing miserably. There just weren't enough people out at that hour for them not to stick out like a sore thumb.

When we got to the house, Adam stopped on the doorstep and looked down at Henry and Boyd and Allegra where they waited awkwardly on the walkway. "Do you think we could have a little privacy, just this night?"

They exchanged glances.

"What do you think is going to happen?" Adam demanded. "Pretty soon she's going to be safe forever. Just let us have this time together, okay?"

Another long pause. "All right," Boyd said at length. "We'll go to my place, since it's only two doors down. We can be here fast enough."

"Good," Adam said shortly. "We'll see you in the morning."

He pulled out the key I had given him earlier—he didn't have my same talent with locks—and opened the door. The house felt oppressively quiet as we entered. Although I'd hated having the bodyguards underfoot all the time, it still felt strange for no one to be there except Adam and me. I realized that I'd never been this alone in the house.

But there were his fingers around mine, warm, reassuring. "Let's go upstairs."

I let him lead me up to the bedroom. Everything was dark here as well, but he waved his hand at the fireplace, and immediately the logs stacked within began to blaze, warming the space, sending dancing light against the clay-hued walls.

My head still spun, and my mouth was suddenly dry. No more delays. He was here and I was here, and we both knew what was going to happen next.

Which one of us moved first, I couldn't tell. I only knew we were suddenly standing very close, and his mouth came down to mine, and I opened my lips, tasting the wine on his tongue as well, feeling the warmth of his body against mine.

Only then it wasn't warm, but cold, as an icy blast seemed to move through the room, and the fire in the hearth snuffed itself. Shadows formed all around us, shadows that resolved themselves into the shapes of people in hooded cloaks. I pulled away from Adam, opened my mouth—not to kiss, but to cast a spell of protection, and then to reach out with my mind to the three who were supposed to be watching over us. I had no idea whether that would work, since that had been Ruby's gift and not mine, but in my desperation I couldn't think what else to do.

But my breath seemed to choke in my throat, even as my body froze, and the words wouldn't come. A blast of light, gray-tinged, and Adam flew backward, fell lifeless to the floor. Because I was choking, I couldn't scream, couldn't do anything but stand there, impotent, as I saw Damon Wilcox's glinting black eyes come closer and closer.

"I told you I wanted you," he said.

Darkness swirled around him, seemed to become one with him, and I fell into it, was sucked down into a lightless tunnel with no end.

All went black.

CHAPTER SIXTEEN

Solstice

LIGHT RETURNED. WELL, NOT LIGHT EXACTLY, BUT A DARK-ness that wasn't absolutely black. My eyelids fluttered open, and I thought I saw the movement of dim shapes around me. Black candles burned behind them, but I could make out no details beyond that.

I tried to sit up, and realized I could not. The surface beneath me was hard, and felt like some kind of a long table, draped in heavy black cloth. When I turned my head to one side, I couldn't see any ropes or any other bonds holding my wrists and ankles in place, but I might as well have been bound for all the good my struggling did.

"Hello, Angela," came Damon Wilcox's voice from off to my left. I turned my head and saw him standing in front of a group of his clan members. They all wore dark robes, some with the hood pulled up, concealing their faces. There seemed to be at least twenty of them in the room, but it was so dark I couldn't tell for sure.

And then I recalled Adam's limp body falling to the rug in my room, remembered how only a few seconds earlier he had been kissing me, and now he was dead. Well, it felt like seconds earlier. I had no idea how much time had passed, how long I had floated in the dark until I awoke in this room.

Tears came to my eyes, but I blinked them away. I would not cry in front of Damon Wilcox. I would *not*.

"Fuck you," I said succinctly.

He just laughed and shook his head. "Soon, I promise."

His words sent another wave of ice through me. Of course I knew exactly why he'd stolen me away from my home, but that didn't make his words any easier to hear. "You're crazy," I told him. "You think my clan isn't going to come after me?"

"They can try, I suppose, but what good will it do? By then the deed will be done." He looked past me to one of his clan members, a woman who had pale streaks of gray in her long black hair. I couldn't tell for sure in the semi-darkness of the room, but something about her features looked vaguely Native American. "Is it time?" he asked.

"Yes," she replied. Her voice was soft and low. "The solstice is upon us. Now is the time for the binding."

He turned back to me and then approached until he stood next to the table where I lay. Although I knew it would do no good, I gritted my teeth and strained against the invisible force that held me in place. I'd never heard of a spell like this, especially one that could subdue the magic of a *prima*, but then, I'd never studied dark magic. It wasn't the McAllister way. History told too many grim stories of those who'd studied the left-hand path, seeking only knowledge, but who then had been seduced by it.

In the gloom I could see Damon Wilcox's grin flash as he stared down at me. "I've been waiting for this a long time."

Then he bent down to me, and I braced myself. Of course I knew how a kiss between a *prima* and a consort was supposed to feel, but I had no idea what this would feel like, this forced contact between the dark power of a *primus* and his victim.

His lips touched mine. I had thought they would be cold, since he seemed to bring the cold with him wherever he went. Maybe he drew his power from it, from the ice and the snow and the long, dark winter nights. But he was warm enough, surprisingly.

I'd been expecting a shock, a chill…something. Not this, only the press of mouth against mouth and nothing else, just the way I'd felt it so many times before with all of my failed candidates.

The black eyes flashed, and then narrowed. He lifted his mouth from mine and stared at me for a long moment, then bent again and pressed his lips to me again, this time forcing my mouth open with his tongue. I shuddered, although he tasted faintly of mint and nothing else. It was just the violation, the feel of this man I had come to despise forcing himself on me in such an intimate way. Nothing compared to what he had planned, I knew, but still….

He pressed his hands against the edge of the table and thrust himself upward, then whirled on the woman who had spoken a few moments earlier. "It's not working!" he snarled. "You said on the night of the solstice she would be mine!"

Face calm, she stared up at him, meeting his angry gaze as if it were nothing. With a shrug she replied, "I said the signs told me that she would be the consort of a Wilcox. They did not tell me *which* Wilcox. You just assumed it would be you."

"Fuck!" Damon Wilcox ran an angry hand through his hair, and glared into the watching crowd. "Connor, come here."

The watching clan members shifted, and a tall man moved forward, but slowly, as if he was reluctant to do as Damon had asked. Unlike the others, he wasn't wearing the dark robes, but what looked like jeans and a sweater.

Even in the dim lighting it seemed as if there was something familiar about him, although I couldn't quite figure it out. Probably my eyes playing tricks on me. After all, how could there be anything familiar about any of the Wilcoxes? I'd never seen any of them before, except that one time in Phoenix when Damon tried to grab me at the Nordstrom Rack.

But then the strange man bent over me, and I stared up into his eyes.

Green eyes. Cloudy jade, just as I'd dreamed a hundred times.

I sucked in a breath, and then looked beyond those eyes to the face of the man who gazed down at me, and that was familiar as well.

"Chris?" I asked, my voice cracking on that one syllable. It couldn't be. Maybe I'd gotten knocked in the head during the kidnapping, and I was hallucinating things that weren't there. No way could Chris Wilson be here, of all places.

Those green eyes didn't seem to want to meet mine. Finally he said, "It's Connor, actually. Connor Wilcox."

No. The room seemed to tilt around me, and I wished I could sit up, wished I could push myself off this table and run, run far away. I shut my eyes, but when I opened them again, he was still standing there.

We might have been the only two people in the room. "You lied to me," I whispered finally.

He pressed his lips together, as if he wanted to say something but couldn't quite manage it. Not with his brother and so many of his clan members looking on.

"Do it," Damon said, his voice harsh with anger and frustration. "You have to bind her to us. Now."

Again Connor hesitated. His hands were shoved in his jeans pockets, and I could practically feel the tension radiating from him as he stood there. At last he took his hands from his pockets, leaned over me, and murmured, "I'm sorry."

His face was very close to mine. I'd dreamed of him kissing me, had wondered what it would be like, but never had I ever thought that we would come to it like this.

Then his mouth pressed against mine.

Heat flooded through me, seeming to set off every nerve ending in my body, as if all my veins no longer ran with blood but molten lava, bright and terrible and alive. That same warmth traveled to my core, making me ache with need. In that moment I wanted him so badly that I think I would have let him take me right there on that table, in front of everyone. Even in front of Damon Wilcox.

Connor felt it, too, I could tell. His eyes widened, and those same hands that had been clutching the table reached up as if of their own volition to cup my face, to hold me tenderly while he kissed me again and again, lips matching perfectly, tongues reaching out to touch one another, the feel and the taste of him better than anything I'd ever experienced. I fought against those invisible bonds, and then it seemed as they melted away, because I was able to reach up and wrap my arms around him.

My consort. The one I'd been waiting for all these years.

A Wilcox.

I gasped then, pushing him away, trying to recover something of my sanity, something of my will, even as my body cried out for him. He seemed to understand, and stepped back, although I could hear his rough breathing and knew he wanted me just as badly.

"It's done," the woman said. "She has bonded to him."

Damon Wilcox made a gesture with one hand, and someone turned on the overhead lights. I could see now that it looked as if we were in someone's basement rec room. There was a wet bar in one corner, and a large flat-screen television on the far wall, fronted by a leather couch and a recliner. As I put my hand out and felt the lip of the surface on which I lay, I realized their makeshift "altar" had to be a pool table.

Incongruously, I wanted to laugh. But even beneath my amusement I could still feel those ripples of arousal. Connor Wilcox was so very close. It would be so easy to reach out and pull him against me, taste his mouth again, let his hands explore my body, push me back down against the table....

No. It was one of the hardest things I'd ever done, but somehow I managed to shove those thoughts away, force myself to think of what the Wilcoxes had done—stolen me from my home, from my clan. And again I saw Adam's lifeless body lying on the Navajo rug beside the bed, and that was enough to flood my veins with ice to replace the heat of a moment ago.

Without thinking, I launched myself off the pool table and at Damon Wilcox, hand raised to deliver the sort of blow I'd dealt Perry in the parking lot of Main Stage, only this time so much more powerful, as I had the strength of a *prima* and the hate and sorrow of a thousand avenging angels to bolster it.

But then he raised his own hand, and it was as if I'd crashed into a stone wall. The breath was knocked out of me, and I staggered. At once Connor was beside me, reaching out to take my arm. I wrenched it away.

"Don't touch me!"

He stopped immediately, fist clenching at his side.

Damon watched me, an odd mixture of anger, frustration, and amusement twisting his features. Now that I saw them together, I thought I could glimpse a slight resemblance to Connor, but Damon's face was harsher, more hawk-like. He smiled, a mere curling of his lip. "Well, she can't stay here now. I'm afraid she's your problem, brother." Then he added over his shoulder, to two of the burlier-looking members of his clan, "Help Connor get his new package home, would you?"

They converged on me. I lifted a hand again, thinking that even if I couldn't attack Damon I could surely take out a few of his supporters. But whatever magic he'd used to subdue me before seemed to be active again, because I found I couldn't move, couldn't do anything except stand there as one bound my hands in front of me, even as the second man fastened a dark cloth over my eyes. I tried to cry out, but my mouth was blocked as well, and I choked on the words I had been about to say.

Rough hands lifted me up and slung me over a shoulder. I could feel the man going up a flight of stairs, and crossing what sounded like a wood floor. The sound of a door opening, and then a blast of freezing wind against me, colder than anything I'd ever felt before. It made sense, I supposed, if we were now in Flagstaff, several thousand feet higher than my home in Jerome and at least twenty degrees colder.

He carried me what seemed to be several yards, and then I was tossed on the back seat of a car or some other vehicle. The man settled himself beside me, even as I heard an engine rumble to life. It sounded powerful. Maybe not a car, then, but an SUV or a truck with an extended cab. We began to move.

It was hard to tell how long that trip lasted. I thought I heard the sound of another vehicle following us, but it was hard for me to know for certain. The tires were noisy, the road beneath them sounding slushy, rough. Neither the man in the seat beside me nor the person driving the SUV/truck spoke, making it that much more difficult to gauge the passing of time. It didn't feel that long, though, maybe fifteen or twenty minutes. Not much more. At least, I didn't think so.

Eventually the vehicle came to a stop. The driver got out, as did the man next to me. He grabbed me and threw me over his shoulder again, but I felt him slip a little, as if the surface he stood on was slick. Again that freezing air hit me, and I wondered if the street or sidewalk was icy. The sound of another door slamming, and we walked a little way before we entered a building and went up a flight of stairs.

A pause, and then I was deposited on the floor, still not able to move except for a slight shivering caused by the chill wind outside.

It was warmer here, at least, although I couldn't begin to guess where I'd been brought. The man who'd been carrying me said, "He'll contact you tomorrow."

"All right." Connor's voice, sounding resigned.

The door opened and shut again. A second or two later, I felt hands untying the knot in the cloth at the back of my head. The dark fabric was lifted away, and I blinked.

I stood in the entry area of what appeared to be a house or apartment. The space was open, with heavy dark wood framing the doorways and windows. One wall seemed to be all brick. The furniture was simple and strong, leather couch and chair, dark wood cocktail table. Most of the walls were covered in unframed canvases, desert landscapes and mountain scenes. The place felt old, maybe of similar vintage to the apartment where I'd grown up. I'd never been to Flagstaff, but I thought I recalled that the only section with buildings this old was the Old Town district.

"Where are we?"

"My apartment," Connor replied, moving out from behind me. I'd noticed as he undid the blindfold he'd been careful not to come in contact with

my hair, as if he were afraid even that small touch
would be enough to set us off again. Maybe it would
have. My aunt had told me what the bond between a
prima and her consort was supposed to feel like, but
I'd never imagined it would be so shockingly strong,
so overpowering in its urgency.

"Your apartment," I repeated blankly.

"Well, Damon had thought you'd be staying
with him, but that didn't exactly work out." He lifted
his shoulders, as if recognizing the impossibility of
the situation. "So here you are."

Alone with him, and away from the rest of his
clan. It seemed like the perfect opportunity to me.

Opportunity for escape, that is.

Without thinking I bolted for the door. I grasped
the knob, but it wouldn't turn. Of course. Deadbolt.
I reached up to turn it, but it wouldn't budge, either.

A strong sun-browned hand descended on mine.
At once my blood began to race, heat washing over
me. I snatched my fingers away as if they'd touched
a flame. Then again, maybe they had.

"You won't be able to open it," Connor said.
"Nor the latches on the windows, so don't bother
with them, either. You're only getting out if I lift the
spell, and that's not happening. Now, do you want
something to drink? Some water, maybe?"

Just to be difficult, I put my hand on the door-
knob again. This time it felt almost as if an electric

spark leapt from the metal to my fingertips, and I jerked my hand back.

"Just as I told you." His voice didn't sound particularly happy. Resigned, maybe, as if he couldn't have expected anything other than me trying to get away from him. "It's a little late for coffee, and I don't think wine is a very good idea, either. Pellegrino? Juice?"

"I don't want anything from you."

His expression hardened. "Don't make this more difficult than it has to be."

"Difficult?" I demanded. "Difficult? When you broke into my house, killed Adam—"

"We didn't kill anybody," Connor cut in. He went into the kitchen and got two glasses out of a cupboard, then poured some sparkling water into each one.

"What?" I'd been through too many shocks that night. My brain felt as if it had given up trying to process them.

Without answering me immediately, he took one of the glasses and held it out in my direction. Just as wordlessly, I took it from him. My throat was dry, so I went ahead and drank. Maybe he was trying to drug me or something, but I sort of doubted it. I'd just watched him break the seal on the bottle of San Pellegrino.

"I doubt it was out of the goodness of his heart, but Damon only knocked your cousin out. Murder is hard to cover up, even for a warlock. There would be too many questions. Possible repercussions. He just wanted to get in, get you, and get Adam out of the way. Simple enough."

I didn't think it was all that simple, even though I let out a mental breath, and the tiniest bit of the tension in my throat seemed to ease. Adam was still alive. He wasn't dead because of me. Hardening my voice, I said, "There are still going to be repercussions. If you think my clan is just going to sit idly by—"

"And how much can they do, deprived of their *prima?* Not to be rude, Angela, but even with you there they weren't exactly a match for us Wilcoxes. And with you gone...."

He let the words trail off. There wasn't much need for him to say anything else. I loved my clan, loved each and every one of them for their quirks and their odd little habits, but I knew they weren't strong enough to take on the Wilcox clan. Not by a long shot.

If I dwelled on that, I knew I might break down. It was so late, and I was so, so tired. I set down my glass on the counter and decided to move to another subject. "So it was all a lie—grad school, and Tempe, and final projects. Everything." I looked up at him, at those painfully familiar green eyes. Maybe I should have been on guard against such a simple glamour, but again, that wasn't the sort of thing the McAllisters did. We were who we were, with no need to hide it. "Even your eye color."

"It was necessary." He shook his head. "Anyway, a lot of what I told you wasn't exactly a lie. I did go to school in Tempe, but that was a few years ago."

"But you did want to know about our trip to Phoenix so you could report back to your brother."

His shoulders lifted. He didn't bother to deny it.

"And you *were* stalking me, showing up at the Day of the Dead festival like that." Angry tears pricked the back of my eyes as I recalled how nice he had seemed, while the whole time he was just collecting data for his brother. Stupid for me to be upset about that part, but I couldn't help it. I'd had an image of this Chris Wilson person in my mind and my heart, and it hadn't been real at all, only a mask he'd put on to conceal himself from me.

He ran a hand through his hair. It needed cutting, and fell back over his forehead. "Look, Angela, it's almost four. Do you think we can hash this over later? Like, in the morning after we've both gotten some sleep? I promise that I'll try to explain things to you then, but you've been through a lot today, and I think it's better if you get some rest. I swear you'll be safe here."

Despite his attempt at reassurance, panic washed over me at the thought of sleeping here in his apartment with him. Even now, angry and frightened and weary as I was, I could still feel the electricity sparking between us. But I couldn't get out. The place was as locked down for me as a vault at Fort Knox.

What he saw in my face, I couldn't say for sure, but his expression softened. "I have a guest room. You'll be fine."

"I highly doubt that," I retorted.

"Okay, then you'll survive." Bending down, he retrieved a dark duffle bag from where it had been sitting on the floor, halfway hidden by the kitchen cabinets. "I have some stuff here for you." He extended his arm, clearly intending for me to take the bag.

"What is it?"

"Some clothes. Boots. Underwear." His eyes glinted, and for just a second he looked a little too much like his brother for my comfort. "It's the stuff you picked out in Phoenix, and some extra. Damon took it with him that day. He needed to know your sizes so he could have some of the women in the clan get some things together for you."

So that was why Damon Wilcox had stolen my bag from Nordstrom Rack. I didn't really want to dwell on him going through it and figuring out my panty and bra size. On the other hand, it meant I at least had a change of underwear. "Thanks," I said grudgingly.

"Let me show you where the spare room is," he replied, seeming glad that I hadn't pushed back on that one.

Just inside the entryway and past the bathroom there was a flight of wooden stairs that doubled back on itself. We emerged in a short upstairs hall. At the end of the hallway was another window, but I couldn't see anything except black night beyond it. On one wall was a single door, while on the other there were two. He opened the second door and flipped the light switch.

"Here you go."

It wasn't very large, maybe ten feet by ten feet. A twin bed covered in a plain brown spread was pushed up against one wall, and there was a table and chair tucked against the opposite wall. More paintings hung in here. A Navajo rug covered the floor.

"The bathroom is next door," he went on, as casual as if I were just a friend stopping by to hang out for the weekend, rather than the girl his family had kidnapped...as if I weren't the one somehow fated to be with him, if our physical reaction to one another were any indication. "And I'm just across the hall, so if you need anything, knock." Not meeting my eyes, he added, "I'll make sure to put on something besides just underwear."

The thought of him wandering around up here in just a pair of boxer-briefs was enough to relight

that flame in my core. I sucked in a breath, reminding myself of Adam, knocked aside like a rag doll,
of my family realizing sometime in that bleak
December morning that I'd been snatched from
under their very noses. For some reason I thought
of all their presents, wrapped and waiting for them
under the tree Adam and I had set up in the living
room, and the realization that I wouldn't be there
to spend Yule with them made the tears start to my
eyes again.

No, I couldn't cry, and I wouldn't let myself think
that way. There was still time. They would come for
me. They had to.

Coldly I said, "Thanks," to Connor, then turned
away from him and set the duffle bag on the floor.

He seemed to hesitate before saying, "Goodnight,
then," and going out to the hallway and shutting the
door behind him.

For a minute I didn't do anything, only stared at
the plain little room, at the oddly masterful paintings
of canyons and mountains and high desert hills on
the walls. Then I went over to the bed and fell rather
than sat down on it, my head spinning.

Connor Wilcox was the man I'd been dreaming
of since I was sixteen years old. He'd awakened the
prima's fire within me, but it wasn't completely alive.
Not yet. We would have to be together fully as man

and woman for that to take place. I couldn't let it happen, though, not here in the heart of their territory. That would mean my powers would belong to the Wilcoxes, and not the McAllisters.

I would have to find some way to resist him.

I just didn't know how.

The story continues in *Darknight*, Book 2 of the Witches of Cleopatra Hill trilogy, releasing in June 2014.